Where
Love Endures

DEMCO

**Crossway Books
by Noreen Riols**

THE HOUSE OF ANNANBRAE ❦ BOOK FOUR

Where Love Endures

Noreen Riols

CROSSWAY BOOKS • WHEATON, ILLINOIS
A DIVISION OF GOOD NEWS PUBLISHERS

Library of Congress Cataloging-in-Publication Data
Riols, Noreen.
    Where love endures / Noreen Riols.
        p.   cm. — (House of Annanbrae ; bk. 4)
    ISBN 0-89107-779-0
    I. Title. II. Series: Riols, Noreen. House of Annanbrae ; bk. 4.
PR9105.9.R56W484 1997
823'.914—dc21   97-27307

07	06	05	04	03	02	01	00	99	98	97
15	14	13	12	11	10	9	8	7	6	5	4	3	2	1

To
Clémence, Marie-Camille, Daphne,
Margaux, Mathilde, Chloe,
Thomas, Quentin, and Louis
who give me so much happiness

PART I
1962

One

"Cristobel's engaged!"

Maxime looked up from his desk with a frown, his mind still juggling figures. Seeing Katharine standing in the doorway waving an envelope in her hand, his frown disappeared. And he smiled.

"A letter from Flora," Katharine went on, her topaz eyes dancing with excitement. "She and Cristobel will be in Paris the week before Easter, and she wants me to meet them there."

"How lovely!" Maxime exclaimed, getting up and putting a match to the logs in the grate as the room darkened. An explosion of thunder momentarily extinguished the light on his desk. The rain that had been threatening all morning suddenly bucketed down and hammered against the tall stained-glass windows.

"Will they be coming here?"

He sat down in his old leather armchair opposite the sofa on which Katharine had curled up.

"No," his wife answered reflectively. "They won't have time."

"Then do go to Paris."

"But it is the boys' school holidays!"

"I'll take them to Gure Etchea, and you can join us there. Easter's late this year. Not until April. The weather should be perfect."

"Oh, Maxime," Katharine cried, "it would be lovely to spend a few days with Flora. She wants help with choosing a dress for Cristobel's engagement reception on—"

She leafed quickly through the thick vellum sheets.

"Saturday, the 23rd of June."

She looked across at her husband in dismay. "Maxime, we can't go. We'll be in America for Philip's wedding. We don't arrive back until the 29th!"

"All the more reason for you to meet Flora and Cristobel in Paris." Her husband smiled. "At least you'll see her dress."

"'It's all rather rushed,'" Katharine read on. "'We had planned to announce the engagement in September and have a December wedding to coincide with Cristobel's twentieth birthday. But Lindsay's regiment is off to Germany at the end of June, so it has been put forward. You will let us borrow Elisabeth for a bridesmaid, won't you?'"

Katharine's voice trailed off.

"There's nothing we can do about it," Maxime soothed. "We can't let William and Lavinia down. They're counting on us to accompany them on their first trip across the Atlantic since the war. And, anyway, you're looking forward to seeing Hope again after all these years."

Katharine sighed. She had been thrilled when Hope had suggested that they attend her elder son's wedding in Charleston and then return to Boston with her and Bill. Katharine had never met Bill, Hope's second husband. And after all these years, she was looking forward to seeing her former sister-in-law and her sons Philip and Ben, Ashley's nephews, again and introducing them to Maxime. She and Hope had shared so much during those traumatic war years when they had both lost their husbands. Philip's wedding was to be a wonderful reunion with William, their former father-in-law, who had been such a bulwark for them both in their time of loss and pain.

But Katharine also wanted to be present on her goddaughter's special day. . . .

Maxime smiled across at Katharine's crestfallen face.

"We'll be able to make it to Cristobel's wedding. Telephone Flora and make plans to meet her," Maxime urged. "You've always enjoyed Paris in the spring, and we so rarely go there nowadays. While you're helping Cristobel choose her frock, you can kit yourself out for the States."

Katharine smiled wistfully, still torn between the two conflicting events.

Maxime rose and went to sit beside her. Putting his arm around her shoulders, he squeezed them reassuringly. "Knowing Cristobel, she'll be so excited she won't even notice who's present at her ball."

Katharine leaned her head against his shoulder. A great wave of love for him swept over her.

"Maman," the twins shrieked as the car drew up in front of Gure Etchea.

Before Maxime, following at a more leisurely pace, had time to open the door, it was almost wrenched from its hinges by three of his sons, who had catapulted down the steps as soon as they heard the vehicle approach.

Katharine stepped out of the car and hugged them.

"Where's Elisabeth?" she inquired, looking round at the clustered group.

As she spoke, a dark-haired elfin child with enormous violet-blue eyes carefully negotiated the steps, helped by Léon. As his little sister's feet touched firm ground, Léon rushed to Katharine.

But Elisabeth ran to Maxime.

"Look who's here," Maxime cried, sweeping her into his arms.

Elisabeth allowed Katharine to kiss her cheek. But she made no attempt to go to her, nestling possessively against her father's shoulder as they walked into the house. He put her down on the cool tiled floor, but she grasped his hand, as if afraid that he would be torn away.

Katharine smiled. "I see my daughter hasn't changed," she remarked.

Maxime glanced at her quickly, detecting an ironic edge to

her voice. "That's why my mother always said she was glad I was a boy." He smiled, taking his wife's arm and leading her toward the terrace where breakfast was waiting. "All little girls are in love with their fathers."

"So it seems," Katharine replied drily.

As the words left her lips, she remembered the years after Léon's birth when their positions had been reversed. She had been so wrapped up in their ailing child that her husband had been slowly pushed into the wings. Their marriage had almost foundered because of her obsession. For the first time she understood the sense of rejection Maxime must have felt. And she determined that no child, that nothing, would ever be allowed to come between them again.

He looked across at her and smiled. "How was Paris?"

"Stifling," Katharine replied.

"It's pretty hot here," Maxime put in.

"Yes, but here there's the sea breeze."

She returned his smile as she handed him his coffee. "Now I want to know everything that's been happening in my absence."

"You've barely been away a week."

"It seems like a year."

Their eyes met across the table. Reaching across, he took her hand. "For me too," he whispered.

"Can we have another breakfast with you?" Jehan inquired, skipping onto the terrace. "And when are we leaving for the picnic?"

"Soon," Maxime replied. "But first Maman and I have a few things to discuss."

"Okay," Jehan chirped affably and ran off to join his brothers playing pétanque in the garden.

"How did the shopping go?" Maxime inquired.

"Darling, it was wonderful. Cristobel's got a dream of a dress, and they made it in record time. Flora left with it packed in a very impressive carton." She paused and frowned. "I don't know how Laura will react to Cristobel's getting married. Flora and I were talking about it one afternoon when Cristobel was having her final fittings. Flora's concerned about her. Laura's such a lonely girl, and her only real roots have been Annanbrae and the Hamilton family. Flora's afraid that after the wedding she might disappear and lose contact with them altogether. She's so shy and sensitive she could easily retreat into that defensive shell she was wearing when Cristobel first brought her to Annanbrae seven years ago."

Katharine shook her head sadly.

"Flora's done her very best to make her feel part of the family. But Laura seems afraid of making attachments to anyone—except Cristobel, who's more like a sister to her. A twin sister even. They're so very close. But once Cristobel has a husband . . ."

"Maybe Laura will find a husband at the wedding," Maxime volunteered.

"Maybe," Katharine murmured. "But I think it highly unlikely. Or perhaps Alasdair will suddenly notice she exists."

"Alasdair?" Maxime frowned inquiringly. "Cristobel's brother?"

"Yes. Laura's been in love with him since she was twelve. And according to Flora, she still is."

Maxime drew his brows together in an amused frown.

"I know it sounds ridiculous," Katharine went on. "I thought so too, four years ago when Flora first told me about it. But now, looking back, I think it *is* possible to feel so deeply—even at that age."

She leaned back pensively in her chair. "Flora thinks Laura is someone who will suffer greatly in life. More than most people. Laura feels things so intensely. She's like a tightly strung violin. Her acute shyness used to irritate me. But now . . . I understand."

She paused, idly crumbling a piece of bread.

"Laura's a brilliant pianist. I wouldn't be at all surprised if one day she makes a name for herself internationally. I suppose the price one has to pay for such exceptional talent is to have nerves that jangle just below the surface."

She smiled mischievously across at her husband. "Not a problem any of our children are likely to suffer from."

"Perhaps she'll marry Alasdair and live happily ever after," Maxime suggested.

"Perhaps," Katharine agreed. "But I'm not sure Laura *could* live happily ever after, *whoever* she married. Every one of life's pinpricks, which most of us ignore, is like a knife turning in a wound for her."

She looked across at Maxime, sadness and compassion mingling in her tawny eyes. "Losing her mother at a difficult age and having a father who seems to show little interest in her hasn't helped."

She thoughtfully folded her napkin and replaced it in its ring.

"I think, Maxime," she sighed, "that Laura is going to need a lot of prayer over the next few months, perhaps even the next few years, to keep her from going under. Flora and I agreed that until she meets Jesus and gives the burden of her fragile sensitivity to him, she will always carry it within her—and be helpless, even collapse, in the face of suffering."

Two

A sudden jolt, followed by the hiss of steam and raucous shouts as heavy metal wheels clattered over concrete broke into Laura's dream. The gentle swaying and rhythmic clackety-clack had stopped. Drifting back to consciousness through veils of sleep, she heard doors slamming and footsteps hurrying along the corridor.

She leaned on one elbow and twitched a corner of the blind, letting a shaft of bright early morning sunlight stream in through the window.

"It's Edinburgh," Cristobel slurred from the bunk below. "No need to panic. We've bags of time."

Pulling the bedclothes over her ears, Cristobel immediately fell back asleep.

Laura, now wide awake, dropped the blind in place and lay back on the hard pillow. She knew every corner of the great echoing Waverley Station. She could picture the frenzied activity as the night train from London stood panting for a few minutes. It was almost two years since she had last accompanied Cristobel to Annanbrae. And the excitement mounting inside her since Cristobel had arrived from Switzerland yesterday afternoon now threatened to burst like an overflowing dam. Sleep was out of the question.

Turning on her side, she watched the shadows flickering on the opposite wall. The train shunted. Footsteps raced along the platform. Doors were hastily slammed, and with a hiss and a snort, they were off again. Laura sighed. But it was a sigh of pure joy laced with tingling excitement. She was going to see Alasdair again. Reveling in anticipation, she drifted into a fitful doze.

"Perth in fifteen minutes," announced the attendant rapping on the door of their compartment as he passed along the corridor.

"Cristobel?" Laura called anxiously.

"I heard." Cristobel yawned.

"Do you think one of your brothers might come to meet us?" Laura asked hesitantly, gingerly negotiating the steep ladder from her bunk.

"Not a hope," Cristobel answered, wriggling into her clothes. "At this hour of the morning the lazy devils will be in bed. I expect Father will send Donald."

She stepped out into the corridor and leaned against the window watching the heather-covered mountains sloping away in the distance.

"It's good to be home again," she mused as Laura joined her.

Laura didn't reply. She envied Cristobel her roots and her family. And she began to wonder about the tenuous links that held herself to her one remaining parent.

Henry Denning had always been remote. Laura brushed a hand across her eyes to prevent the tears, stinging behind her eyelids, from spilling over. Her mind turned to Cristobel's father. Robert Hamilton was so different, so very much a presence in his home and in both their lives.

Cristobel lurched against her as the train rounded a bend.

"Do you remember that first day at Rosemead?" Laura reflected, as they staggered to regain their balance.

"*Do* I!" Cristobel grimaced. "Those archaic mistresses and bossy prefects. I wondered what on earth I'd been dumped into."

"Me too," Laura mused. "I don't think I'd have survived if I hadn't met you."

Cristobel slipped her arm through her friend's.

Meeting Cristobel on that first day when they were both new girls had forged a friendship that, when she was invited to

Cristobel's home the following summer, had become an anchor for Laura. She had returned every year and slowly recaptured that feeling of security she had lost the day her mother died. Cristobel's family had become her family and Annanbrae her home. And Cristobel's four brothers her brothers. All except Alasdair. Her feelings for him had been different.

Alasdair had danced with her at her first ball when she was sixteen. That evening at Annanbrae had been engraved on her memory ever since.

"You've got freckles on your nose," he'd teased.

And she had felt mortified.

Now she was going to see him again, and she wondered what her reaction would be. The train snaked around a corner and began to slow down.

"Here we are," Cristobel announced, leaning out the window and waving frantically.

Laura's heart tripped and missed a beat. Could it be Alasdair on the platform waiting for them?

But it was only Donald. He greeted them as they stepped down.

"Has everyone arrived?" Laura asked diffidently.

"Mr. Ninian and Capt. Fraser will be arriving tomorrow, and Mr. Alasdair is expected this evening," Donald replied.

"I'll bet Sandy's there," Cristobel groaned. "How are we going to stand him? Has he improved, Donald?"

"He's much taller," Donald hedged.

"Oh, you know what I mean," Cristobel spluttered. "Is he still as *ghastly?*"

"He's certainly full of life," Donald replied evasively.

"I hope he hasn't brought an appalling friend with him."

"No, Miss Cristobel, not this time." Donald smiled.

As they drove in through the open wrought-iron gates and swept up the tree-lined drive, Sandy, brandishing a catapult, leaped out of a bush and flung himself at the car.

"Sandy!" Cristobel shrieked as Donald swerved.

Sandy grimaced at her through the window before leaping back into the bushes.

"I don't think I can stand it," Cristobel wailed. "Not for a whole week."

"If you'd ever spent your holidays in Oxford with my father," Laura remarked drily, "you'd appreciate Sandy. At least with him around you know you're still alive."

"Can't imagine *anyone* appreciating Sandy," Cristobel replied, as the car drew up in front of the house.

She jumped out and ran through the open door into the hall's dim interior.

"Dogs," she called. "I'm home."

There was a scuffle and a slither of feet as three black labradors, snoozing on the half-landing, hurtled down the wide oak stairs, barking and whining for joy.

Laura, who had never owned a pet, was mystified by the Hamilton family's passion for their dogs.

Cristobel dropped to her knees and hugged the three excited beasts as they clawed at her hair and licked her face, howling with delight.

"Where's Sara?" she inquired, looking up.

At the sound of her name, a very old dog limped painfully down the stairs. Cristobel sat on the bottom stair cradling the matriarch's head in her arms.

A growl sounded from a small turret at the side of the front door, and an elderly white West Highland terrier waddled out. He growled again as Cristobel turned to pat him.

At that moment a shadow, moving very slowly, glided across the landing, and a lined, parchment-colored face framed with white hair peered over the bannister. Cristobel looked up and, releasing Sara, suddenly rushed up the stairs.

"Morag!" she cried, hugging the frail figure.

The diminutive woman smiled, sending wrinkles swarming across her face, as her eyes rested on Cristobel.

Laura walked slowly up the stairs. "Hallo, Morag." She smiled diffidently.

The old woman turned and offered her withered cheek.

As Laura bent and brushed her lips across its cool, dry surface, she felt once again that apprehension in Morag's presence.

Morag was like the frowning portraits lining the walls of Annanbrae, arrested in time. She had been nanny not only to the Hamilton children but to their mother before. No one knew or dared to ask her age. But she was now very old and had become woven into the fabric of Annanbrae, gliding along the galleries, silently watching.

"Laura, Cristobel, you've arrived!"

Lady Flora, a large, flat basket brimming with fresh-cut flowers over her arm, walked in from the garden.

The two girls leaned over the bannister and then ran down into the hall.

"Darlings," she cried warmly, putting the basket on a dark oak table and embracing them warmly. "Let me look at you both."

"Isn't breakfast ready?" Sandy bellowed, skidding into the hall. "I'm starving."

"You smell *disgusting*. I'll bet you haven't washed since you arrived," Cristobel accused.

"There's talk of a drought," Sandy replied smugly.

Cristobel caught his arm and pinned it behind her young brother's back as he attempted to brush past her and into the dining room. But he wriggled free and ran up the stairs, Cristobel and the dogs in hot pursuit.

"They don't change, do they?" Lady Flora smiled, bending to pick up the West Highland terrier as he ambled past.

"I love it," Laura answered dreamily.

She turned impulsively to her hostess. "You don't know what it means to me, coming here. I feel part of a family."

"We consider you as part of the family," Lady Flora said gently.

Laura's blue eyes filled with tears. She turned and fled up the stairs.

Would she one day really be part of this family? she asked herself. And Alasdair's face embedded itself in her mind.

Three

The following day dawned with a perfect blue sky hanging low over the mist-capped mountains. Laura woke in her turret room next to Cristobel's and, slipping out of bed, walked over and knelt on the cushioned window seat. Leaning her elbows on the wide sill, she wondered whether Cristobel was awake. But nothing stirred. Propping her chin in her palm, she looked along the line of mullioned windows. Behind one of them Alasdair was sleeping.

Abruptly the stillness was shattered by Sandy's high-pitched laugh, followed by shrieks and dire threats from the kitchen. Sandy darted round the corner of the house, a plate of ice cream in one hand and a large piece of cake in the other. Looking over his shoulder, he blew kisses to the invisible cook. Laura smiled, imagining cook's angry face. The woman looked like Mrs. Noah—bright red cheeks, stiff black hair plastered on her head, teeth like tombstones, and a moustache.

"Master Sandy," the cook shrieked, "I'll no' ha' ye comin' into ma kitchen an' helping yerself. Ice cream's no good fer a body at this hour o' day."

"It's all right, Cookie," he shouted back. "I've got a cast-iron stomach."

"Och, ye'll be the death o' me," the cook retorted as the kitchen window slammed shut.

But Cook's tone had softened. No one could resist Sandy for long. Laura watched as he flopped into a wicker chair, planted his feet on the table, and began stuffing enormous amounts of chocolate ice cream and cake into his mouth.

The door leading onto the terrace opened, and Alasdair strode through. Picking Sandy up by the scruff of his neck, he yanked him to his feet, sending the plate crashing to the ground.

"Now look what you've done," Sandy howled.

"Get that mess cleared up immediately. Then go and apologize to Cook, you little blighter," Alasdair barked, giving his unfortunate young brother a shake.

Sandy howled even louder.

"And you can shut that row," Alasdair concluded.

Sandy escaped and leaped down the terrace steps.

"Sandy," Alasdair menaced.

Leaping after the boy, Alasdair grabbed him and frog-marched him to the kitchen.

Laura's heart was thumping. Getting up, she walked across to the mirror and carefully studied her reflection. The freckles were gone. The image that gazed back at her was of a slight blonde girl with deep blue eyes, fair skin, and a soft upward-curving mouth. She was pinching her cheeks to give them more color when the breakfast gong sent thundering blows echoing round the house.

Opening her door, she bumped into Cristobel.

"Did you hear that fearful row between Sandy and Alasdair?" Laura asked.

"Didn't hear a thing." Cristobel yawned. "But that's nothing new. Everyone's always having a row with Sandy. He's so obnoxious."

Lady Flora glanced up from her place at the end of the table and smiled vaguely when Laura and Cristobel entered the dining room. Robert was at the sideboard helping himself to smoked haddock.

"Come along," he said jovially. "Big day ahead."

He stopped and peered at them, his bushy eyebrows bristling. "You're not on a diet, I hope."

Cristobel rushed across and kissed him, and his ginger moustache quivered with pleasure.

"Of course we are, Father," she teased. "We only ever touch black coffee in the morning."

"I'll have your share then," Sandy remarked, already back at the sideboard for a second helping.

"No, Father," Cristobel laughed. "Just teasing you. Here, Sandy, leave something for the rest of us."

"The rest of us have almost finished." The newspaper rustled as Graeme's voice came from behind it.

Laura glanced surreptitiously around the table. Alasdair's napkin in its silver holder lay unopened beside his plate. A wave of disappointment swept over her.

"There's an invitation here from the McFaddens," Lady Flora announced, sorting through her letters. "They are having a ball for Catriona on the 21st of July."

She looked at Laura and Cristobel. "Would you like to go?"

"Lindsay will be in Germany," Cristobel answered.

"Never mind," Lady Flora replied. "Graeme can take you, and Alasdair can escort Laura."

Laura choked on her toast.

Graeme groaned. "I thought now that we'd palmed her off on Lindsay, we'd no longer have to cart little sister around."

"PIG!" Cristobel spat across the table, her gray eyes dancing with laughter.

"Why must you children always bicker?" Lady Flora remarked absently. "Sandy, dear, don't gulp."

She smiled across at her daughter. "There's a card here from your godmother, Cristobel. She's in Boston."

"Katharine?" Laura queried. "Isn't she coming for the ball?"

"No," Cristobel grumbled. "She and Maxime had already made plans to go to America for Katharine's nephew's wedding."

Laura frowned. "I thought Katharine was an only child."

"She is," Cristobel explained. "It's her first husband's nephew—Ashley's. Katharine and Maxime are accompanying her Aunt Lavinia and Canon Paget, Ashley's father. Poor Mr. Paget—he lost both his sons in the war. Guy, the elder one, was killed at Dunkirk. Guy's wife was American, and after the war she went back to Boston with her two little boys. It's Philip, her elder son, who got married this month."

"I see," Laura mused, slightly confused by Cristobel's woolly explanation.

"But Katharine and Maxime will be here for my wedding in September." Cristobel dimpled. "And Elisabeth, their daughter—she's two and a half and absolutely gorgeous—will be my youngest bridesmaid."

Lady Flora gathered her pile of letters together. "Such a busy day," she said dreamily, getting up from the table. "I must go and see Cook about lunch. Malcolm is sure to be already in the kitchen fussing about flowers and vegetables."

She smiled vaguely around the table at them all. "We'll talk about the McFadden ball later. By the way, who's here for lunch?"

Her voice was drowned out by a commotion in the hall. It sounded as if a male choir had arrived, accompanied by a pack of howling beagles.

"No one," a voice roared.

The dining room door crashed open, and Hamish stormed in. Hamish, who lived in a house on the other side of the lake, was a bachelor, a caricature of his elder brother Robert. Hamish was almost as tall as Robert, six-foot-five, and twice as broad. His nose had been broken countless times during unofficial boxing bouts and had spread over his face in every direction, giving him a froglike look of permanent surprise. Wearing an ancient pair of greenish tweed plus-fours and a brass helmet, and for no obvious reason carrying an axe, he now stood like Boadicea, his vast form entirely blocking the dining room doorway.

"Hallo, Hamish dear," Flora said brightly. "Have you been practicing?"

"Rehearsing," he corrected sternly.

Hamish was in charge of the local fire brigade, which rehearsed with great pomp and much shrieking and ringing of bells every Saturday morning.

"Down, Archie, down," he hollered, brandishing his axe at his black and white spaniel, who was leaping and howling, turning somersaults around his master.

24

"I've come to invite you all to lunch," he announced.

Producing a large red-spotted handkerchief from his over-flowing pockets, he proceeded to blow his nose with a series of explosive honks.

Cristobel rushed from the table and hugged him around his vast waist. "Lovely, Uncle Hamish," she cried delightedly.

Graeme slowly lowered his newspaper. "It's not one of your picnics, is it?" he inquired suspiciously.

Hamish was addicted to picnics, but for reasons known only to himself, he never organized them between April and October.

"Picnic!" he spluttered, his blue eyes snapping. "Most certainly not!" He glared out the window at the brilliant June sunshine. "Not the weather," he muttered. "Most unsuitable. Now then, how many of you? Jeannie will want to know."

"Well," Flora replied, "I don't think I'd better come. Cook is sure to have one of her fits if I do. Robert?"

"I'll stay with you, my dear," he answered. "You might need some help."

"Laura, Cristobel, Graeme, Sandy, Alasdair," Flora began ticking Hamish's guests off on her fingers. She looked up. "Where *is* Alasdair? He hasn't come down to breakfast."

"I saw him earlier on," Sandy remarked casually. "He was going toward the wood carrying a gun. I think he went to commit suicide."

"He drove over to the Farquharsons," Robert broke in, glancing sternly at Sandy. "I met him as I was coming in for breakfast. Said he wouldn't be here for lunch."

"I expect he's gone to see Colin," his wife remarked.

"To see Fiona more likely," Graeme put in. "Colin's just a smoke screen."

Laura's heart began to thump against her ribs.

"Oh, do you think so?" Lady Flora replied. "How nice."

"So that makes how many?" Hamish roared.

"Four." Flora smiled. "It *is* kind of you, Hamish."

"Nonsense," he said gruffly.

He glared back at them all, his hand on the doorknob. "That young fella o' yours arrived?" he growled at Cristobel.

"Not yet, Nunkie darling," she replied.

"Very decent sort," Hamish grunted. "I like him. Knew his grandfather well. We were at school together."

Hamish cleared his throat loudly and then delved into his voluminous pockets. "Thought this might come in useful," he muttered. His great fist shot out and pushed something into his niece's hand.

Cristobel cried out in delight as she snapped open the faded blue velvet box and held up a heavy gold locket. Slipping the clasp, she caught her breath at the miniature of a young woman lying on her palm, the delicate oval face surrounded by pearls intertwined with locks of dark brown hair.

"Uncle *Hamish*," she whispered, gazing up at him, her deep gray eyes misty.

Looking as though he were trying hard not to burst a blood vessel, Hamish noisily cleared his throat again. "Belonged to your great-grandmother," he muttered. "Dunno how I came to have it."

"You know perfectly well how you came to have it," Lady Flora said softly, coming to her daughter's side. "That locket means a great deal to you. Your grandfather wore it on his watch chain for most of his life. When he died, your grandmother had it made into a pendant and gave it to you for your future wife."

Hamish, now puce in the face, positively squirmed with embarrassment as his niece reached up on tiptoe and kissed his perspiring cheek.

"Yes, well," he growled, glaring furiously at everybody, "not much hope of that now. Cristobel might as well have it. Archie," he roared, desperate to escape, "Archie, you dratted hound, where are you?"

There was a scuffle, and Archie appeared from under the table where Sandy had been feeding him bacon rinds.

"Now he'll be thirsty on the walk back," Hamish hollered, his protruding eyes shooting daggers at Sandy. Stomping angrily over to the table, Hamish grabbed a large jug of milk and poured the contents onto the parquet floor.

"There, boy," he said, pointing to the opaque puddle rapidly spreading in all directions.

No one batted an eyelid. Robert did exactly the same thing each evening for his dogs with the milk and biscuits left behind a screen in the drawing room after dinner. Laura never ceased to be astonished every time she saw this extraordinary gesture, which everyone else appeared to consider perfectly normal.

Archie lapped noisily, chasing the milk as it spread across the floor until every trace was gone. Then, leaping and yapping, he waltzed to the door in a grotesque ballet with his master.

"Quarter to one then," Hamish bellowed, turning to glower at them in the doorway. "Don't be late."

Lady Flora had already drifted into the hall, murmuring about lists and vegetables and refreshments for the band.

"Mother," Graeme called after her, "is Morag coming downstairs this evening?"

His mother turned with a startled look on her face, as if her eldest son had just announced that he intended to go and live on a raft in the middle of the North Sea.

"Oh no, dear," she said earnestly, collecting her thoughts with an effort. "Morag's very frail now. The noise would be too much for her."

"Then can you lock her up somewhere?" Graeme went on. "Otherwise she'll be roaming around the galleries like Banquo's ghost, terrifying all the guests."

His mother opened her mouth to protest, but Graeme forestalled her. "Or poor old Morag might get killed in the crush. Especially if some of the young bloods mistake her for the Phantom of Annanbrae and chase her into a turret."

"Graeme," Lady Flora wailed, "I *do* wish you wouldn't discuss our ghost in front of the servants. You *know* how it upsets them. Now where was I? Oh yes, refreshments for the band."

And she wafted off with her lists through the green baize door leading to the kitchen.

Four

L et's go and sit in the old schoolroom," Cristobel suggested as she and Laura left the dining room. "It's always full of sunshine in the morning."

She put her arm briefly around Laura's waist and hugged her. "I'm so happy," she confided as they wandered along one of the many galleries that meandered through the old house. "And I'm so pleased you're here to share it."

Laura looked at her friend and smiled.

"I just wish you had someone," Cristobel brooded, pushing open the schoolroom door and flopping down in an armchair.

Laura walked across and looked out the window. "My turn will come, I suppose."

"But I want it to be someone I know," Cristobel insisted. "I'd hate for us to lose touch. We've been friends for so long."

"We won't," Laura reassured her.

And she hoped it was true.

"Perhaps there's someone invited tonight who is just right for you," Cristobel speculated, swinging her slim legs over the arm of the sagging chair. "Let me see now . . . there's the Buchanans, the Chisholms, the Scott-Campbells. No, they're none of them any good."

"Oh, Cristobel, stop it," Laura interrupted irritably.

Cristobel's wide gray eyes opened even wider.

"I'm sorry," Laura apologized, turning around. "But you can't just organize marriages like that."

"No, I suppose not," Cristobel sighed. "But if you did meet someone, perhaps we could have a double wedding."

"Perhaps you can have a double wedding anyway," Laura answered tightly.

Cristobel, busy checking eligible bachelors off on her fingers, looked up in surprise.

"From what Graeme said at breakfast, it seems that Alasdair is pretty involved with the Farquharson girl." Laura paused, breathing deeply. "He must be to have rushed off to see her without even having breakfast," she ended bitterly.

"Maybe," her friend replied vaguely. "It would be fun if you married one of my brothers. Then you'd be my sister."

She looked up, smiling brightly at the idea. Then she shrugged her shoulders. "But not a hope. They're all so horrible."

In spite of the knot that had tied itself inside her stomach, Laura couldn't help laughing. "You don't mean that!"

"I *do*," Cristobel replied airily. "They're all right. But not good enough for you."

She tilted her head on one side. "I can hear hammering," she shrieked delightedly, leaping up and grabbing Laura's hand. "Let's go and see what's happening."

They arrived, breathless, in the sunlit drawing room just as Lady Flora put her head around the door. "Has anybody seen Sandy?" she asked, stooping to pick up Laird who was whining and pawing at her feet.

"The last time I saw him he was at the end of the long gallery kicking a football against the wall in between the portraits of the Marquess of Bute and Great-uncle Willie," Graeme remarked matter of factly, still deep in his newspaper.

Lady Flora sat down abruptly on the piano stool, absently stroking her pet. She looked bewilderedly across at Laura and Cristobel, who were rolling on the sofa with laughter.

"There are times," she sighed, shaking her head sadly, "when I simply don't understand you children."

And with Laird still wriggling in her arms, she went back to wandering through the house reciting her lists.

The two girls crossed the lawns and entered the wood, sauntering around the lake shining in the morning sunlight. Laura breathed deeply. As she gazed up at the mountains, a feeling of pure joy surged through her. Suddenly from somewhere deep in the hidden recesses of her subconscious mind, words long buried floated into her mind. She stopped abruptly.

Cristobel looked around.

"The mountains," Laura said breathlessly. "They're so beautiful. Seeing them reminded me of some verses we had to learn by heart at school."

She sat down on the grass at the side of the lake, her eyes fixed into the distance. "'I will lift up mine eyes unto the hills, from whence cometh my help,'" she recited. "Do you remember?"

Cristobel nodded and flopped down beside her.

"Old Glory in divinity lessons," she remarked. "Wasn't she a sight?"

Laura smiled, her eyes still riveted on the distant mountains.

"She always reminded me of a worn-out hymnbook," Cristobel giggled.

Laura giggled too.

"Weren't her lessons boring?" Cristobel went on. "She made everything sound as if it had been doused in vinegar."

"But those words are beautiful," Laura murmured. "And so appropriate this morning."

"I suppose so," Cristobel remarked. "But Old Glory really put me off Christianity. Didn't you feel the same?"

"I don't know," Laura mused, fiddling with a clover leaf.

"If being a Christian means wearing dusty, old black skirts and a porkpie hat skewered with a pin," Cristobel announced, lying back and closing her eyes against the warm rays of the sun, "I'd rather be a heathen."

Laura looked at her friend reflectively. "I don't think anyone with Lady Flora for a mother could ever be a heathen," she said quietly. "To me she epitomizes everything a Christian should be."

"What do you mean?" Cristobel inquired, a frown creasing her brow. "Mother doesn't go around handing out texts or spouting verses from the Bible. She doesn't even expect us to go to church with her anymore."

"No," Laura replied. "She allows you to be yourselves and doesn't try to force you into her way of thinking."

"Oh, Mother lives in another world," Cristobel declared.

"That's just it," Laura went on. "A world I've often thought I'd like to explore, but I've never found the way. Your mother seems to have the key." She sighed. "I wish I could explain it."

"So do I," Cristobel remarked nonchalantly. "Maybe Mother's got this key you're looking for. But she's certainly not Old Glory's idea of a Christian."

An ear-splitting shriek startled them, and they saw Sandy shoot out of the wood, followed at a more leisurely pace by Graeme. It was obvious they had been having a row.

"Wish I were an only child," Sandy grumbled, braking to a halt.

"So do we," Graeme cut in, coming up behind.

"Oh, come on, Sandy," Cristobel laughed. "Cheer up. Jeannie's bound to have cooked all your favorite dishes. For some obscure reason she likes you, though I can't think why."

"There you go again," Sandy wailed. "Everybody's at me." With an agonized howl he raced around the lake and out of sight.

"I can understand Sandy in a way," Laura put in quietly, getting to her feet.

"You always were his champion," Cristobel interrupted. "Accompanying him on the piano while he pierced our eardrums with that ghastly trumpet."

"It wasn't ghastly," Laura protested. "He plays rather well and . . . I enjoy accompanying him. Perhaps later on he'll follow in my footsteps and study music full time."

Both brother and sister looked at her in amazement.

"It's not always much fun being the youngest," Laura continued. "You're bait for everyone."

"Bait?" Graeme hooted. "Mother dotes on him."

"And you all take it out on him because of it," Laura replied. "Perhaps he wishes she *didn't* dote on him so much."

"Oh, Sandy's unique." Cristobel grinned, brushing strands of grass from her frock as she scrambled to her feet. "I'm going to run ahead and say hallo to Jeannie."

Graeme held out his hand to help Laura to her feet, giving her one of his slow, rare smiles.

Falling into step beside her, he walked with her through the shining green mist hanging over the clustered trees leading to Hamish's house.

Hamish lived in Findlay's Fortress, a jumble of old gray stones quite unlike anything Laura had ever seen before. It had been built a few centuries earlier by an eccentric Hamilton ancestor who had modeled it on the Norman castle William the Conqueror, his hero, had abandoned when he crossed the Channel to subdue the English.

When Findlay Hamilton's wife had presented him with a fifth daughter, he had retired to his fortress in a fury and remained there for the rest of his life—after installing twin cannons on either side of the massive front door to discourage visits from his female relatives. Since then the second son had always inherited the place, though few of them had actually lived in it until Hamish retired from the army and took up residence.

From the outside it resembled a fortress in a fairy tale—inhabited by giants and ogres and wicked witches spinning devilish charms and brewing evil potions. Inside it was chaos. No two rooms seemed to be on the same level, and endless stairs meandered up and down without appearing to have any clear idea of where they were meant to go. If countless stories told about the Fort, as it had become known, were to be believed, skeletons clanked in cupboards the minute the sun set.

Although under Flora's gentle urging some improvements

had been made, basically it hadn't changed over the centuries. It was just as drafty and uncomfortable, even menacing, with the cannons rusting in situ, as the 1066 fortress on which it had been modeled. Getting through to the Fort on the telephone was more difficult than having a direct line installed to the Dalai Lama.

Over this confusion Jeannie, Hamish's housekeeper, reigned supreme. She looked a little like an understanding goat, with her boot-button eyes and a tuft of whiskers bristling on her chin. Oblivious to anything that might be happening in the world outside, she appeared to spend her days boiling dusters. She and Hamish lived a strange, disconnected existence inside the Fort's massive walls, yelling at each other all winter in an attempt to make themselves heard above the howling gales that rattled under every door and window.

But on that June morning when Graeme and Laura approached it, the old stones were mellowed by the shimmering light radiating from a transparently blue buttermilk sky. The windows winked a welcome in the sun's flashing rays, and a gentle cooing of doves drifted on the still air.

Graeme pushed open the immense studded door, and they entered the lofty dark hall. It was crammed with stags' heads, trophies of all kinds, bits of armor, a selection of assegais and blowpipes, dusty family portraits, and faded prints of faithful spaniels panting through the rye with glassy-eyed hares dangling from their jaws. The floor sloped precariously, giving the impression that the furniture was about to collapse.

From Hamish's study came the crackle of his prewar wireless set, tuned to full blast. It had just finished wheezing out its lunchtime entertainment of massacres, bombs, riots, tribal wars, and financial disasters. As Laura and Graeme entered, a chirpy voice announced that tomorrow morning the temperature would be minus ten in Stornaway and the rest of the country blanketed in thick fog by noon.

Ensconced in a sagging leather armchair, Hamish puffed away at his pipe. The study looked like the headquarters of the War Graves Commission with turbaned, battle-scarred heroes scowling down from every available space on the walls. The room was so cluttered that all furniture had disappeared from view. Hamish rose from amid a toppling pile of old newspapers, a broad smile on his face, his extraordinary nose and sandy-colored moustache twitching in unison as he greeted them. Laura noticed that he had discarded his ancient tweed jacket for an even more decrepit shapeless woollen cardigan of vast proportions, the corners of which drooped almost to his knees.

"Down, Archie, down," he roared, as the dog yapped excitedly, leaping frantically in an attempt to catch one of the corners of the cardigan and drag it even further down.

Hamish fished in his waistcoat pocket and pulled out a large gold hunting watch. "Jeannie's late sounding the gong," he muttered irritably.

"That's Cristobel's fault," Graeme informed him, as his sister appeared. "She went on ahead to receive her congratulations."

"Oh, I see," Hamish grunted. "Then I'd better sound it myself."

He ambled across the hall and struck three thunderous death blows at an ancient Burmese gong hanging on the wall.

Laura didn't really see the point of sounding the gong since they were all there. As the echoing booms trembled in the distance, Sandy surfaced, and, with Hamish leading the way, they trooped across the hall.

The dining room smelled of mutton. Laura doubted whether Jeannie, who had served as cook-housekeeper to Hamish for as long as anyone could remember, ever opened a window. The immensely long table, at the head of which Hamish usually sat in solitary state, was overshadowed by an enormous sideboard resembling a Buddhist temple. It groaned with silver salvers, decanters, and an assortment of bottles all jostling for space. The walls were covered in what must once have been red brocade. But time, dampness, and cigar smoke had weathered them to a color somewhere between slime and mold.

Hamish enjoyed his food and ate voraciously, not wasting time in small talk. He totally ignored Sandy's appalling table manners, adopted in the hope of provoking one of his uncle's choleric outbursts.

At one point during the meal a flock of geese nosed their way through a long window that Graeme had surreptitiously opened. Flapping their way to the floor, they honked madly before lining up in formation and waddling solemnly around the table to the accompaniment of shoos from Cristobel and frantic napkin-waving from Sandy, who was hugely enjoying the parade. Hamish didn't appear to notice anything amiss until the weird procession arrived back at its point of departure. Looking up, he nodded toward the window.

"Let 'em out, Graeme—there's a good fellow," he remarked in a tone implying that this was a normal occurrence.

Graeme rose from the table and thrust up the window sash. With a final flapping and squawking, the geese made their exit. As they disappeared, Laura felt that she wouldn't have been in the least surprised had Hamish suddenly leaped up and balanced on his head in the middle of the table.

But the unexpected interlude must have triggered something in Hamish's brain. Looking up, he glared at Cristobel. "D'you know which band your mother's engaged for this evenin'?" he growled, chomping on his roast beef.

"'Fraid not," Cristobel replied.

"Not one of those Sassenach groups, I hope," he snorted.

They all stared at him in astonishment.

"Uncle *Hamish*," Cristobel spluttered. "I didn't know you felt like that about the English."

"I don't," he muttered. "Nice chaps most of 'em. But don't care for their music. Had one of their newfangled bands at the Farquharson girl's comin'-out ball last month. Terrible show, terrible."

Even Sandy stopped eating and stared at him.

"Dunno what came over 'em," Hamish mumbled on. "Though old Farquharson always was a queer sort of fella. We were at school together."

Hamish appeared to have been at school with everybody's grandfather and to have missed out on the intervening generation. And their worth had obviously been assessed at that time and not revised since.

"Must've passed his odd ideas on to his son," he grumbled. "All that heathen dancin'."

Hamish glared around the table and threw a lump of gristle to Archie.

"Wouldn't be surprised if there wasn't something between Alasdair and Fiona Farquharson," he spluttered. "Never left her side all evenin'. Jiggin' around with her in a most improper manner."

Laura looked down at her plate, desperately hoping that no one would notice the slow blush she could feel creeping up her neck. She suddenly felt hollow.

"So it was true what you said this morning about Alasdair and Fiona?" Cristobel gaped incredulously, turning to Graeme.

"Looks like it," he replied.

Hamish lifted his napkin and furiously scrubbed his moustache.

"Only hope we have the old dances this evenin'," he trumpeted, "not those modern things. Never saw anything like it. Women hoppin' one way, wavin' things—men hoppin' the other way, stampin'."

Sandy began twirling his napkin around his head, ignoring Graeme who was semaphoring across the table, ordering him to behave himself. But Sandy's antics were interrupted by the arrival of a wobbly pink blancmange. As it was ceremoniously placed before Hamish, he glared down at it and then gave it a poke with a spoon.

"Dunno what this is," he grunted. "Jeannie produces the most extraordinary puds these days."

He sniffed disgustedly. "All the fault of that pig!"

Four pairs of eyes swiveled toward him in surprise.

"The pig?" Cristobel repeated.

Hamish snorted.

"Her nephew, dratted fella, gave it to her. A throw-out from his last litter."

He glared ferociously around the table, as if his guests were responsible for the pig's arrival.

"Rickety looking thing. She keeps it in a basket by the kitchen fire. Most unhealthy."

"But what has a pig got to do with the pud?" Cristobel giggled.

Hamish raised his eyes mournfully, his haycock of a moustache drooping.

"Mind's no longer on her cookin'," he answered plaintively. "Spends her time singin' to the wretched thing."

An explosion of laughter from his guests rocked the table. Hamish stared at them uncomprehendingly.

"Can't think what you all find so amusin'," he growled. He gazed unhappily at the sagging blancmange. "Used to enjoy her puds." He held up a large spoon inquiringly. "Anybody want any?"

Nobody did. Not even Sandy.

"May as well ring for cheese," Hamish concluded, picking up a small Hindu cowbell and agitating it furiously.

The meal over, Hamish retired to his study, and Laura and Cristobel wandered into the garden. Flora called it the Shakespeare garden, probably because it looked as if nothing had been done to it since the time of the bard.

"Oh, bliss," Cristobel sighed, sinking down onto a curved stone bench covered with moss. "Perhaps when we get back, Lindsay will have arrived."

"What time do you expect him?"

"Around teatime, I think," Cristobel replied dreamily. "He's coming with Ninian."

She stretched her arms voluptuously as Laura sat down beside her. Once again that awful feeling of envy crept over Laura.

"I always thought Lindsay was a girl's name," Laura remarked in an attempt to fight it off.

"It's both," Cristobel answered, her eyes closed. "His first name is Ewen, but no one has ever called him by it. Lindsay is his mother's maiden name, and, as she's an only child, Lindsay, being the second son, will inherit Grandfather Lindsay's estate."

"Does that mean he'll leave the army?" Laura asked.

"I suppose so." Cristobel yawned. "And we'll go and live in the beautiful Highlands and have lots of children and live happily ever after." She laughed delightedly. "Isn't life *wonderful*?" she breathed.

Laura smiled but didn't reply.

"Let's go home," Cristobel cried, jumping up and dragging Laura to her feet.

"Already?" Laura frowned. "It's only a quarter to three."

"Never mind." Cristobel grinned. "I'm so excited I can't stay still."

When they entered the hall, Hamish was in the corridor leading to the gun room, energetically practicing golf shots into a large net strung across the entrance to the butler's pantry. His niece rushed perilously into his line of fire and flung herself at him, causing the ball to catapult into the glass eye of a stag's head staring from the opposite wall.

"Darling Uncle," she cried, "it was a lovely, lovely lunch, but you will excuse us if we're awfully rude and rush off. Laura and I must look our best for this evening, and it will take hours and hours."

"Of course, of course," he muttered. "Baths in asses' milk and all that, I suppose." Hamish snorted in delight at his own joke. "I'll drive you back."

"No," Cristobel protested. "We'll walk."

"Wouldn't dream of it," he snorted. "I insist. Where're the other two?"

"Don't worry about us," Graeme's voice came out of the depths of an armchair in the drawing room. "We'll walk back later. I want to keep Sandy out of the way as long as possible. Mother's got enough to do without having to wonder what he's up to. And, with any luck, he might exhaust himself and fall into a coma by this evening."

"Oh," blurted Hamish, startled, "where is Sandy?"

"Best not to ask," Graeme replied.

Hamish grunted and handed his golf club to Jeannie, who appeared to have been keeping score. Then, walking over to a heavy brass hat stand to which caps, deerstalkers, bowlers, and straw boaters clung for dear life, he carefully selected a brightly colored tam-o'-shanter perched like a triumphant poppy in their midst. Anchoring it firmly on his head, he ushered them through the front door.

Settling the two girls on the backseat of his car, Hamish insisted on smothering them in a mohair rug despite the brilliant sunshine. Then, having carefully tucked it around them as if they were made of Bohemian glass, he eased his vast frame into the driving seat and started the engine with an explosion that might have shattered the Eiffel Tower.

Laura and Cristobel stifled their giggles as the car leaped from the front door with a series of epileptic jerks, only to collapse with a shattering bang in the middle of the drive.

Hamish glared angrily through the windscreen. Grabbing a shooting stick from under his seat, he stamped around to the front of the car, jerked open the bonnet, and peered intently at the engine. Then giving it a tremendous blow with the shooting stick, he slammed down the bonnet and returned to his seat. With an appalling smell of burning and clouds of dust, the car roared into action.

Hearing the series of explosions, Sandy thrust his tousled red head through the kitchen window and then galloped after the car, yelling frantically for them to stop. Hamish took not the slightest notice. Sweeping majestically on, he deposited the two girls, with a loud screeching of brakes, at Annanbrae.

"Won't come in," he grunted, yanking open the door for them. "Give my regards to young Fraser."

And with a great slamming of doors and another volcanic explosion, the car roared back down the drive.

Laura and Cristobel sauntered into the silent hall.

Sounds of hammering and of furniture being heaved around came from the ballroom at the far end of the house. From downstairs Cook's wails and the scuffle of feet could be heard as everyone raced frantically around.

When the girls entered the drawing room, Lady Flora was kneeling in front of the huge fireplace carefully arranging an enormous sheaf of flowers in its wide black aperture. She looked up with that vague air of inquiry she always had, as if she wasn't quite sure where the two of them had come from or why they were there at all.

"Any news of Lindsay?" Cristobel asked.

"Yes, darling," her mother answered absently, tweaking some ferns into position. "He arrived about half an hour ago. But as you weren't here, he's gone to Killistrathan to see his parents."

"Oh no," Cristobel wailed, sinking into a chair.

"But Ninian's here," her mother went on brightly, as if that would dispel any disappointment her daughter might feel at just missing the fiancé she had not seen for almost three months. "I think he's in the old schoolroom. I've ordered tea to be sent up there. Everywhere else seems to be in a state of siege."

Laura looked around her. The drawing room did not appear to be in a state of siege. In fact, she thought she had never seen the gracious room looking lovelier—its long windows open to the dazzling sunshine, the turrets at either corner with their cushioned window seats bathed in the golden afternoon haze.

Leaving Lady Flora to her floral arrangements, the two girls wandered up to the schoolroom. Despite all she had heard during the day about Alasdair and Fiona Farquharson, Laura's heart was jumping like a frightened sparrow at the prospect of seeing him again.

But Alasdair did not appear for tea.

Toying with a scone, Laura's spirits slowly sank. As soon as she could, she made her excuses and escaped.

"I'd better come too," Cristobel sighed. "Perhaps if I try to sleep, the time will pass more quickly. You *will* call me the *minute* Lindsay arrives, won't you, Mother? Promise?"

"Of course, my darling," her mother soothed.

"I'll be in my room, so don't let anyone pretend they can't find me," she threatened.

"Try to sleep," Laura said as they parted outside her bedroom.

"I'll try," Cristobel grumbled, "but I don't think I'll be able to. Every time I hear a car in the drive, I'll hurtle down the stairs, just in *case* it's Lindsay."

She dimpled and, with a lighthearted laugh, skipped into her room and closed the door.

Five

To her surprise Laura fell asleep. She woke to see a shimmer of midges dancing across her open window in the evening haze. Slipping off the bed, she checked to see if the bathroom she and Cristobel shared was empty. A thin film of condensation over everything told her that her friend had already had her bath. Leaning over, she turned on the taps and stood watching the water gush out, her thoughts once again on Alasdair.

"You're being ridiculous," she told herself as she slid into the foamy depths. "It's almost three years since you last saw him. You're infatuated with an idea."

But as she swirled her toes around in the perfumed bubbles, she knew that it wasn't true. Alasdair's face had never ceased to haunt her.

"Laura," Cristobel called from the adjoining room, "are you nearly ready?"

"Won't be long," she called back, stretching for a fluffy white towel hanging on the wooden stand beside the huge, old-fashioned bath. "Has Lindsay arrived?"

"No," Cristobel groaned. "What *can* he be doing?" Her head appeared around the bathroom door. "You don't suppose he could have changed his mind?"

"Not a hope," Laura laughed.

From one of the turrets a clock chimed the hour.

"Gracious!" Laura exclaimed. "I'd better hurry."

The soft folds of the blue shantung dress slid over her slim, young body. Smoothing it into place across her hips, she had a strange feeling. She turned this way and that in front of the long mirror, reveling in the way the dress glided around her, flowing over her ankles in ripples like sparkling blue water.

As she sat at the dressing table, the apricot light of the early summer evening streamed in through the window and touched her long blonde hair with gold. There was a knock on the door, and, with a rustle of tulle, Cristobel stood framed in the doorway, a thousand diamonds shining in her eyes.

"Cristobel," Laura breathed, "you look *lovely*."

Cristobel walked slowly into the room, the flowing folds of white tulle whispering around her, emphasizing her tiny waist, her creamy shoulders rising from the froth of satin.

"What a gorgeous dress," Laura enthused. "Wherever did you get it?"

"In Paris," Cristobel answered, sitting down gingerly on the side of Laura's bed, the dress flowing around her, almost entirely covering the narrow surface. "When Mother came over to Switzerland to spend Easter with me, we rushed to Paris for a few days to meet Katharine, and she introduced us to the most wonderful fashion house. They were marvelous. Made it in record time, and Mother brought it back with her."

She stood up and twirled around, her head thrown back, her dark hair caught up in a soft fold at the back with a beautiful old pearl comb.

"I was going to wear the pearls Father gave me for my eighteenth birthday," she confided. "But I decided to wear the locket instead." She opened it and looked once again at the delicate miniature inside.

There was another knock, and Lady Flora entered. The color of her lilac silk dress suited her classical beauty, highlighting her silver-gray eyes and soft dark hair. At her throat she wore a fine web of gold filigree sprinkled with diamonds, like a cluster of dewdrops sparkling in the rain. Laura was struck, not for the first time, by the remarkable likeness between mother and daughter.

"I thought I'd find you here." She smiled. "Lindsay has just arrived. He's waiting for you in the library."

"Lindsay!"

Cristobel's hand flew to her mouth, and the diamonds shining in her beautiful gray eyes suddenly leaped and flashed.

"Oh, Mother," she gasped.

Picking up her skirt in both hands, she ran from the room.

"Be careful not to trip on the stairs," Lady Flora called after her.

But Cristobel had already turned the corner of the long corridor, oblivious of everything but Lindsay.

Lady Flora smiled across at Laura. "How lovely you look, my dear," she murmured, sitting down on the bed her daughter had just vacated.

Laura turned on her dressing table stool. "Has everyone arrived?" she ventured hesitantly.

"Everyone?"

"Well . . . all the family. Graeme and Sandy and . . . and Alasdair," she stumbled, her eyes glued to the carpet on which her small blue silk shoe was slowly describing concentric circles.

"Alasdair." Lady Flora frowned. "No, I don't think he has. At least I haven't *seen* him. Oh dear, how tiresome. I wonder what's keeping him?"

Laura had a very good idea what, or more especially who, was keeping him. She bit her lip in an attempt to hold back the tears.

"Do come down whenever you're ready," Lady Flora said gently, getting up.

"Thank you," Laura replied in a strangled voice without looking up. "I won't be long."

Lady Flora smiled her sweet, vague smile and drifted through the doorway, leaving the scent of summer roses lingering behind her.

At that moment Laura wished she hadn't come. All she wanted was to run out of the house and away from them all. From far below came the sounds of the band tuning up, followed by soft, lilting music and a man's voice throatily crooning, "They say that falling in love is wonderful. . . ." As the refrain drifted up, a great surge of loneliness swept over Laura, and she burst into tears.

"Oh, no," she choked, looking into the mirror as her weeping subsided. "Now I'll have to make up my face all over again."

When she finally appeared, most of the guests had already arrived, and the sound of voices, laughter, and the swish of feet dancing across the ballroom floor rose to meet her.

Cristobel waved her hand excitedly. "Laura," she cried, "where *have* you been? You were ready when I came down."

She broke off and gazed adoringly at Lindsay, standing tall and erect beside her in his kilt. "You remember Laura, don't you?"

"Yes, of course," he answered politely.

Laura wondered whether he really did.

"My adopted sister," Cristobel trilled. "We've got to find someone for her this evening."

"Cristobel!" Laura protested, feeling her cheeks turn crimson.

"Look," Cristobel squealed, holding out her hand at arm's length. A large diamond surrounded by tiny rubies glittered on the third finger of her left hand. "Isn't it *gorgeous?*"

Laura bent to examine the ring. "It's beautiful!"

"That's why Lindsay couldn't stay this afternoon," Cristobel confided. "He had to rush home to collect it."

She held out her arm again as the ring flashed on her finger.

"It belonged to Lindsay's great-grandmother," Cristobel babbled on, turning her hand this way and that to catch the light. "His grandfather arrived with it yesterday evening. You haven't met Grandfather Lindsay, have you? You must. He's a *darling.* Graeme's in the ballroom. He'll introduce you."

She abruptly broke off.

"Catriona, how lovely!" Cristobel exclaimed to a tall, young woman with flaming red hair, who swished into the hall holding up her long skirts.

Laura moved toward the ballroom as a car decanted more guests. The floor was already crowded with dancers, and she stood in the doorway admiring the scene. Ever since her first ball at Annanbrae when she was sixteen, Laura had been fascinated by the way the men in their colorful swinging kilts and velvet jackets, lace ruffles peeping at throat and wrists, far outshone the women.

She noticed Graeme leaning over the back of a delicate sofa, listening politely to Lady Entwhistle, whose large frame flowed across both seats. She looked like a beer barrel draped in yellowing lace, through whose folds a half-submerged diamond glittered helplessly, flashing SOS signals for survival every time its owner breathed. A glittering tiara was clamped down on hair the color of Dundee marmalade. In her plump, bejeweled fingers she agitated an ivory fan.

Graeme looked up and saw Laura. He waved and then offered Lady Entwhistle his arm.

Her small satin-shod feet, dangling in midair, tentatively felt for terra firma. Stretching up, she grasped Graeme's proffered arm and shuddered to the floor, her body wobbling like gelatin. With her tiara bobbing somewhere in the region of his waist, they began a lopsided two-step across the floor.

Graeme steered her toward Hamish, standing stiffly to attention in his vast kilt, glowering at everybody. Lowering his charge onto a more substantial piece of furniture, Graeme made entreating signs to his uncle above Lady Entwhistle's head—signs Hamish chose to ignore. As the sofa sagged beneath her weight, Lady Entwhistle glanced coquettishly up at Hamish and patted the seat beside her invitingly. But he stared stonily ahead, muttering to himself like an angry volcano. Hamish was so ill at ease at parties that he either shut up like an oyster or said all the wrong things, warbling like an aging prima donna in a series of high-pitched yelps.

Graeme escaped and hurried over to Laura. "There you are at last!" he exclaimed. "Now whom don't you know?"

Looking around her, Laura felt she didn't know anyone. In a sudden panic, she decided she didn't want to know anyone. She fiddled nervously with the little blue tasseled pencil dangling from her dance card.

"Oh, forgive me," Graeme said contritely. "What dances have you left free?"

Laura had every dance left free.

"May I have this waltz?" Graeme inquired as the band struck up again.

The dance over, he led her toward a group of young people and made the introductions. Then excusing himself, he returned to entertaining the many elderly ladies scattered on sofas around the room. Laura's ball card rapidly began to fill up.

And when a quick step was announced, one of the kilted young men led her onto the floor. Over her partner's shoulder, Laura caught sight of Alasdair, Fiona Farquharson in his arms. And suddenly she felt as if the ground had been snatched from under her feet.

At that moment Alasdair wheeled in her direction, his head thrown back laughing at something Fiona had said. And their eyes met. For a second Alasdair looked blankly at Laura. Then a spark of recognition shot into his hazel eyes, in which the green and gold lights were shining brightly this evening. He inclined his head in a slight bow.

"Splendid party, isn't it?" Laura's partner remarked conventionally, looking down at her.

"Yes," Laura replied weakly. "But would you mind if we sat out the rest of this dance?"

"Not at all," he replied. "Let me get you something to drink."

He took her elbow and led her to a sofa as the music stopped. From beneath her eyelashes she saw Alasdair escort Fiona back to their party. Excusing himself, he made his way across the ballroom toward her.

Oh, God, Laura pleaded, *please don't let him come.*

But Alasdair arrived at her side at the same time as her partner. Taking the glass from his hand, Alasdair handed it to Laura and then sat down beside her. "It is little freckle-nose, isn't it?"

Laura's partner discreetly disappeared as tears of humiliation smarted behind her thick lashes.

Alasdair put one finger under her chin and drew it upward until she was looking directly at him.

"They've gone," he announced, smiling his crooked, quizzical smile. He tilted his head to one side. "What a transformation," he said softly. "Cristobel's little school friend has turned into a beautiful princess!"

Laura averted her eyes, mortified by his teasing. The band broke into another waltz, and she heard the swish of a kilt as her next partner came to claim his dance. She half rose, but Alasdair gently pulled her back into her seat.

"Hang on a moment, Angus," he said to her hovering partner.

Removing her ball card from her gloved hand, he began to scribble his name against most of the free spaces.

"Please," Laura began.

But he silenced her. "I want all the dances you have left." He smiled.

"I've promised to save one for Sir Adam," she cried desperately. "And I must dance with Lindsay's father and his brother, and Cristobel wants me to meet Lindsay's grandfather. I want to save one for him too."

"Well," Alasdair replied smoothly, "pencil me in for the rest."

"All right, Angus," he said, getting up and reaching down to help Laura to her feet. "Sorry to have encroached on your time with your enchanting partner."

Laura danced woodenly, unable to think of anything to say.

Suddenly there was a peal of drums. The dancers melted to the sides, and, to a whisper of violins, the happy couple entered. The band began to play "I'll Be Loving You Always." Turning to his fiancée, whose head barely reached his shoulder, Lindsay swept her into his arms and waltzed dreamily around the deserted floor. They had eyes only for each other and hardly seemed to notice when other couples gradually joined them.

The music gently wound down as the ballroom's double doors were flung open, and supper was announced.

Out of the corner of her eye, Laura, now being twirled by another Angus, saw Fiona Farquharson crossing the ballroom floor clinging possessively to Alasdair's arm. The excitement she had felt pulsating through her when Alasdair had asked for all her dances drained away, and she wished she could drop through the floor. This dream evening, so eagerly anticipated, had turned into a nightmare.

Alasdair had only been teasing his little sister's friend after all—just as he teased Cristobel. He hadn't really wanted all her dances. Perhaps he hadn't even wanted any. Pressing her lips tightly together to hold back the tears of humiliation, Laura determined never again to be deceived by his charm.

She was to be escorted into supper by Niall Fraser, Lindsay's elder brother, who now came to claim her. He would introduce her to his grandfather, and after that she would make sure that her ball card was filled before Alasdair had a chance to approach her again.

Six

It was a perfectly lovely ball," Lady Flora said dreamily as Cristobel and Laura, bleary-eyed, sat down to breakfast the following morning. "What a pity Katharine and Maxime weren't here."

She sighed nostalgically.

"Reminded me of our engagement, Robert."

Her husband's face appeared from behind the Sunday paper, and he smiled affectionately across at her.

"And so wonderful to have the house full and the ballroom in use again."

There was no post to occupy Lady Flora this morning, so she had taken to reminiscing.

"I imagine you're going to have another busy day, darling?" She raised her eyebrows inquiringly at her daughter.

"Lindsay's coming for me after breakfast," Cristobel sighed happily. "We're having lunch with his parents. And then . . ." She broke off, her eyes clouding. "What time do you have to leave, Ninian?"

"Not late," her brother replied. "Got to be back on duty first thing in the morning."

"The night train?" Cristobel wailed.

"Oh, earlier," Ninian answered, looking around the corner of his newspaper. "The 8:30."

"Oh *no*," Cristobel groaned.

"'Fraid so, little sister." Ninian grinned. "But cheer up, you'll soon be married. Then you can come with us." He lowered his newspaper. "Have you decided on a date?"

"Helen Fraser and I were discussing it last evening," Lady Flora broke in. "We thought mid-September."

"Should be possible," Ninian replied thoughtfully. "The regiment's moving off before the end of the week. That'll give us almost three months. Oh yes, I should say, go ahead."

"We've tentatively suggested the 22nd," Lady Flora informed him.

"I don't suppose that was the date of Katharine's first marriage, was it?" Cristobel inquired. "We became engaged two days after the anniversary of her marriage to Maxime. It would be funny if we chose another special date for her."

"No, dear," Lady Flora replied. "I remember Katharine's wedding to Ashley *very* well. It poured rain. I think it must have been in February."

"Well, we can't wait *that* long."

Graeme pushed back his chair. "I'll leave you to your nuptials," he remarked. "I'm off to play golf." He smiled inquiringly at Alasdair. "Doesn't give you any ideas?"

Alasdair looked up. "What, golf? No, not today, thank you."

"Not *golf*," Graeme chortled. "*Nuptials*."

Alasdair grinned. "Not for the moment."

"Seeing you last night," his brother went on slyly, "I rather thought it might."

"Seeing's not always believing," Alasdair answered enigmatically, picking up the newspaper Graeme had discarded.

Graeme strolled toward the door. "I won't be here for lunch, Mother," he said, pausing with his hand on the knob.

"Neither will I," Ninian added.

Lady Flora looked inquiringly at Alasdair.

"I'll be here," he announced, wiping his mouth with his napkin.

"How strange," Graeme commented. "Thought you'd be racing over to the Farquharsons' again."

"They're having a family party to celebrate Grannie

Farquharson's seventy-fifth birthday," Alasdair replied, unperturbed.

"And you're not considered family?" Graeme taunted.

"Not yet." Alasdair grinned.

"Can I come and play golf?" Sandy shouted, jumping up from the table with a clatter.

"No, you can't," his brother said firmly.

"Miserable blighter," Sandy growled, flopping back into his chair. "Might as well have some more haddock then."

"Come to church with me instead," Lady Flora soothed.

Sandy looked at his mother as if she'd just made a lewd suggestion. "No thank you, Ma, not today." He was the only one of the children to call Lady Flora "Ma" and get away with it.

Laura looked anxiously around the table. Graeme had gone. Robert and Ninian were just leaving. Lindsay would be picking up Cristobel any minute. Sandy was still munching ravenously but would soon be bounding off. And she panicked at the thought of being left alone with Alasdair, who didn't seem to be in any hurry to leave the table or to have any plans for the morning.

"I'd like to go to church with you, Lady Flora," she said, hastily pushing back her chair.

"How lovely, Laura," Lady Flora replied. "Let's meet in the hall in half an hour and walk over. It's such a beautiful morning."

Laura followed her hostess out of the room. She hadn't the slightest desire to go to church, but anything was better than being left alone with Alasdair.

Sitting in the drawing room after lunch, Laura tried to concentrate on the Sunday crossword.

"I can never fathom those things," Lady Flora remarked, looking up from her embroidery. "Perhaps Alasdair could help you."

Alasdair glanced inquiringly over the edge of his newspaper.

"Laura's having trouble with the crossword," his mother explained.

Putting down his paper, Alasdair crossed to Laura's side and picked up the puzzle. He thoughtfully stroked his chin as he studied the squares, and Laura held her breath. Except for their one dance the previous evening, he had never been so close to her. The touch of his hands brushing hers as he held the paper sent her heart scurrying. Then she remembered Fiona Farquharson, and she stiffened.

Alasdair looked down at her with that same crooked smile, and a blush slowly flooded her cheeks.

"I do hope Cristobel's wedding won't mean we'll lose you," Lady Flora remarked.

"Of course it doesn't," Alasdair assured her, quickly penciling in a few letters. "Laura's part of the family."

"Will the wedding be here?" Sandy butted in from the turret where he was hunched on the window seat, watching dark clouds form and race across the sky, waiting for the first drops of rain to fall. The glorious promise of early morning had gradually deteriorated.

"Of course it'll be here," Alasdair replied without looking up. "Where did you expect it would be? At the Edinburgh zoo?"

Lady Flora leaned forwards and threw a handful of pinecones from a basket on the hearth onto the fire.

"Did you say something, Sandy?" she queried.

"Only asked where Cristobel's wedding would be," he answered sulkily. "And Alasdair informed me it would be at the zoo."

Lady Flora turned her bewildered gaze on him. "Oh no, dear, it will be here. In the garden."

"Perhaps this time we can have *my* band," Sandy grumbled, swinging his long legs off the window seat and strolling over to the fire.

Alasdair looked up in amazement. "Your band? Heaven help us, the monster's not running a band now."

Sandy lunged out at him with his foot, but Alasdair skillfully caught it.

"Ow, lemme go, you blighter, lemme go," Sandy yelled, hopping furiously up and down while his brother held him in a viselike grip. Without warning Alasdair let go. Sandy staggered backwards, ending up on the floor.

Lady Flora looked from one to the other of them in total bewilderment. Then she held out her hand to her youngest son. "Sandy darling," she exclaimed, "what *are* you doing on the floor?"

"Ask him," Sandy bawled, scrambling to his feet.

Alasdair laughed and, sticking his pencil behind his ear, leaned back on the sofa. "I want to hear about this band," he teased.

"I believe it's very good," Lady Flora said. "Sandy took up the drums as well as the trumpet at school last year. Now four of them have formed a small orchestra."

"Band," Sandy corrected.

"To think we could have reeled to the rhythm of the Gordonstoun Goons last night," Alasdair teased. Throwing back his head, he roared with laughter.

"Been better than that lousy lot from Perth," Sandy spat.

"Sandy, they were very good," his mother chided.

"So are we," Sandy spluttered indignantly. "And we'd have been cheaper."

"You even expect to be paid?" Alasdair challenged, going off into another laughing fit. "Mother, do tell me what else the young get up to at school these days."

"We could have had my band as well as the other one," Sandy sulked.

"But, darling, there simply wasn't room," Lady Flora comforted.

"It wouldn't have taken up any more room than Lady Entwhistle," Sandy blurted out, standing in the doorway letting in a draft.

"Perhaps not, dear," Lady Flora replied mildly. "But she's such a darling." She added as an afterthought, "Sandy, do please shut the door."

Sandy did. And shut himself out.

Alasdair looked at Laura, the green lights in his hazel eyes dancing with merriment. "He's probably right." He smiled.

The tension momentarily leaving her, Laura smiled back.

"By the way," Alasdair asked, looking across at his mother, "what was the matter with Grace Entwhistle last evening? She didn't seem pleased at all."

"Oh, dear," Lady Flora sighed. "Is she still cross?"

"Cross?" Alasdair frowned. "What about?"

"I'm afraid it's Sandy," his mother answered.

"Not surprised," Alasdair sniffed.

"You remember those marvelous fancy dress balls she gives every New Year's Eve for her grandchildren? You all used to go. Well, this year she invited Sandy."

"He's hardly old enough to go to that sort of thing," Alasdair put in.

"No," Lady Flora continued. "But her youngest grand-daughter, Rose Livesey, who's the same age as Sandy, was there. Grace felt it was hard for Rose to be the only one not to go, so she asked if Sandy would partner her."

"And?" Alasdair raised an eyebrow inquiringly.

Lady Flora sighed and put down her embroidery. "He can be terribly stubborn. He insisted on going as a radish."

"A radish?" Alasdair threw back his head and laughed. "I can't believe it."

"I didn't take much notice at the time," his mother said mournfully, because I knew we'd never find a radish outfit at the costumers in Perth. "So I ordered a Bonnie Prince Charlie one, which is what Grace expected. Rose was going as a Quaker maid."

"So how did he get it?"

"The radish suit? Oh, he persuaded Janet to make it. You know how she dotes on him. I can't tell you how frightful he looked."

Janet was the teenage nanny who had arrived to help Morag in the nursery when the children were young. She had since married Donald and now lived at the gatehouse.

Alasdair was rocking with laughter, and Laura found herself joining in. Lady Flora looked at them both as though they had broken into a bawdy song at a funeral.

"I can assure you it wasn't funny," she said sternly. "When I went to tell him we were ready to leave, there was this ghastly apparition. He'd even persuaded Janet to tie his feet together in an enormous white sock. Getting him down the stairs was a feat in itself. And you can imagine the effect he had on everyone when we arrived! He ruined the evening for poor Rose, jumping around like a demented frog."

Alasdair was by now convulsed.

"Not only that," his mother continued, "Janet had made some waving foliage for his head as he'd told her he wanted to be a living radish, not one in a salad. You know how tall he's grown. The wretched thing got entangled in the chandeliers. It was quite dreadful. And poor Rose ended the evening in tears. I'm very surprised Grace accepted our invitation for last evening. If it weren't that she's so fond of Cristobel, she certainly wouldn't have. Or perhaps it's because she's a distant cousin of your father's."

"Hardly that," Alasdair said drily. "Everyone's related in some way to Lady E. She's got cousins receding into the distance almost to vanishing point."

Alasdair got up, walked over to a basket beside the hearth, and threw two large logs onto the fire.

"I don't know how you managed to produce such a monster." He grinned, kicking the logs into place with his foot.

But before his mother had a chance to reply, the drawing room door burst open, and Sandy, who had obviously been listening behind it, thrust around his shock of red hair. "Old seed," he announced triumphantly.

Speechless, they all three gaped at him as he sauntered into the room, hands thrust jauntily in his pockets.

"Old seed," he repeated pompously, gazing loftily down at them. "Don't forget Dad was nearly fifty-nine when I was born."

Laura felt Alasdair stiffen.

"Alexander," Lady Flora said weakly, using his real name for the first time in years.

"Sandy," Alasdair barked, "that's enough!"

He took a step menacingly in his brother's direction. But

Sandy was too quick for him. Darting through the door, he slammed it loudly in his brother's face.

"That little bounder needs teaching a lesson," Alasdair said angrily.

"Oh, Alasdair," his mother whispered, bending to pick up Laird, who was sitting on a tapestry cushion at her feet, gnawing an ivory bone. "I don't understand Sandy. You others never behaved in such an atrocious fashion. I can't think what the school's coming to. Things must have changed dramatically since Mr. Harris retired."

"The school's got nothing to do with it," Alasdair replied curtly. "Sandy is one on his own. Even old Harris would have found his match in him."

Lady Flora got up and looked around her with a vague, troubled expression. "Shall I ring for tea?" she suggested hesitantly.

She consulted the fob watch hanging around her neck. "No, it's only half past three." She paused, bewildered. "I think I'll go up and see Morag. Everyone has been so busy these last few days she may be feeling neglected."

"You do that, Mother," Alasdair soothed, knowing that Morag had always been Lady Flora's bolt-hole in times of stress.

He got up and opened the door for her. "I'll take Laura out for a drive, and we'll stop and have tea somewhere. That little blighter Sandy can live on his hump."

As Alasdair closed the door behind her, Laura's calm evaporated. "I've got rather a headache," she lied, struggling to her feet. "I think I'll go up to my room and sleep it off."

Alasdair glanced out the window at the darkened sky, now curdled and menacing, strewn with ashen clouds slowly turning a ragged anthracite-gray.

"It's not raining yet," he said slowly. "Don't you think a drive would help blow your headache away? We could walk a little and then drop in somewhere for tea."

"Th-thank you," Laura stammered, averting her eyes from his. "But not this afternoon."

Alasdair caught her arm as she made for the door. "Laura," he said softly, "are you avoiding me?"

At his touch Laura felt the blood rise behind her ears and spread slowly across her cheeks.

"Why should I avoid you?" she answered tightly, pulling her arm away.

"I don't know," he challenged, willing her to meet his gaze. "Only one dance last evening. And now this sudden malaise."

As the first drops of rain began to patter against the window panes, she hesitated. Then she remembered Alasdair's laughing face as he held Fiona Farquharson in his arms.

"I'm sorry," she faltered. "But all I feel like doing at the moment is sleeping."

Alasdair opened the door for her. He said nothing. But his lips were pressed together in a tight line. As she passed through, he gave her a strange look.

Laura walked heavily up the stairs, feeling as if her legs were about to give way beneath her. Reaching the half-landing, she stopped as the woman blossoming inside her struggled to escape and fight for the man she loved. In that instant Laura almost spun around and raced back down the wide staircase into the drawing room where Alasdair was standing, one elbow on the high mantel of the great fireplace, staring moodily into the leaping flames. Her instinct told her to grasp his hand and run with him, laughing and carefree, across the silent, echoing hall, through the great oak door, and out into the rain.

But then the frightened twelve-year-old still lurking inside her took over. The pain and rejection she had felt when the bedroom door had closed on her mother's lifeless body once again enveloped her. Her mother had been her refuge and her anchor. And now that she was gone, Laura could only see herself trapped forever on an endless treadmill of despair. These violent adolescent emotions rose to the fore, insisting that she could not face the pain of rejection again. And the young woman crying for release from her traumatic childhood was brutally pushed below the surface.

"How can I compare with Fiona?" she muttered bitterly, gripping the heavy bannister as she rounded the bend in the stairs. "She's so vivacious and amusing. And she's a wonderful sportswoman. Hunts and shoots and does all the things Alasdair enjoys."

She sniffed back her tears.

"Not like me. I can't bear the thought of handling a gun, and I've never fished in my life. I must have been mad to think that Alasdair could be interested in me. They all marry amongst themselves. Cristobel has known Lindsay all her life. Katharine's first husband was Fiona's father's cousin. And her Aunt Lavinia was once engaged to Robert Hamilton's elder brother, who was killed in World War I. It's a closed circle. I'm just an outsider in their world."

Miserably turning the corner of the corridor leading to her bedroom, Laura heard the front door slam. She glanced through the turret window. Huge brooms of rain swept across the lawn as Alasdair, hands thrust deep into his pockets, his head bent against the rising wind, strode hatless down the drive. She assumed that, having been relieved of any further duty toward his little sister's friend, he was off to see Fiona Farquharson.

Seven

Laura did not appear for the rest of the day. At about half past six Lady Flora tapped tentatively on her bedroom door. "My dear, I do hope it's merely tiredness," she called softly, "and you're not becoming ill."

"No," Laura called back, not inviting her hostess to enter. "I drank too much champagne last night. My tum's queasy, and I've got a headache. I just want to sleep it off."

She turned on her side and closed her eyes. Her mind drifted back to the last time she had seen her mother, that warm July evening when Edwina had taken her to the sickroom to say good night. Margaret Denning's pinched white face had smiled at her daughter from the mound of pillows, and her emaciated hand had felt for Laura's. Her mother's long illness seemed to have brought her into a new spiritual dimension. And in spite of the pain, she had never lost her peace.

"Don't worry, Laura darling," she had whispered, as if sensing that this was good-bye. "Your heavenly Father will look after you."

Laura had looked bewilderedly toward her aunt. Then bending hastily to kiss her mother's paper-thin cheek, the young girl had backed away.

As these memories inexplicably surfaced, she recalled the conversation she had had with Lady Flora as they walked back from church that morning.

"Do you mind going to church on your own every

61

Sunday?" Laura had inquired. "Wouldn't you be happier if some of the family came with you?"

Lady Flora had smiled. "I'm delighted to have you with me this morning, Laura," she had replied. "But faith is a personal commitment between God and each one of His children, not something we can inherit. The children must each come to Him in their own way and their own time. I have shown them the way, but I cannot force them."

For a split second Laura was tempted to ask how she could get to know this God who seemed so real to Lady Flora, how she could have this faith. But at that moment, frantically ringing the bell, Sandy raced past them on an ancient bicycle almost scattering them into the bushes.

And the moment had passed.

Laura opened her eyes and stared out of the window. The mountains were almost obliterated by a thick mist that hung damply over everything. The downpour had ceased, but dark sullen clouds threatened in a leaden sky heavy with rain. The whole outlook was bleak and menacing, in tune with Laura's present mood. For a brief moment she contemplated ringing the bell and asking if Lady Flora would come and talk to her, continue the conversation Sandy had so abruptly terminated that morning. But her innate reserve and shyness made her hesitate. And once again the moment passed.

Closing her eyes, she reflected on how quickly light can change to darkness, happiness to despair. It didn't seem possible that her window, which now had a rain-sodden wind rattling angrily at its mullioned panes, could only twenty-four hours before have been wide open to admit the gentle, perfumed breeze that had danced through it in dazzling sunshine. Even the long northern twilight had vanished, replaced by a curdled gray patchwork of clouds.

A car door slammed, followed by Cristobel's voice and her footsteps running up the stairs. Cristobel hesitated as she passed Laura's door. But, unable to face her friend's woebegone face now that she had parted from her fiancé, Laura did not move. And, as the great house finally settled down for the night, Laura felt the sleep that her tired brain craved creep over her.

"Tomorrow is another day," she murmured, veils of darkness slipping before her eyes. "Alasdair will have gone, and life will return to normal."

The next morning when Laura opened her door to Cristobel's tentative knock, Cristobel found her friend looking pale and jaded.

"Are you feeling better?" Cristobel inquired.

"I'm perfectly all right now," Laura said, forcing a smile. "But you're the one who looks as if she needs a doctor."

Cristobel grimaced. "Miseryitis," she wailed. "Never thought it would be so hard to say good-bye to Lindsay."

"Not for long," Laura comforted, slipping her arm through Cristobel's as they walked along the gallery.

"Long *enough*," Cristobel answered mournfully. "And just *look* at the weather. It doesn't help!"

They stopped and peered through the turret window. The rain-sodden sky looked as if it were perched on top of the mountains, darkly outlined against it.

"Ugh!" Cristobel shuddered. "Looks the way I feel." She turned to Laura wistfully. "Do you think it's easier to be miserable if you live in a hot climate like Italy or the south of France? Someplace where the sun always shines."

"According to Philippa, the sun *doesn't* always shine in Italy," Laura laughed.

Laura's eldest sister was with her husband at the embassy in Rome.

"Anyway, Philippa says she sometimes wishes it wouldn't, and she often longs for a rainy day."

"Oh, how can she?" Cristobel wailed.

But it was difficult for Cristobel to be downcast for long. The tempting smell drifting from the open dining room door as they reached the bottom of the stairs immediately revived her spirits.

"In Italy we wouldn't be having eggs and bacon and sausages for breakfast, would we? Just coffee and an old roll. I suppose there are *some* compensations for living in the Arctic."

Grabbing Laura's hand, she skipped across the hall.

As they entered the dining room, Laura froze. There, carefully wiping his mouth with his napkin, was Alasdair. He looked up and smiled. Then picking up his cup, he raised it to them in a mock salute. "Hail to thee, blithe spirits," he quoted.

"Hail," Cristobel replied, helping herself lavishly at the sideboard.

Laura felt a blush mounting behind her ears. Turning swiftly, she began fiddling with dish covers. But suddenly she didn't want anything to eat. Pouring a cup of coffee, she sat down and reached for the toast rack.

Lady Flora looked up from her letters. "Laura dear," she reproved, "is *that* all you're having? You've eaten nothing since yesterday's lunch."

Laura kept her eyes glued to her plate. "I think my stomach's shrunk," she joked.

Getting up to pour herself some coffee, Cristobel appeared to notice Alasdair for the first time. "Hallo," she chirped. "What are you doing here on a Monday morning?"

"I've been here all the time," he answered. "I even greeted you when you arrived, and you replied."

"Oh, did I?" Cristobel said airily. "How long are you staying?"

"Not long. I've got an appointment in Perth at eleven, so it wasn't worth going back to Edinburgh last night."

"Perth!" Cristobel exclaimed, brightening up. "Can Laura and I cadge a lift with you? A day in town is just what we need to clear Laura's headache and blow away my doldrums."

Laura opened her mouth to protest, but Cristobel forestalled her. "Lovely," she cried, turning to her friend. "We can do some shopping, have lunch at the Royal Oak, and see a film afterwards."

"I wonder if going to the pictures is a good idea if Laura has just recovered from a nasty headache," Lady Flora interrupted.

"Oh, *just* the thing," Cristobel replied gaily. "Come on, Laura, let's put on our best bibs and tuckers and dazzle the local yokels."

"Shall I send Donald to meet you later on?" her mother called as Cristobel danced out of the room, all signs of depression gone. "No, Mother, don't bother. We'll take the bus."

She caught Laura's hand and dragged her across the hall.

"I love that old country bus," she cooed happily. "It takes hours and stops everywhere, but it's such fun."

Half an hour later, with a heavy heart Laura walked back to the hall where Alasdair was shuffling papers into his briefcase.

"All ready?" he inquired, as Cristobel pirouetted down the wide staircase, holding out her left hand and admiring her ring yet again.

"Good-bye, Mother," he called, snapping his briefcase shut.

Lady Flora appeared at the door of the morning room, Laird cradled in her arms. "Oh, good-bye, darling," she said vaguely as her son bent to kiss her cheek.

"By the way," Alasdair inquired, straightening up, "what's happened to that brat Sandy? He's kept a pretty low profile since yesterday afternoon."

"He's behaving very strangely," Lady Flora sighed, idly fondling Laird's ears. "Came down to breakfast very early wearing a yellow kimono and announced that he intends to become a Buddhist monk." She shook her head sadly. "Your father sent him to his room, and now he's sitting cross-legged on the bed meditating."

"Mother," Alasdair said, barely concealing his amusement, "I despair of your youngest offspring."

He placed his hand affectionately on her arm, and Laird promptly bit him.

"You sit in the front," Cristobel said to Laura, jumping into the back of the car as her brother held the doors open for them.

"No," Laura panicked.

"Oh, go on," Cristobel insisted. "Don't fuss. I'm going to lie down and dream of Lindsay, so there won't be room for you."

As they bowled down the drive, Alasdair waved out the side

window to his father striding toward the house with the dogs. Then, gathering speed, he drove into the deserted road.

"She hasn't wasted much time," he remarked, jerking his head toward the backseat where Cristobel was curled along its length, eyes closed.

Laura glanced into the overhead mirror. "I expect she's tired after all the excitement," she replied stiffly.

"And you?" Alasdair said, looking quickly at her. "Are *you* completely recovered?"

Laura thought she detected a hint of irony in his voice.

"Yes, thank you," she answered primly, staring woodenly in front of her.

Alasdair slowed down and maneuvered over a small bridge crossing a rushing stream that was swollen with yesterday's rain.

"So I'm to be your escort to Catriona McFadden's coming-out ball," he casually remarked, pressing his foot down on the accelerator.

Laura looked at him, her eyes wide with fright. "I don't think so."

"That's what Mother said last night."

He paused. And she panicked again.

"Graeme as the eldest son is to give his arm to his betrothed sister, and I'm to offer mine to you." He smiled down at her. "Will you accept?"

Laura could think of nothing to say. A week ago she would have been deliriously happy at the mere suggestion of being escorted to a ball by Alasdair. But in the last few days everything had changed.

"I-I don't think I'll be here," she stammered.

"What do you mean?" Alasdair inquired. "I thought you were staying for the summer?"

"Not this time," Laura rambled on, words dropping haphazardly from her lips without her seeming to have any control over them. "I've promised to go to Italy to stay with my sister Philippa."

"But I thought she was in Cairo."

Laura was taken aback. How could he possibly have remembered?

"She was when I was twelve," she replied coldly. "They've been in Moscow and Paris since then."

Alasdair smiled across at her. "And how old are you now?" he asked softly.

Laura felt herself on the brink of tears. "I'm three months younger than your sister," she bristled.

Then abruptly they fell silent. She knew that if she attempted another word, the tears would gush out and pour down her cheeks.

The narrow mountain road began to climb, and Alasdair kept his eyes fixed on it. Staring through the side window into the valley below, willing the tears not to flow, Laura caught her breath. A ray of sunshine had burst through the clouds and flooded a little chain of blue tarns twinkling below like a many-faceted sapphire necklace. But almost immediately, the road twisted, and they vanished from sight. As the descent began, Alasdair relaxed his grip on the wheel.

"You can't go to Rome in July," he stressed. "The heat's appalling."

"I shan't be going to Rome," Laura answered, swallowing hard before she spoke. "Philippa is taking the children to the Lakes, and I shall join them there. I haven't seen my nieces since Christmas."

"Your family seems to specialize in girls," Alasdair commented. "Does your other sister have only daughters?"

"Mary and Edward don't have any children," Laura replied.

"We'd make a good couple." Alasdair smiled. "Break the terrible bias in the Hamilton family toward male offspring."

Laura felt a swift, hot blush stain her cheeks. She turned back to the window, annoyed that she had allowed herself to be upset by his teasing.

"That blush is entrancing," Alasdair went on, ignoring her embarrassment.

She averted her eyes, her mind spinning.

"You'll come back in August for the shoot, won't you?" he went on, as the outskirts of Perth came into view.

"I don't shoot," Laura replied tightly, her face still glued to the window.

"How refreshing!" he exclaimed.

"Do you fish?" he inquired after a pause.

"No," she answered coldly, picturing Fiona standing knee deep in an ice-cold lake. "And I'm not sure Cristobel will be here in August. She mentioned something about Lady Fraser taking her for a trip on the Rhine and Lindsay joining them for a few days."

"But you don't always have to be Cristobel's guest," he blurted out.

Laura looked at him in surprise.

"You could be mine," he coaxed, flashing that quizzical crooked smile on her.

For a brief moment he took his hand off the steering wheel and placed it lightly on hers, lying clenched in her lap.

"And we don't have to fish or shoot," he said softly.

Once again that voluptuous feeling she had felt at his touch the previous afternoon raced through her. She felt captured, flooded with its warmth as rippling sensations trembled through her body. She half turned toward him, then remembered his eyes gazing into Fiona Farquharson's laughing face. And the warm feeling drained away, leaving her stiff and frozen once again.

Alasdair had sensed the warmth. Now he felt the abrupt change in this bewitching girl. Puzzled, he slowly removed his hand and fixed his eyes on the road ahead.

"I'm tied up in Edinburgh next week," he said as they entered Perth. "And the following weekend I've promised to escort Fiona to her cousin's wedding in Aberdeen. But in three weeks I'll be back at Annanbrae." He paused and glanced down at her. "I hope you'll still be there," he ended softly.

Laura could scarcely believe her ears. For one wild moment when his hand had touched hers, she had allowed her hopes to soar. Now she was totally bewildered. How could Alasdair ask her to stay at Annanbrae as his guest, yet flaunt his relationship with another woman? She opened her mouth to make a scathing remark, a remark that, had she only known it, would have cleared the air.

But at that moment Cristobel awoke. "Yippee," she cried irrepressibly, bouncing up on the seat. "We're running into Perth. Can you drop us at the Royal Oak, Alasdair? We can have a quick cup of coffee and book a table for lunch."

Taking a small gold powder compact out of her handbag, she peered into the mirror. "Heavens, what a sight! You *must* drop us at the Royal Oak even if it means you're late for your appointment. I can't face the town looking like this."

She snapped the compact shut and ran her hands through her thick dark hair, yawning as the car drew up in front of the hotel.

"I'd like to invite you both for lunch," Alasdair said as he opened the door for Laura. "But I'm afraid this meeting will run into lunch."

Laura sent up a quick prayer of thanks.

"Don't worry, big brother," Cristobel chirped, stepping out onto the pavement.

"I'll see you in three weeks," he said softly as he bade Laura good-bye.

"No," she hissed.

He looked taken aback. "Well, I hope you'll deign to come to Cristobel's wedding," he replied stiffly.

"My wedding?" Cristobel queried, as he climbed back into the driver's seat. "Whatever are you talking about? Of course you'll see Laura before then. She's here for the summer."

"I wouldn't count on it," Alasdair observed drily.

Turning the key in the ignition, he waved through the side window as the car glided smoothly away.

"What's bitten him?" Cristobel remarked, taking Laura's arm as they walked into the hotel.

"Cristobel," Laura began, meaning to get this settled once and for all.

"Oh, weddings," Cristobel cooed excitedly. "Let's order some coffee, and I'll tell you about mine. We organized just about everything yesterday. All that's left to do now is make sure Lindsay can have leave and that I have his colonel's approval."

She grinned.

"It would be a funny wedding if he couldn't get time off," she laughed. "But I charmed his colonel at the New Year's Eve ball, so there won't be any opposition there. Lindsay tells me I'm approved. Even by Mrs. Colonel."

Eight

The *Queen Elizabeth* sounded its mournful horn as it curved around the Needles. Passing St. Katharine's Point, the ship headed toward Shanklin. Then it slowed down at the approach to Nab Tower to allow the pilot, chugging toward them in a small launch through the narrow Nab Passage, to climb aboard and guide the great ocean liner safely into Southampton Water.

"I've always thought sea travel so romantic," William reflected. He stood at Katharine's side studying a lacy mantle of foam trailing behind the speedboats in the gray-green water. "So much pleasanter than climbing into an airplane."

Katharine leaned on the rail gazing at the yachts lazily sailing out of Cowes and smiled dreamily.

"Everything goes at such speed nowadays," William sighed. "Even ocean liners. Before the war it was a holiday just getting there." He grinned mischievously at Katharine. "In those days some people's cabin trunks contained nothing but evening dress and night wear."

Katharine's eyes widened in surprise.

"One could dance till dawn or even later," William explained, "have breakfast, then sleep until it was time to dress for evening."

"Is that what you and your wife did?" Katharine teased.

"No, Catriona and I were past our dancing days by 1935,

though we had met doing the Gay Gordons at a ball at Annanbrae back in 1906."

William stared reflectively over the side, listening to the steady hiss of the sea as the great ship slid across the flat surface.

"How times have changed." He smiled nostalgically. "I imagine in a few years traveling like this will be a thing of the past, with ocean liners the stuff of storybooks. And we shall all be skimming around the world in giant zeppelins."

Katharine dimpled up at him. "That dates you horribly," she teased. "We've had another war since zeppelins. Or don't you remember?"

She raised her eyebrows, a mischievous smile on her face. She knew all too well that, like her, William had ample reason to remember.

He placed his heavily veined hand over hers but didn't reply.

"I remember the last time I sailed into Southampton," William mused, as they turned into the Solent, and a vague outline of the town shimmering in the afternoon sunlight came into view. "Catriona and I were returning from Guy's wedding."

"Did you marry Hope and Guy as well?" Katharine queried.

William nodded.

"Yes, in St. Michael's Episcopal Church where I married Philip. Both times the vicar was very gracious and allowed me to take the service."

Katharine leaned her chin on her arms, propped on the rail.

"I was sorry to miss Cristobel's engagement ball at Annanbrae," she remarked. "But I'm so glad Maxime and I came with you and Lavinia to Philip and Cindy's wedding." She paused, frowning slightly. "I wonder why they call her Cindy? Cynthia is such a pretty name."

William smiled but offered no explanation.

"Philip's marriage seems to have rounded something off," Katharine went on pensively. "In some strange way it makes up for the terrible carnage the war produced in all our lives. I realize now that something of Guy will live on in his grandchildren—that there is a continuity, a pattern to it all, if only we will let God pick up the pieces and help us start again."

She paused, suddenly overcome by emotion. "I sometimes wonder what difference it would have made to my life had Ashley's baby lived," she ended, watching intently as the pilot edged the liner cautiously around Bramble Point.

"As I told you then, Katharine," William said gently, "God can make beauty out of ashes. And He has done so with your life."

Katharine squeezed his hand. His fingers felt flaky, like shells of dry flesh, beneath her touch. She looked closely at him and realized with a shock that William was growing old.

"I'm surprised you and Lavinia never married," she ruminated, removing her hand. The realization of William's mortality had given her a shock.

"It didn't seem necessary," William replied. "We have both been alone for a long time and have gotten used to our independence. We see each other almost daily when we are in Goudhurst and greatly enjoy each other's company. But we decided that, at our age, it was best to each keep our own homes."

He smiled. "Perhaps when I get old and crotchety, we will marry. Then I'll have someone to warm my slippers and help me up the stairs to bed." His eyes twinkled down at her.

"What do you two find so amusing?" Maxime inquired coming up behind them.

"Just a private joke," William declared. He turned. "Isn't Lavinia with you?"

"She's having a cup of tea in her cabin. She'll be here in a minute."

Maxime slipped his arm through his wife's. "Pleased to be home?"

"This isn't home," she murmured as the town outlined against the achingly blue sky became more distinct. "Home is where the heart is. And my heart's at Le Moulin."

"Won't be long now," Maxime assured her.

He waved his hand as Lavinia, anchoring a straw hat in place against the gentle breeze that was ruffling their bare heads, walked gingerly along the deck toward them.

"I imagine you are missing your children," William

remarked. "Especially your little daughter. A month away is a long time."

Katharine gave an almost imperceptible sigh. "I doubt whether my little daughter is missing *me*," she replied drily. "Elisabeth has eyes only for Maxime."

"Like all little girls," William put in.

"No, William," Katharine went on, her face serious, as Maxime left her side and went to help Lavinia. "It's more than that. Ever since Elisabeth was born, her father has been the only person who counted for her. She *adores* Maxime. It's as if I didn't exist."

"She'll grow out of it," William soothed.

"I hope so," Katharine said slowly. "But I'm not so sure."

"Just passing Castle Point," Lavinia remarked, putting a stop to any further confidences as she and Maxime joined them at the rail. "And there's Fawley Refinery. We'll be docking very soon."

"It's all very somber, isn't it?" she went on as the blurred outline of upturned faces waiting on the quayside danced into view. "Weren't there military bands and bunting greeting arriving passengers in the old days, William?"

William's brow creased in thought. "I think it was only when we left, Lavinia, not when we arrived. But it's almost thirty years since I last crossed the Atlantic, and I honestly can't remember."

"We didn't even have them when we left," Lavinia remarked.

"It was seven o'clock in the morning," William reminded her.

The ship had slowed almost to a stop, and enormous anchors and clanging chains were being thrown overboard. As they watched, a gangplank clattered into position, and a line of officials trooped on board.

"Well, that's the end of the holiday," Maxime remarked. "A few days in London to see to some business, and then we'll be home again."

"Will you have time to come to Goudhurst for the weekend?" Lavinia asked.

Maxime raised his eyebrows inquiringly in Katharine's direction.

"Not this time," she replied. "We've been away for over a month . . . and I can't wait to see the children."

Lavinia smiled affectionately at her great niece. "You should have gotten off when we docked at Cherbourg," she teased. "And left Maxime to do his business on his own. That way you'd be almost home by now."

Maxime clicked his tongue in annoyance. "How stupid of me. I should have realized you were dying to see the children again after so long and suggested it, instead of dragging you to London with me." He smiled ruefully down at his wife. "Can you forgive me, darling?"

Katharine smiled back, taking his arm as they moved away. "I can't wait to see the children," she whispered. "But . . . I couldn't bear to be away from you."

As their eyes met, they spoke volumes. And Katharine knew that Elisabeth's obsession with her father, which so irritated her, was not important beside the fact that she loved Maxime. Nothing was important, nothing mattered except her love for her husband and his love for her.

Reaching up on tiptoe, she lightly kissed his cheek.

"How *could* you desert me like this?" Cristobel wailed. "And on our last summer together."

She looked at Laura with such gloom etched on her delicate features that Laura burst out laughing. "Oh, come on, Cristobel," she chided. "You're not going into purdah!"

Cristobel dimpled. It was difficult for her bubbling spirits to remain downcast for long.

"Promise you'll be back in London by the beginning of September," she cajoled. "Mother and I are coming down to see about my dress and the bridesmaids' outfits. You need to be there for fittings."

"Cristobel," Laura sighed, "do you *really* want me to be a bridesmaid?"

Cristobel sat down abruptly, her enormous gray eyes like saucers. "Of course," she answered in astonishment.

"But I'm going to look ridiculous in the middle of that flurry of small children," Laura continued lamely. "Lindsay's niece and nephew who can barely toddle, plus all your little Sutherland cousins who are scarcely any older. I'll be like a runner bean in a field of daisies."

She sat down beside Cristobel, knowing that this remark had hurt her friend. What she meant was: *I don't want any official role that could bring me into close contact with Alasdair.* But, in spite of her close friendship with Cristobel, a certain reticence she had inherited from her father prevented her from revealing her true feelings.

"You're like a sister to me," Cristobel wailed. "It never occurred to me that you wouldn't want to be my bridesmaid."

Laura sighed, entangled not only in her own emotions but now also in Cristobel's. "I just thought . . . ," she began helplessly, "it might be better to have only small pages and bridesmaids."

Cristobel began describing circles on the carpet with her foot. "Laura," she pleaded, her brow creased in a puzzled frown, "what's the matter with you all of a sudden? We always said that whoever married first would have the other as a bridesmaid."

"That was when we were sixteen," Laura retorted.

"We're only *nineteen* now!" Cristobel exclaimed. "Does it make such a difference?"

She leaned toward Laura. "Is something the matter?" she asked gently. "You've been strange ever since we arrived."

Laura forced a smile. She longed to share with Cristobel, the one person with whom she had shared so much in the past. She hesitated. Perhaps Cristobel could explain her brother's strange behavior. A ray of hope squeezed its way into Laura's mind, and she opened her mouth. But the words wouldn't come. In her frustration she clamped her lips firmly together. "It's nothing," she lied. "You're imagining it."

"Then you *will* be my bridesmaid," Cristobel wheedled.

Laura nodded dumbly.

"Cheers," Cristobel exulted, clapping her hands like an excited schoolgirl.

Laura knew that she had lost.

But over her departure, ignoring Cristobel's melodramatic face, she stood firm. Alasdair was due to arrive at Annanbrae the following Friday evening, so Laura insisted on taking the afternoon train. She didn't want to run any risk of meeting him again.

If Edwina was surprised to see her niece return so soon, she made no comment. She welcomed her as warmly as ever to her Kensington home which, since Laura's mother's death, had also been Laura's home.

"I'm afraid you'll find London dreadfully hot after Scotland," she declared, kissing her lightly on the cheek.

She held Laura at arm's length, frowning slightly. "You seem tired," she said gently. "Would you like something to eat, or do you just want to go to bed?"

Laura smiled at her aunt, grateful not to be plied with questions. "If you don't mind, I think I'll go straight to bed."

Edwina gave her niece a shrewd glance and then led the way to the small room overlooking the courtyard. "Philippa telephoned yesterday evening," she remarked, walking across to the window and drawing the curtains. "She wanted to know when to expect you."

"I'd like to stay here for a few days before going to Italy," Laura answered listlessly. Her mind and her heart were still at Annanbrae where she was imagining the family sitting on the terrace after dinner watching the midges dance in the northern twilight haze.

Her aunt's gaze rested on her thoughtfully for a few seconds. "You'll feel better after a bath and a good night's sleep," she said practically, removing the apple-green silk coverlet and turning down the sheet.

Laura's eyes suddenly filled with tears, and she longed to throw her arms around Edwina's neck and cry her heart out, tell her about the misery of the last few weeks and the emptiness she was now feeling.

Edwina stood silently waiting for the outburst. But it didn't come. Once again the words dried up inside Laura. Kicking off her shoes, she turned away.

"I thought we might drive down to Oxford for lunch on Sunday," Edwina suggested. "I'm sure your father would be pleased to see you."

Laura wasn't so sure. Since his wife's death, Henry Denning hardly seemed to be aware of the world outside his books. He was thankful that his two elder daughters had their own lives and grateful to his sister for taking his youngest off his hands. Remembering Robert Hamilton, Laura's tears brimmed over.

"I'll run you a bath," Edwina put in quickly, squeezing her niece's arm affectionately.

Laura lowered her body into the fragrant suds, assured that now that she was back in London, she would see things differently. Alasdair would once again become a distant dream. There was her visit to Philippa to look forward to. The Donkey Derby in Connemara and the Dublin Horse Show with Edwina. Life was full of excitement, and she was young—on the brink of adventure. She did not need Alasdair.

Lying back in the perfumed waters, she relaxed. As she did so, Alasdair's face seemed to rise up out of the warm steam, smiling his crooked, quizzical smile.

And Laura knew, without a shadow of a doubt, that she did need him.

Nine

Lady Flora and Cristobel arrived in London at the end of August. Laura was not there.

"Where've you been?" Cristobel shrieked over the telephone when she finally managed to track down her friend.

"In Ireland," Laura replied. "I told you."

"But," Cristobel spluttered, "I've been ringing for ages, paralyzed with fear thinking you'd deserted me."

"You said you'd be here around the beginning of September," Laura interrupted. "It's only the 3rd."

"Oh, is it?" Cristobel sounded surprised. "Can you come around this very minute?"

"Yes. But where to?"

"Madame Zoe's. She's getting *frantic*. Says your dress will *never* be ready on time."

"Sounds very French," Laura commented.

"Yes, but the most *marvelous* dressmaker," Cristobel cooed. "My dress is a *dream*—"

"It would help if you'd tell me where to come," Laura cut in. "Madame Zoe's."

Cristobel sounded as surprised as if she'd suggested meeting her friend in front of the Eiffel Tower and Laura had asked, "Eiffel what?"

"It's a small street off Piccadilly, almost opposite the Ritz, not far from Old Bond Street."

"Please, Cristobel," Laura cut in exasperatedly, "just give me the address."

"Oh, horrors," Cristobel chirped. "I don't know it. Look, I'll pass you to one of these nice assistants."

"Goodness knows where I'd end up if I had to rely on Cristobel for directions," Laura remarked to an amused Edwina as she put down the telephone. "Probably in a back street on the other side of Wapping!"

The next few days flashed by at lightning speed. It was impossible to hold a conversation with Cristobel or hope to receive a coherent answer if one tried. And fittings became a major ordeal for the dressmakers.

Lady Flora smiled sweetly at everyone, twittered about lists and flowers and invitations, oblivious of the frantic activity going on around her as she drifted gracefully through the whole procedure. When they at last were ready to return to Scotland, Laura was exhausted.

"I really don't see *why* you can't come with us," Cristobel sulked. "To come the day before the wedding is positively *cruel*."

"I promise I'll be there in time for the rehearsal on Thursday afternoon," Laura soothed.

But after a series of wailing telephone calls from Cristobel, Laura capitulated and took the night train on Tuesday so as to give them what Cristobel described as a final day of giggling together before the last-minute countdown. To her great relief she discovered at breakfast on the morning of her arrival that Alasdair would not come until the following afternoon.

"Does he *have* to rehearse?" Laura inquired. "He's not the best man."

"No, but we need him for the procession after the service," Cristobel announced, her eyes shining. "The verger wants to make sure everyone knows whom they'll be walking with, to avoid all the family scrambling about in the aisle looking for partners."

Laura sighed and tried to put the whole thing out of her mind.

The wedding party gathered in the old village church, already beautifully decorated for the following day's ceremony.

"Now," intoned the verger nasally, when they had all trooped down the aisle with one partner, done a quick swap and about-turn, and were waiting to troop back up it with someone else.

Nobody took the slightest notice of him. He coughed discreetly. Then more loudly. And finally he clapped his hands, eyeing the milling mass of pages and bridesmaids with distaste.

They had all spent a delightful morning making a thorough nuisance of themselves, racing around the galleries at Annanbrae, sliding down bannisters, thoroughly upsetting Laird and Sara, with the help of the three younger dogs who had added their barks and yelps to the children's ear-piercing shrieks. The youngsters were now trying to recreate the earlier pandemonium.

"If you *please*, ladies and gentlemen," bleated the verger, as Robert grabbed a handful of wriggling, giggling small attendants and sorted them into pairs once more. "For the processional march after the ceremony, Lady Flora will walk with Sir Charles directly behind the bridal party."

Lady Flora and Sir Charles Fraser took up their positions once more in the aisle. Everyone else either walked backwards or shuffled up.

"Now Lady Fraser and Mr. Hamilton."

But Robert had gone back to threatening the pages, who were starting to fight. Lady Fraser looked helplessly around, and the group disintegrated again. The whole thing was turning into a farce when suddenly Cristobel slipped her hand from Lindsay's arm and assumed command.

"Mr. McIntyre," she soothed, firmly pushing the perspiring verger into a pew, "we are all being *quite* dreadful. You sit there and tell me what you want us to do."

And, completely ignoring him, she took over. "Listen, everybody," she called, clapping her hands for silence. "After

Father and Lady Fraser, Grandfather Lindsay and Grannie Sutherland."

Lady Fraser began frantically semaphoring to Cristobel. "Grandfather Lindsay doesn't want to be in the procession," she mouthed. "He has trouble with his hip."

"But won't he look very odd standing there all by himself in the front pew?" Cristobel queried. "It'll look as if we've forgotten him." She shrugged. "Never mind. Just leave him there for now. We'll work something out later. Graeme, you'll have to walk with Grannie Sutherland."

She turned to the verger, giving him one of her sweetest smiles. "I don't think there's anything else, is there, Mr. McIntyre?" she cooed. "We're all in line. Now the wedding march can begin."

The organist, who had been hanging over the organ loft waiting for a signal from someone, climbed thankfully back onto the seat. He had just broken into a loud chord when there was a piercing shriek from Cristobel. "Stop, everybody. Stop!"

Mr. McNabb's hands fell abruptly from the keys, and the organ gave a tortured groan.

"It's Laura," Cristobel wailed. "We've forgotten Laura!"

All eyes turned to the chief bridesmaid standing in splendid isolation.

"Ninian, as best man, should be walking with the chief bridesmaid," Cristobel sighed dramatically. "But he'll be outside organizing the guard of honor. Now what do we do?"

Everyone looked around hoping someone else would come up with a solution. Everyone, that is, except Hamish who had been prowling up and down the aisle all afternoon in the opposite direction from everyone else. Now that the wedding party was facing the door, he was standing to attention facing the altar.

"That leaves only Alasdair," Cristobel said thoughtfully, grabbing Hamish and anchoring him firmly in the pew beside the distraught verger. "Darling Laura, do you mind? Alasdair's all that's left."

She suddenly looked around. "By the way, where *is* Alasdair?"

As she spoke, they heard a scrunching of brakes, and Alasdair dashed into the pool of sunshine flooding through the open church door. "Sorry," he said, hurrying up to his sister. "Got held up at the last minute. Am I very late?"

"Yes," she answered. "We're just about to process out. We processed in before you got here."

Cristobel spun around and grabbed a small bridesmaid, pushing her firmly back into place.

"Now," she said, frowning in concentration, then broke off again. "Oh, *do* stand still, Kate," she snapped at the protesting bridesmaid. "It doesn't matter if Nigel stepped on your foot. Now where was I? Laura, you should be in front of Mother and Sir Charles, immediately after all these little horrors. And, Alasdair, good thing you turned up, because you walk with Laura."

Laura looked up in a panic and caught Alasdair's amused gaze on her. Walking to her side, he offered her his arm as, like a pack of cards, they were all shuffled into place again.

"Ready?" Cristobel called, putting a restraining hand on Hamish who was about to resume his prowling.

"Now do stay there with Mr. McIntyre, Nunkie darling," she pleaded. "Or go and talk to Grandfather Lindsay if you must change places. Now, off we go."

Mr. McNabb, who by now had also joined the ranks of the punch-drunk, slid around on the organ seat again. With majestic chords thundering above them, they all began to march down the aisle.

Tentatively, as if she were touching red-hot coals, Laura placed her hand on Alasdair's arm. He looked down at her, and she felt the muscles tighten inside his gray pinstriped jacket. As the music echoed around the empty church, Laura closed her eyes. She felt safe and secure on Alasdair's protective arm. And for one wonderful moment she imagined it was the two of them heading the procession out of the dimness of the church into the sunshine of a new life together.

"We've reached the steps," she heard him whisper.

Opening her eyes, she looked up to see him smiling down at her.

"Don't know where you were," he went on, "but with your eyes closed you risked catapulting us both headfirst into the graveyard."

Laura felt a blush creeping up from her neck and quickly let go of Alasdair's arm.

"Hey, wait a minute," he cried, pulling her back. "Not so fast. We've got to maneuver ourselves through this arch of swords. Or is it only the bride and groom?"

"Only the bride and groom," Graeme called from the back. "Now we have to hang around and say 'cheese' for the photographers."

As there was no photographer present to capture the bride in her old tweed skirt and faded twinset standing beside the groom in crumpled cavalry twills, the little group broke up on the steps of the church.

"Listen, everybody," Cristobel called, again clapping her hands for silence. "Are you *sure* you all know your places for tomorrow? We don't want a rugby scrum, do we, Mr. McIntyre?"

The verger nodded bleakly, obviously convinced that tomorrow would be a disaster.

The group responded in the affirmative, led loudly by the pageboys who had been standing still long enough and had now begun a hilarious game of hide and seek among the tombstones.

"Oh, someone catch them and tie them up," Cristobel groaned.

She broke off and bent down to sweep a tiny, dark-haired girl who was crying bitterly into her arms.

"Darling," Cristobel exclaimed, "whatever's the matter?"

But the child only sobbed more loudly, pathetically repeating, "Papa, Papa."

Cristobel's concerned expression slowly faded. "Katharine," she called, standing on tiptoe and looking around. "Mother, can you see Katharine?"

"She and Emma are still in the church," Flora replied. "They're putting the last touches to the flowers."

But at the mention of her mother's name, the child's wails

of "Papa, Papa" became louder and more insistent. She struggled to release herself from Cristobel's grasp.

"She doesn't seem to want her mother," Cristobel went on. "Better get hold of Maxime."

Flora took the struggling child from her daughter's arms and set her on the ground, firmly holding her hand.

"I'm afraid the excitement's proved too much for Elisabeth," Cristobel confided. "She's wet her knickers."

Ten

D o you think Lady Entwhistle will wear the Red Indian headdress she sported at the Buchanan wedding in June?" Alasdair asked his mother halfway through breakfast the next morning. "She looked as if she'd been on a duck shoot and was carrying the booty home on her head."

"Will I have a chance to meet her?" Maxime cut in from the other end of the table, interrupting his conversation with Robert. "She sounds enchanting."

"Won't be able to miss her." Alasdair grinned. "She'll probably butt you in the midriff with her 'Save the cuckoo' hat."

"Does everyone know about the arrangements for this evening?" Lady Flora inquired, skillfully changing the subject. "It's always such an anticlimax for the younger members of a wedding party once the bride and groom have left, so the Farquharsons have very kindly invited you all for dinner and an informal dance afterwards. I think Dorothy said she was hiring a pianist. Graeme will escort Laura. Ninian . . ."

Her third son peered around the corner of his newspaper.

"As you're the tallest, I've arranged for you to escort Catriona McFadden. One has to be so careful whom one chooses for her, otherwise she ends up with a partner who only comes up to her hip."

"Thanks," Ninian retorted drily.

Crumbling a piece of toast between her fingers, Laura kept her eyes fixed on her plate. No mention had been made of

Alasdair's partner. But since the party was to be at the Farqu-harsons', it was obviously a foregone conclusion.

Reaching for the marmalade, Alasdair smiled across the table at Laura. "Why can't Graeme take Grannie Sutherland to the party and leave me Laura? After all, the chief bridesmaid is my wedding partner, not his."

"You can have Catriona McFadden if you like," Ninian put in without taking his eyes off his newspaper.

"Ninian!" Lady Flora cried. "I've told Catriona you're so looking forward to accompanying her."

"Thanks again," Ninian muttered. "I love escorting lamp-posts."

"Oh dear," Lady Flora sighed. "Why do you all have to be so difficult?"

"Is something the matter, my dear?" her husband inquired, lowering his newspaper.

"No, yes, oh, Robert, now that everything's arranged, they all want to start changing partners."

Her husband smiled—a smile so like Alasdair's.

"Even Cristobel?" he teased raising his bushy ginger eye-brows.

Flora stared at him helplessly.

"Don't worry, my dear," he comforted. "Everything is always all right on the day."

At that moment Sandy looked up from his plate, his mouth full of kipper. "What about me?" he blurted out, showering everyone around him with half-masticated bits of fish.

"Sandy, you're *disgusting*," Alasdair exclaimed angrily, wiping lumps of Sandy's breakfast off his sleeve. "Mother, can't he be locked up somewhere out of sight at mealtimes?"

"I had thought of asking him to have breakfast upstairs with the little bridesmaids and pages," Flora replied, which remark brought further howls from Sandy. "But it slipped my mind."

"Heaven forbid!" Graeme exclaimed. "Goodness knows what tricks he'd teach them. They'd probably all go trotting down the aisle disguised as turnips and cucumbers."

"But what *about* me?" Sandy insisted loudly. "I'm ushing too. I should be invited to the party."

"Not a hope," Alasdair said firmly. "Who in their right mind would want to partner you?"

"We could always ask Rose Livesey," Graeme said innocently.

Alasdair burst out laughing.

"I went to Cristobel's engagement ball," Sandy pouted.

"Merely because it was safer to have you where we could keep an eye on you," Alasdair replied.

"But why should I have to come home to a rotten boiled egg when you all will be stuffing yourselves with caviar?" Sandy protested, waving his fork in the air.

"Sandy dear," Lady Flora put in mildly, looking up from her conversation with Katharine, "don't be so tiresome. You know perfectly well that no one goes to grown-up parties at fifteen. And leave your fork on your plate."

As the wrangling and repartee echoed around her, Laura wondered at Robert Hamilton's seeming indifference. He was a man of authority, and yet he rarely intervened in these frequent altercations between his children. Perhaps he realizes it's all just a game, she thought. Once again she felt a pang of envy for Cristobel's good fortune at being part of this teasing, happy family.

Looking up, she caught Katharine's eyes on her. And Laura blushed. Laura had seen that same compassionate look in them three years earlier when Katharine had found her crying her heart out on a bench in the walled garden. Laura had given no explanation of her distress, but she felt that Katharine knew. Her eyes held Laura's. It was as if Katharine were trying to say, "I understand."

Carefully replacing her napkin in its holder, Katharine rose to her feet. "I must go and have a word with Janet about Elisabeth."

She smiled down at Flora. "We don't want a repeat performance of what happened after the rehearsal yesterday afternoon."

"I hope Elisabeth has gotten over her little upset." Flora smiled back.

"I've no idea," Katharine replied airily. She smiled quizzically at her husband as he rose from the table and came to stand beside her. "Ask Maxime. He's the only person Elisabeth ever communicates with."

"Elisabeth's all right," he reassured her, throwing an arm lightly around her shoulders. "I looked into the nursery on the way down to breakfast, and Janet said she'd slept the clock around. It was the excitement of having so many children to play with. She must have gotten overtired."

"All the same, I'll just go up and make sure," Katharine murmured.

"I'll come with you," Maxime said quietly.

"They're talking about our little lass," Graeme announced, shaking the pages of the *Scotsman* as, arm in arm, Katharine and Maxime walked from the dining room.

"Ooh," squealed Cristobel, "let me see."

Leaping up, she flew around the table to grab the newspaper from her brother's hands.

"Hey, steady on," he chided as she impatiently rustled the pages, searching for the announcement. "Let me find it for you." Taking the newspaper, he pointed out a paragraph.

Cristobel gazed enchanted at the black print announcing her wedding and sighed with delight. "I can't believe it," she purred. "It's really happening. . . . It's today!"

Throwing down the paper, she grabbed Graeme from his chair and whirled her eldest brother around the table until he begged for mercy.

"If you want me to ush," Graeme gasped, "then you'd better let go, or I won't even be able to stand up, let alone show your illustrious guests to their seats."

Cristobel dropped her arms and stood stock-still. "Oh, *why* isn't it half past eleven now?" she spluttered.

"It soon will be." Robert Hamilton smiled affectionately at his only daughter.

Laura looked at him and thought she detected a note of sadness in his voice. He caught her glance and, perhaps sensing that she had understood the undertones behind his remark, quickly masked his face with the newspaper.

Cristobel grabbed Laura, hauled her to her feet, and danced out of the dining room with her.

"The bouquets have just arrived," Lady Flora announced, joining the two girls on the half-landing. "They are absolutely lovely. Jock insisted on coming back and organizing the flowers."

"Darling Jock," Cristobel breathed, her arm around Laura's waist. "Is he downstairs now?"

"No, he's gone home. But he'll be here when you arrive back from church."

"Isn't he going to the church?" Cristobel asked in surprise.

"Darling, he *is* ninety-two," her mother reminded her. "He might find the crowd and the standing too much. But he wants to be the first to congratulate Lindsay when you return."

Cristobel's luminous eyes filled with tears. Jock had come to Annanbrae as an apprentice gardener before Robert was born. He had risen to head gardener and taught Malcolm and a succession of younger men their skills. He was now very frail but had sworn that he would not die until he'd seen his Miss Cristobel married.

A terrible caterwauling echoed from the floor above.

"Oh dear," murmured Lady Flora. "I do hope Alasdair isn't being too unkind to Sandy. He's supposed to be helping him get ready."

Laura and Cristobel looked at each other and grinned.

"You will stay until Lindsay and Cristobel come back from their honeymoon, won't you?" Lady Flora asked Laura as they walked up the wide oak staircase together.

"I'm afraid I have to go back to London," Laura mumbled. "My classes start next week."

"You're returning to the Royal Academy of Music?"

"Yes, and I'm studying the harp as well this term," she added. "I can't possibly arrive late."

"Oh, Laura, how sad," Lady Flora remarked. "I was hoping you would be able to stay on. Robert and I will find the house terribly empty once Cristobel has gone."

Laura knew this was not true. Lady Flora and her husband were utterly wrapped up in each other. But the lonely child inside her was pleased to feel wanted.

"We're only going to be away a week," Cristobel complained. "Lindsay has to be back on duty in Germany on Monday, so we shall be leaving here on Sunday morning and taking the boat from Hull to somewhere or other over there. Then we drive to our new home."

Lady Flora looked intently at her daughter. "I do hope you won't be too disappointed," she said thoughtfully. "Married quarters can sometimes be rather primitive."

"Disappointed?" Cristobel exclaimed, her eyes shining. "Oh, never. I'd be in heaven living under the bacon counter at Sainsbury's as long as Lindsay was there."

Her mother and Laura exchanged amused smiles.

"Oh, *do* change your mind," Cristobel wheedled, grabbing her friend around the waist. "You *must* stay. You can practice your old scales twice as hard the week after. The entire family will be here," she added. "And we're going to have a lovely wedding party all over again next Saturday evening. Only this time with Lindsay and me present."

They had reached the long gallery, and Cristobel began dancing Laura from side to side. Had Laura been wavering, this last remark would have decided her. She had no desire to be part of any more family gatherings as long as Alasdair was around.

"Say yes," Cristobel coaxed as, breathless, they slithered to a halt.

Laura smiled and said nothing. Cristobel assumed that she had won. *When she returns, she'll have other things to occupy her mind*, Laura thought. *She won't even notice I've gone.*

"Your dress has been laid out on your bed, Laura dear," Lady Flora said coming up behind them. "It's *so* pretty. The same blue as your eyes. You'll look enchanting."

Laura smiled and opened the door to her room.

"Mother, I want you to help me," Cristobel squealed, pushing open her bedroom door. Then she gasped, "Oh, Laura, come and *look*."

She reappeared in the gallery holding a frothing mass of ivory satin and old lace against her.

Lady Flora started to follow her daughter as Cristobel waltzed back into her room. But pausing in the doorway, she saw Laura standing in the long gallery. Sensing the bitter-sweet emotions that mingle in the mind of every chief bridesmaid when she sees her best friend go to the altar before her, Lady Flora turned back.

"Do call if you need any help," she said softly. She drew Laura to her in a warm embrace.

In spite of the pandemonium at the rehearsal, as Robert had predicted, everything was all right on the day. Cristobel's wedding was the wedding every young girl dreams about.

A perfect September morning dawned, the autumn foliage brush-stroked with glorious wild slashes of rust and gold against a cloudless blue sky. Shimmering sunbeams filtered in through the open church door as Lindsay and Cristobel walked back down the aisle as man and wife. The organ boomed, the great bell pealed, the waiting crowd cheered, and, Alasdair's arm against her hand, Laura felt the flame of the bridal couple's happiness blaze in her.

"That dress exactly matches your eyes," Alasdair whispered as they stood in the sunshine posing for the photographer. "Has anyone ever told you that they are the color of forget-me-nots?"

Laura felt that revealing blush rise up and stain her cheeks.

"But this morning they're shining like deep blue unfathomable pools."

He pressed her hand against his arm. But at that moment Fiona Farquharson ran toward them. "Laura," she called, "you're to go with Lady Entwhistle in her car. Alasdair, you're coming with us." She possessively grabbed his hand.

Laura felt like an unwanted parcel with "not known at this

address" written boldly across it in Fiona Farquharson's hand-writing.

"Just one minute," Alasdair protested, retrieving Laura's hand and tucking it back under his arm. "I'd like to see Laura to her car."

"All Mother's carting arrangements seem to have gone hay-wire," he remarked as they walked to where Lady Entwhistle's chauffeur was waiting.

He laughed. "But that's Mother. Unfortunately out of the lottery you've picked an unlucky number. Only hope the old girl doesn't bite you!"

Laura looked up at him, not understanding.

"Her fancy dress," he explained. "She's swapped her Hiawatha headpiece for a bright purple brush festooned with feathers. Looks like a cockatoo that's been left out in the rain."

Squeezing her hand, he helped her into the waiting car.

"It won't make any difference to our friendship," Cristobel whis-pered, dodging an avalanche of confetti. She hugged Laura. In a moment she would be whisked away by her handsome bride-groom to the Lindsay estate in the western Highlands, which would one day be theirs.

As soon as the hugs, the kisses, the good wishes, and the frantic waving had subsided, and the leftover kippers and old boots thoughtfully provided by Sandy had been untied from the car bumper and the culprit hauled from the trunk, Laura escaped to her room.

Sitting on the wide cushioned window seat, she looked out over the lawns that had so recently teemed with more than 300 people. This would be her last visit to Annanbrae, she decided. Unless her feelings for Alasdair died or were replaced by some-thing stronger. But as she watched the last guests straggling across the lawn, she knew that this was unlikely.

Her adolescent infatuation had changed into a deep certainty that he was the one man who could bring her to that awakening she had seen in Cristobel's eyes. But now all she could see was Alasdair dancing into the distance, Fiona Farquharson in his arms. Plunged in gloom, Laura determined that no matter what pressure was put on her to stay, she would return to London the following morning.

"What a pity Maxime and Katharine rushed off so early," Lady Flora remarked at breakfast the following morning. "But they've always wanted to visit the Hebrides, and this was the ideal opportunity." She smiled. "And I'm delighted to have Elisabeth to myself for a week. She's an enchanting child and so like her great-great-grandmother. Didn't you notice the resemblance, Laura?"

Laura looked up, a puzzled expression on her face.

"That portrait of the empress hanging in the drawing room at Le Moulin," Flora explained. "I couldn't think who Elisabeth reminded me of when they arrived. But it suddenly came to me in the church when I saw her standing so solemnly behind Cristobel and Lindsay as they exchanged their vows. She has the same mysterious expression one sees in the Winterhalter portrait—that depth, almost melancholy, in those amazing eyes. The resemblance to the Empress Elisabeth is almost uncanny. I must mention it to Katharine when they get back. Though I'm sure she's noticed it too."

Lady Flora's eyes strayed to the long windows.

"It's another beautiful day," she sighed dreamily. "And we're all going to Pitlochry for lunch."

Laura was tempted to let herself be drawn into this post-wedding family gathering. It would be fun, she reasoned, to dissect the events of the previous day. Looking up, she saw Alasdair remonstrating with Sandy, who was wolfing eggs and bacon as if he'd had warning of a famine. And she knew that, as far as her emotions were concerned, the sooner she got away, the better. Every glance he cast in her direction she misinterpreted. Every kind word he uttered gave her hope. And although he had been attentive the previous evening, she knew that she was only building up dreams that would in the end be shattered. For Alasdair, she was merely his little sister's friend.

"I'm afraid I have to leave this morning," she announced, taking her courage in both hands.

"Going already?" Alasdair teased, grinning across at her. "I was just beginning to enjoy walking down the aisle with you."

Laura colored and felt wretched.

"Maxime and Katharine are coming back especially for our post-wedding party next Saturday," Lady Flora coaxed. "I had hoped you'd stay at *least* till then. Katharine was saying only yesterday evening that she hadn't seen you for ages."

"I'd love to stay," Laura replied. "But I really must get back to my studies. I'd like to take the lunchtime train."

"Oh, Laura, I was so looking forward to our taking little Elisabeth for walks and reading her bedtime stories," Lady Flora chided. "Perhaps even giving her her first piano lessons. I'm sure she's musically gifted." Noticing Laura's embarrassment, she stopped. "But you'll come back very soon, won't you? We've come to regard you as one of the family."

Lady Flora gathered up her letters, and everyone left the table to go their separate ways.

As Laura made for the stairs, Alasdair was standing in the hall glancing through a copy of *Horse and Hound*.

"It's possible I may be in London in a few weeks' time," he said casually, lowering the magazine. "Perhaps I could have your address. It would be nice if we could meet."

Laura was taken aback. "I-I don't have an address," she stammered stupidly. "I live with my aunt."

"I know," he went on. "Edwina. Cristobel told me."

Laura looked at him in surprise.

Alasdair smiled his tantalizing smile.

"But she must live somewhere," he pursued, putting the magazine on the table and walking toward her.

"Y-Yes, she does," Laura stammered. "In Kensington. Cristobel will give it to you."

Alasdair barred her path, his head on one side.

"Won't *you?*" he asked softly.

Taking a small leather-bound notebook from his breast pocket, he stood there, pen aloft, looking at her inquiringly.

Eleven

Laura stared out the train window at the countryside flying past, her mind in a turmoil. Not only was she physically tired, she was also emotionally drained. The hectic few days she had spent at Annanbrae had been like a violent thunderstorm pierced by intense flashes of lightning, only to be immediately followed by sudden plunges into darkness. And Alasdair's behavior toward her was now even more of an enigma.

By the time the train finally steamed into King's Cross, Laura wanted only one thing—to wipe Annanbrae from her memory. But, as she wearily dragged her suitcase from the rack and stepped down onto the grimy platform, she knew that even if she could wipe out the past, Alasdair's smile would still haunt her.

In the ensuing days she plunged into her music, spending long hours in front of the harp Edwina had had installed for her in the drawing room next to the grand piano. Every time the telephone rang and Effie announced that it was for her, Laura's heart missed a beat. But it was never Alasdair.

Occasionally she found Edwina watching her, and she longed to tell her aunt about the ache in her heart. But something always held her back. Again Laura would envy Cristobel the easy intimacy between her and her mother, an intimacy that seemed alien to Laura's family.

"I was wondering whether you would like to go to Vienna

for Christmas," Edwina remarked one evening as Laura sat improvising at the piano.

Laura looked up. "But what about Father?"

Since her mother's death, she and Edwina had dutifully spent the two festive days in Oxford with him. But they were anything but festive. Henry Denning, after welcoming them cordially, usually seemed relieved when the time came for them to say good-bye.

"I really don't think he'd notice whether we were there or not." Edwina smiled. "You've been looking very pale recently. You need a change. And you'd enjoy Vienna. There are always wonderful concerts in the winter."

Laura shrugged. "If you think it would be a good idea," she replied halfheartedly.

"I do think so," Edwina replied firmly. "I'll write to the Bristol this evening to reserve rooms and see about our train reservations in the morning. We could leave on the—" She suddenly broke off. "Laura, you're not listening!"

With an effort Laura jerked herself back to the present. She had been thinking of Annanbrae, wondering whether Lindsay and Cristobel would be there for Christmas, seeing in her mind's eye the enormous Christmas tree twinkling with colored lights in a corner of the great hall, the dining room decorated with garlands of holly and mistletoe, and the laughter.

"I'm sorry." She blinked. "Do go on."

"Never mind," Edwina said serenely. "We'll talk about it in a few days when you're less tired."

Laura twisted around on the piano stool. "Yes, if you don't mind. I *am* rather tired. I think I'll have an early night."

"You need to go out more," Edwina said fondly as Laura closed the piano. "There's a Polish pianist playing at the Albert Hall tomorrow evening. I'll book tickets. And it might be a good idea for you to get away from London at the weekend and breathe some country air."

Her eyes followed Laura as she crossed to the door.

"You could put on a little weight as well," she added. "Since the summer you've become positively wraithlike."

The following evening as Laura dropped her music case in the hall, Edwina greeted her with an unexpected piece of news. "I had a telephone call from a friend of yours this afternoon," she announced, walking out of the drawing room. "Cristobel's brother. He's in London for a few days, so I asked him to dinner this evening."

"But I thought we were going to a concert at the Albert Hall," Laura protested.

"We were. But he's agreed to accompany you in my place."

Laura stood stock-still, her throat suddenly dry. "But none of the Hamiltons are musical," she blurted out. "Except Sandy."

"You do surprise me," Edwina answered smoothly. "He seemed delighted by the idea."

Laura stared blankly at her aunt, not daring to voice the question uppermost in her mind. It could be Ninian in London for a few days . . . or it could be Graeme. But neither had asked for her telephone number.

"Do you know which b-brother?" she finally stammered.

"Yes," Edwina replied calmly. "He announced himself as Alasdair Hamilton."

Laura fled to her bedroom, frantically searching for an excuse not to appear at dinner. But she knew that even if she found one, her aunt would not be deceived. Edwina realized that her niece's listlessness since her return from Scotland was not due to overwork. Inviting Alasdair to dinner and offering him her place at the recital was a calculated move on her aunt's part.

"Oh, why did he have to telephone?" Laura groaned.

Why had he come to break into the musical fortress she was determinedly building around herself? Then, remembering the look in his eyes when he had asked for her address, her heart momentarily soared—only to sink again like a bird felled by a hunter's bullet.

"I suppose he doesn't know many people in London," she muttered bitterly, "and thought his sister's little friend might fill an evening."

Laura heard his voice in the hall as she sat stiffly in the drawing room with Edwina. Her heart began to beat unreasonably fast. But by the time Effie announced him, she had set her lips into a hard, straight line.

Edwina was charmed by Alasdair. Good hostess that she was, she made up for Laura's silence, keeping the conversation flowing smoothly throughout dinner.

"Your aunt is delightful," Alasdair murmured as they sat side by side in the taxi on their way to the recital.

"Yes, she is," Laura replied woodenly.

"Odd that she hasn't married," he went on after an uncomfortable pause.

"Perhaps she didn't want to," Laura cut in aggressively.

"Perhaps," he answered, and then lapsed into silence.

"Are you like her, Laura?" Alasdair inquired as the taxi drew up in front of the Albert Hall.

For a moment she didn't understand. Then, realizing that he was merely finishing the sentence he had started a few minutes ago, she flushed. "I don't know," she mumbled as they walked up the steps and into the crowded foyer. "Yes, I suppose I am."

When they walked back into the dark night, it was raining. Standing among the milling crowd waiting for a taxi, Laura looked away from him, looking at anything rather than risk meeting his eyes. The glistening wet pavement, from which red double-decker buses, their streaming windows solid with heads, were lumbering away, spread out before her like a shining wet macintosh. The lights from passing cars dazzled with raindrops as they glided by into the darkness.

"Here we are," Alasdair said as a taxi stopped beside them.

"I have to return to Edinburgh at the weekend," he remarked casually, leaning back against the leather cushion. "But it would be lovely if we could meet again. Would you, by any chance, be free to have dinner with me tomorrow evening?"

Laura's heart was beating a tattoo inside her dress. Her defenses were beginning to crumble. Everything within her longed to shriek yes. But she remembered the last time they had met. And Fiona Farquharson once again came and stood defiantly between them.

"I'm afraid not," she answered tightly.

"Oh dear," he replied, shrinking into the corner of the cab. "What a pity."

Alasdair stared intently out the window for a few seconds. "Perhaps Thursday?" he ventured.

"I'm awfully busy at the moment," she said stiffly. "And on Friday I'm going down to the country for the weekend."

He did not pursue the matter further. They sat in wooden silence as the taxi maneuvered through the web of streets.

"I have the offer of a transfer to London," Alasdair mentioned as they turned into her quiet road. "That's why I'm here. To nose out the pros and cons." He cleared his throat. "I have to decide fairly quickly whether I shall accept it or not," he went on as the taxi drew up in front of Edwina's block of flats.

Laura was in an agony of apprehension. She knew that courtesy demanded that she invite Alasdair in for a nightcap. But, as he sat beside her, the slight damp smell rising from his clothes brought with it an odor that emphasized his masculinity. She didn't know how much longer she could keep up this pretense of indifference.

"I would like to ask you in for a drink," she said awkwardly, as he prepared to pay off the driver. "But it's late, and I know you have a busy day tomorrow with all these important decisions to make. And I have an early lesson. So I'll say good-bye now."

Alasdair looked at her in surprise, too polite to comment. Signaling to the driver to wait, he took her arm and walked with her to the door.

"It's been delightful seeing you again, Laura," he breathed. "May I telephone you when I'm next in London?"

Flashes of electricity shot up Laura's arm and throughout her body. "I-I am very busy," she stuttered, plunging her hand into her little velvet evening bag, searching blindly for her key.

Alasdair held out his hand and inserted the key into the lock. The door swung open, and an elderly porter shuffled out of his lodge. "Good evening, Miss Denning," he said with an approving look at Alasdair. "Good evening, sir. Nasty night."

Alasdair took Laura's hand in both of his as the lift glided to a standstill. "Thank you for this evening," he said softly.

He leaned toward her. Laura felt his breath on her forehead, and for a second she leaned toward him. Then abruptly she stiffened and withdrew her hands. She felt him stiffen in his turn. Without a word, he opened the lift door, and Laura entered. Alasdair closed the gates, and, as it mounted and she disappeared from view, he walked back across the hall and out into the street.

Laura stood frozen as the lift ascended, longing to call him back. But her lips seemed to have locked themselves once again into that hard, straight line. When it stopped at the third floor, she jerked back the door and ran to the window.

Alasdair was climbing into the waiting taxi. She watched it draw away from the curb and disappear around the corner of the road. Tears began to tumble down her cheeks, spattering her dark blue velvet coat in sympathy with the rain spattering the window panes.

"Alasdair," she wept softly. "Oh, Alasdair, why did you come back just as I was beginning to make some sort of pattern out of my life?" Entering the quiet flat, she crumpled, sobbing, onto the hall chair.

When the storm of weeping subsided, Laura became aware of the muted strains of a Beethoven symphony coming from the drawing room. Edwina had not gone to bed. Quickly wiping her face, she put her head around the door. The room was in darkness except for the roseate tints of the logs glowing in the grate and a pool of golden light streaming from the lamp beside which her aunt sat reading. Edwina looked up as Laura appeared.

"What a charming young man." She smiled, wisely ignoring her niece's red-rimmed eyes. "I do hope he enjoyed the recital."

"Yes," Laura mumbled. "Yes, I think so. I've just come to say good night."

"Good night, darling," Edwina said gently. "Sleep well."

As Laura closed the door behind her, Edwina sighed. Switching off the peach-shaded reading lamp, she rose to her feet and stood gazing into the fire's glowing embers. She had heard the lift stop, the front door quietly open, and the brokenhearted sobbing. Her mind returned to that July morning when she had sat beside Laura's bed wondering how to tell her twelve-year-old niece that her mother's long battle with cancer had finally ended.

Laura had shed no tears, shown no outward sign of emotion. In fact, she had never spoken of it. But, always a shy, introverted child, from that day she had seemed to withdraw further into herself. Edwina wondered whether the storm of weeping might be tears that had been stored for over seven years, waiting for release.

As these thoughts crossed her mind, Laura's words to her on that fateful July morning seven years ago took on a new meaning. "Were *they* there?" her niece had asked, referring to her two older sisters.

Recalling that moment, Edwina recognized for the first time the resentment in the young girl's voice and knew the rejection Laura must have felt. Perhaps she even felt that she was unwanted or unworthy, or in some way to blame for her mother's death.

"We thought it best to let you sleep," her aunt had replied.

Now she knew that they had been wrong. They had cut Laura off from the help and healing she needed in this traumatic time, leaving her alone to cope with a pain that had never been worked through and released.

Edwina sighed again. For the first time in her life, she felt helpless. She remembered the last words her sister-in-law had spoken to her youngest daughter: "Your heavenly Father will look after you." At the time Laura had been bewildered by them. But now Edwina wondered whether there was something to be said for having a faith. Had she been a churchgoer . . . but she dismissed the idea. She knew dozens of churchgoers, and she was convinced they would have been as much at a loss as she had been. But, as her elegantly shod foot poked idly at the few remaining embers, Edwina recognized that she had met people who had a transparent quality, a radiance about about them such as her sister-in-law had had during the last few weeks of her life. They had been different.

Edwina straightened up, desperately hoping that her niece would meet one of them, someone who could help her where she herself felt helpless. Who could give Laura the security she so desperately needed and perhaps even the answers to life's problems?

Could this young man, Edwina mused, *be the catalyst for the torrent of pent-up emotions to be released?* She fervently hoped so. Gone were the days when she could make Laura's pain better with a hug and a kiss. Her niece was a woman now. And as far as her aunt could make out, a woman deeply in love.

As she walked across the gracious white-paneled room and into the silent hall, Edwina smiled sadly. She was out of her depth before life's great mystery.

Twelve

It's amazing the way Elisabeth has taken to that pony," Maxime remarked, stretching his neck and peering into Katharine's dressing table mirror as he knotted his tie. "She's a born horsewoman. Today was only the second time I'd taken her out, and she sat in the saddle like a queen."

"Or an empress," Katharine added drily.

Maxime raised his eyebrows quizzically.

"Just something Flora said when we were at Annanbrae," his wife explained. "She remarked on how like her great-great-grandmother Elisabeth is." Katharine sighed. "I hope being a born horsewoman is the only trait she has inherited."

Maxime's mind went back to the night Elisabeth was born and his misgivings when Katharine had insisted on naming their precious daughter after her tragic great-great-grandmother, misgivings he had quickly dismissed in the euphoria of the moment. Now they rose to confront him again, and, not for the first time, he saw what Flora had meant. Elisabeth did resemble her ancestor Elisabeth, the tragic empress. A cold hand of fear for his beloved daughter clutched at his heart.

His eyes met Katharine's in her mirror. Seeing his own anxiety reflected in his wife's gaze, he quickly brushed it aside. "Elisabeth's very like *my* mother also." He smiled.

"Who was like her paternal grandmother," Katharine reminded him. "I remember Armand telling me that. He said it was possibly one of the reasons the empress was so attached to her." A shadow crossed her face. "Oh, Maxime," she cried, turning agonized eyes upon him.

In spite of his own apprehensions, Maxime smiled. "She's inherited her great-great-grandmother's beauty," he soothed. "That's not a bad thing. And possibly her superb horsemanship. But as for the rest . . ." He shrugged. "Our Elisabeth will have a totally different life, and I'll make sure she doesn't choose an ogre for a mother-in-law—or live in a cold-comfort palace."

He brushed Katharine's curls with his lips, feeling her relax under his touch. "I was thinking," he went on, "that perhaps we could spend a couple of days in Bordeaux next week."

Katharine removed the sapphire earrings her husband had given her on their wedding day from their velvet box. Leaning forward and peering into the mirror to adjust them, she raised her eyebrows inquiringly.

"I have to be there on Wednesday morning for a meeting," Maxime explained. "So if you have nothing else on, we could take the lunchtime train on Tuesday, go to the theater in the evening, and stay the night at the Royal Gascogne. You could even make a start on your Christmas shopping the next morning if you wished."

He placed his hands on her shoulders. "How does that sound?"

"It sounds like a lovely idea," Katharine murmured. "But I've already got your Christmas present. In fact, I was going to give it to you tonight after we got back."

Maxime frowned. "Isn't it a bit early? Christmas isn't for another three weeks."

Katharine smiled mischievously at his reflection, her earlier anxiety evaporating as she relished the news she had been nurturing for the past few hours.

He leaned forward and their eyes met. "You're looking very mysterious about something," he teased.

"Not very *beautiful?*" she queried. "If I remember rightly, that's what you said once before when we played this scene."

Maxime's eyebrows drew together in a puzzled frown.

She dimpled up at him, and suddenly his brow cleared. "Katharine," he gasped, "you're teasing me!"

"I'm not," she breathed.

Leaning back against him, she sought his hand and held it lovingly against her cheek. "I always told you there was something magical about the Hebrides."

Maxime sat down abruptly on the stool beside her and, grasping her shoulders, turned her toward him. "If you mean what I think you mean . . ."

"I do." She smiled. "A little sister for Elisabeth. I saw Dr. Massenon this afternoon."

Katharine sighed, her eyes dreamy. This time she was convinced that the child she carried would be the little daughter she had longed for when Elisabeth was born, a daughter with whom she could share as she grew up and be a friend and companion, as her mother had been to her.

"She'll be arriving on the 25th of June."

Maxime's hands dropped to his side, and he rose from the stool. "Katharine," he groaned.

"I know what you are going to say. My age. Dr. Massenon mentioned it too."

"And—"

"He said that after this one, I'd better concentrate on having grandchildren."

Maxime shook his head in bewilderment. Suddenly the joy that had lit a soft glow in Katharine's eyes disappeared. "Darling," she cried, "we have this same performance every time. You panic when there's absolutely no need."

She caught his hand again. "I'm so happy about the baby," she pleaded. "Say you are too."

Maxime's expression softened. "Of course I'm happy, darling," he assured her. "But I'll be happier still when he or she is safely delivered . . . and I know you're still with me."

"I'll always be with you, Maxime," she whispered.

The turret clock ponderously chimed eight.

Maxime picked up Katharine's velvet cloak from the bed and held it out for her.

"I could do without dinner at the Polignac's this evening, couldn't you?" Katharine yawned, rising from her stool. "I feel so gloriously sleepy."

"I should have recognized the signs," Maxime teased.

She slipped her arm through his.

"I'd love to come to Bordeaux with you next week," she whispered. "But don't expect me to give you another Christmas present!"

Thirteen

Laura awoke the next morning with a splitting headache. Remembering Alasdair's nearness the previous evening, reviving emotions she had struggled to subdue since her return from Scotland, she felt a sense of hopelessness. Mercifully, Edwina always breakfasted in her room, so, apart from a brief greeting to Effie, Laura was spared conversation.

When she returned from school to Kensington that afternoon, Edwina was standing by the drawing room fire reading a card. "Aren't they lovely!" she exclaimed, pointing to a beautiful spray of winter roses in a tall vase on the piano. The orange-gold petals blended perfectly with the autumnal shades of the furnishings. "There's a delightful posy for you beside them."

Laura crossed to the piano and picked up a bunch of forget-me-nots tied with blue satin ribbon. Removing the card from its envelope, she felt her knees buckle under her. Abruptly she sat down on the stool.

"The color of your eyes," it read. It was signed: "A."

She remembered her intense moment of happiness at Cristobel's wedding that perfect September morning. Her body tingled, and she began to tremble.

"Such a charming young man," Edwina repeated, sitting down on the deep sofa as Effie came in with a tray. Edwina picked up the silver teapot and began to pour.

"How very thoughtful of him," she went on. "Those roses are exquisite." She glanced across at them, standing erect and regal in

111

the crystal vase. "And wherever did he find forget-me-nots in London in December?" Her eyes carefully avoided her niece's face.

Laura hurriedly put down her cup. "I-I'll ask Effie to put them in water," she stammered, picking up the posy. "I have some theory to work on for tomorrow. I'd better get down to it."

Edwina looked at her intently over the rim of her cup. "For a young girl not yet twenty," she remarked, "you do not seem to be having a very exciting life. It's all work and no play."

"I went out yesterday evening," Laura bristled.

"Merely because I suggested it," her aunt replied smoothly. "When I was your age, we took life a great deal less seriously . . . and enjoyed it a great deal more." Edwina shrugged. "However, that was another generation. Run along, darling, and do your theory. But, remember, there *are* other things in life besides music. Don't become so wrapped up in it that life passes you by."

Leaning back among the satin cushions, Edwina innocently picked up the evening paper and glanced at the headlines.

Throughout the following day, Laura was distracted, unable to concentrate. Her mind kept drifting to Alasdair, wondering whether he had decided to move to London or stay in Edinburgh. Leaving the Academy that afternoon, she felt weary and drained.

But Friday was even worse. She knew that by then Alasdair would have made that vital decision. The idea that he might reappear in London, even live nearby with Fiona at his side, sent her into paroxysms of anguish.

She was now convinced that his telephone call and visit, even his request to see her again, had been merely a means of passing the time and that once back in Scotland, Fiona Farquharson would occupy his thoughts. Indeed, perhaps she had occupied them during the evening he had spent with her.

As these thoughts chased each other around in her tired brain, the notes on the partition in front of her constantly faded, to be replaced by Alasdair's face. With an exasperated sigh, she closed the piano, gathered up her music, and left the little cubicle.

Hailing a taxi, Laura gave the address in Kensington. But suddenly she had an overwhelming desire to see Alasdair again, if only from a distance. Hardly realizing what she was doing, she leaned forward, tapped at the dividing window, and asked the cabbie to drive through St. James. They would pass in front of Alasdair's club, and perhaps she would catch a glimpse of him entering or leaving or even striding across the park.

But although the driver slowed down as they approached the club, there was no sign of Alasdair. Two businessmen wearing bowler hats stood talking on the steps. For a second Laura's heart leaped. But as the taxi crawled by, she realized that neither man in any way approached Alasdair's imposing stature.

Laura closed her eyes to hold back the tears, angry with herself and hating Alasdair for coming back into her life and reducing her to this state of slavery.

As she let herself into the flat, Effie appeared. "Madam asked me to let you know that she won't be in for tea," she announced, "and that there's a gentleman waiting to see you in the drawing room."

Laura frowned. The last thing she wanted was company. Dropping her coat and gloves on the hall chair, she glanced into the gilt mirror.

"What a sight," she moaned as her pale heart-shaped face stared back at her.

Twilight lay like a purple cloak over the drawing room, casting deepening shadows on the silhouette of a tall, well-built man. He was standing framed in the window, looking down onto the mews below. But as the door opened, he turned.

It was Alasdair.

"Laura," he said softly.

Stunned, she remained standing in the doorway, her hand gripping the knob. The room seemed to be filled with his masculinity.

"I'm sorry," he said lamely. "I wanted to see you before leaving for Edinburgh." He paused. "I had to see you. I rang Miss Denning, and she said you would be home around five."

Laura looked pointedly at her watch. "It's only just after four," she remarked stiffly.

"I know. I couldn't wait."

Alasdair took a step toward her, but she remained rooted to the spot.

"Won't you come and sit down," he pleaded.

Her legs like cotton wool, she advanced slowly into the room. Then, carefully avoiding the deep sofa, she quickly sat on a delicate tapestry-covered chair.

He sat down opposite her, his clasped hands hanging loosely between his knees. Neither seemed to know where to go from there.

Laura stole a glance at him from beneath her thick lashes. Alasdair's eyes were fixed on a square of pale gold carpet. His face was almost in darkness, with only his rugged profile visible, reflected in the dancing firelight.

"Laura," he murmured at last, without looking up.

But at that moment the drawing room door opened. Effie entered and set the tea tray on a small table in front of Laura. Crossing to the window, the maid drew the heavy velvet curtains against the early winter's night. Suddenly Alasdair's dim features were plunged into obscurity. Effie switched on a lamp behind him, and he leaped back into view. Laura noticed that his lips also were pressed tightly together.

Lifting the heavy Georgian teapot, Laura began to pour. As she handed him the delicate fluted cup, Alasdair looked up. She tried to recapture the anger toward him she had felt in the taxi. But it had gone. Their eyes met briefly, and she noticed that the green and gold lights that usually danced so merrily in his had vanished.

"Crumpets?" she asked prosaically, avoiding his eyes as she lifted the lid from a silver salver.

He took one and placed it on his plate untouched. Laura did the same. The oppressive silence returned.

Abruptly Alasdair put down his cup and looked appealingly

at her. But she was studiously cutting her untouched crumpet into postage-stamp-sized squares.

"Laura," Alasdair said hoarsely, "did you get my flowers?"

"Thank you, yes," she answered hurriedly. "I'm sorry, I should have written—"

"I didn't want thanking," he interrupted. "I just thought that perhaps forget-me-nots might . . . that you would remember . . ." He made a helpless gesture with his hands.

"Remember what?" Laura asked frostily. And she hated herself.

He suddenly seemed crushed.

Laura picked up her cup and pushed aside her mutilated crumpet. She could feel herself weakening, and she knew she had to steel herself against this man or be submerged in the avalanche of love roaring through her.

"Have you made your decision?" she inquired with a false brightness.

He looked at her blankly.

"Whether to stay in Edinburgh or move to London."

He shook his head.

"But I thought you had to do so before you left," she pursued, still in that same false tone.

"I have. I'm playing golf with the chairman tomorrow morning and lunching with him afterwards. He expects an answer then."

Laura could feel her heart hammering beneath her silk blouse. Reaching up, she pulled her cardigan closely around her. "And do you know what it will be?" Her voice sounded in her ears like a ventriloquist's doll.

A log dropped in the fire, then toppled into the grate. Alasdair bent forward and, picking up the tongs, retrieved it, placing it carefully back on the pile.

"No," he answered dully. "That's why I'm here."

He got up and stood looking down at her.

"Laura," he pleaded, "*please* tell me. Is there anyone else?"

She looked up at him blankly, her blue eyes darkening as she saw the misery in his.

"I *have* to know," he insisted. "At first I thought if I were patient, it would work out. I knew you were shy and reserved, but when we met again last June, you seemed to be as drawn to me as I was to you. And then . . . you became so strange."

He ran his hands through his hair distractedly. "For the last six months you've been avoiding me. Every time I tried to see you . . . you ran away."

Laura sat breathing deeply, unable to believe, much less understand, what she had just heard.

"When I first met you," Alasdair went on, sitting down again, "you were just Cristobel's friend. But that evening of her engagement ball when I saw you dancing with Angus Dunbar, you took my breath away."

He paused, his eyes back on his clenched hands, his voice almost a whisper. "I didn't recognize you at first. Then I suddenly realized who you were. Shy little Laura with the big blue eyes who'd turned into the most beautiful woman I'd ever seen."

Laura leaned back in her chair, the tension melting away as a ripple of happiness trickled through her. She knew that this was only a dream. Her tired brain had given up and was playing tricks, feeding into her mind a scene she had imagined so many times in the past six months, which had now taken over and replaced reality. Closing her eyes, she willed the world to stop so that she could savor and record every moment.

"Since that day I haven't been able to get you out of my mind," she heard Alasdair say in this beautiful dream. "But whenever I tried to approach you, you froze."

He sighed his eyes once more on his clenched hands.

"And yet there were moments," he went on, as if talking to himself, "like the morning of Cristobel's wedding as we left the church when I felt an answering spark in you. And I dared to hope that perhaps you did care." He looked up and smiled his crooked smile. "That I wasn't just Cristobel's big brother."

Laura did not open her eyes. She knew that once she did, all she would see would be the familiar room, the crackling fire, the curtains cozily drawn—and Alasdair's empty chair.

"Laura," he begged, "please say something. Whether I stay in Edinburgh or move to London depends on you."

Alasdair got up and, taking both her hands in his, gently drew her to her feet. She opened her eyes and saw him looking down at her, his eyes pleading.

But at the same time she saw Fiona Farquharson's face. With a sharp cry Laura wrenched herself free. Anger replaced the joy that had filled her only seconds before.

"How *dare* you!" she cried. "How dare you!"

Alasdair stood looking helplessly down at her.

"How dare you come here and make a fool of me!"

Laura breathed deeply in an attempt to control herself. "Has Fiona Farquharson thrown you over, and you're looking for a replacement?"

Fuming, she strode across to the window and fiercely pulled the curtain aside, glaring down at the lighted mews below.

"Fiona?" Alasdair gasped at last. "Fiona? What on earth has *she* got to do with it?"

Laura clutched the curtain for support. Were his conquests so numerous that he had lost track of them?

She knew she had to remain calm, steel herself for long enough to see him out of the flat. Taking a deep breath, she attempted to control her voice. But her words, when they came, sounded like gasps. "Everything," she managed to get out, her hands tightly entwined in the curtain's thick folds. "If you don't know what your relationship with her is, you must be the only one who doesn't. Your family was practically ringing wedding bells for you both the last time I was at Annanbrae."

Once again that terrible electric tension flashed between them. Then a tiny gold clock on the mantelpiece began to tinkle the hour . . . and Alasdair threw back his head and laughed.

Fourteen

As his laughter echoed around the room, Laura stood stiff and tense, willing him to go, longing only to hear the door close behind him. But Alasdair did not move—just continued to laugh helplessly.

Letting the curtain fall from her hand, she half turned from the window. And as she did so, he held out his arms. Striding quickly toward her, he grasped both her hands, pressing his face into her upturned palms.

"Oh, Laura," he gasped, raising his head and looking down at her, the green and gold lights once again dancing in his hazel eyes. "So *that's* what it was."

For a few seconds she remained stiff and taut. Then she struggled desperately to free herself, but he held her hands in a viselike grip.

Still laughing, he tried to draw her to him. With all her strength she resisted, pounding her clenched fists against his broad chest.

"Let me go!" she cried, tears streaming unchecked down her cheeks as Alasdair caught her in his arms. He held her even closer so that her hands were imprisoned, and she felt as if all breath was being squeezed from her body.

"Laura," he murmured, his face buried in her long golden hair. "Little Laura with the forget-me-not blue eyes. What a fool I've been."

He brushed his lips across her forehead. Then, tilting back

her head, he gazed into those blue eyes now swimming with tears. "Darling," he whispered, kissing her hot, wet cheeks, "you're even more beautiful when you're angry."

And bending down, he kissed the tip of her nose.

She was now sobbing uncontrollably, totally bewildered, but wanting never to move from this moment. She was in Alasdair's arms, and the rest of the world seemed to evaporate.

He let her go and drew her toward the sofa. "Laura," he said, sinking down beside her and taking her back in his arms, "I'm *so* sorry. So desperately sorry. I didn't realize that you weren't aware of the situation between Fiona and me." He laughed drily. "Almost everyone else was!"

She looked up at him, her eyelashes wet and glistening against her pale cheeks.

Alasdair let his lips wander across her hair, idly running his fingers through the silken strands.

"I love you," he said softly. "I've loved you ever since I caught sight of you dancing with Angus Dunbar. It just hit me then right between the eyes. I couldn't believe what was happening. Do you remember how I rushed over and tried to book every dance on your ball card?"

Laura nodded dumbly, as he tenderly stroked her cheek with his fingers.

"I won't pretend I haven't been in love before," Alasdair went on. "As you probably have."

"No," Laura whispered, snuggling up to him. "There's only ever been you."

He stopped stroking her hair and tentatively placed his lips on hers. With a sigh Laura closed her eyes and yielded to his embrace.

But suddenly she broke away. "Fiona! What about Fiona?"

Alasdair drew her head onto his shoulder, cradling her in the crook of his arm. She nestled close, tingling as she felt his masculine strength.

"Yes, Fiona," he went on. "But first I want you to know that I've never known anything like this before. I thought it might fade with time, especially as you seemed so indifferent to me. But it hasn't. If anything, it's grown stronger and convinced me that this time it's the real thing. Laura, you are the only woman I could ever ask to be my wife."

Laura leaned against him and began to cry again.

"Darling," Alasdair cried, fumbling in his pocket for a handkerchief. "Darling, what's the matter?"

"I don't know," she mumbled. "I'm just so happy."

"But I thought you wanted to know about Fiona and me," Alasdair teased.

"Not anymore." She smiled, her tearstained face radiant with happiness. "It simply doesn't matter."

"It does to me," Alasdair laughed. "To think that this has been standing in our way for six months when we could have been together. Why ever didn't that idiot Cristobel tell you?"

"Tell me what?"

"Fiona has been dotty about Graeme ever since she was at school," Alasdair explained. "And hedging off all other admirers, always hoping he'd come to heel. So Colin, Fiona's brother, and I worked out a plan to rouse Graeme's jealousy. My pretending, whenever Graeme was around, to be dotty about Fiona. We put the plan into action at the McFaddens' ball. And the evening I fell in love with you we were in full swing."

He grimaced.

"Doing a pretty good job, by the sound of things. We called a halt after Cristobel's wedding since the old bounder wasn't in the least perturbed by our supposed devotion. And, as neither Fiona nor I was even remotely romantically interested in the other, it all seemed rather pointless."

His brow rutted in a puzzled frown. "I can't think why Cristobel didn't mention it to you and put your mind at rest. She knew and thought the scheme hilarious."

"But wasn't it a secret?" Laura inquired.

"Yes," Alasdair answered. "But it never occurred to me that she kept anything from you. You two were always twittering together in corners like a couple of sparrows."

Laura smiled slowly. "Cristobel didn't know how I felt about you," she whispered. "She was even trying to find someone suitable to marry me off to at the ball because she wanted to keep me around. Said she'd love to have me as a sister-in-law, but there was no hope of that because her brothers were all too horrible."

"Did she now?" Alasdair mused, holding her away from him. "And do you agree?"

"No," she whispered, holding her face up to be kissed. "I am dreaming, aren't I? This can't really be happening."

Alasdair fondled her hair. "We're both dreaming. I can't believe it's really happening either."

Laura gazed up at him, and Alasdair noticed that her eyes had darkened to violet blue.

"Oh, Laura," he cried, "you *will* marry me, won't you?"

She searched for his hand, too overcome to speak.

"When?" he whispered. "Say it can be soon."

"Whenever you wish," she exulted.

She closed her eyes, and they clung to each other. Gently releasing her, Alasdair sat watching the firelight dancing on her now rosy cheeks, his eyes serious again. "But what about your music?" he asked. "Doesn't it mean an awful lot to you? Am I asking too much, wanting to marry you without waiting till you finish your studies?"

As he spoke, Laura suddenly realized that in the past half hour everything in her life except Alasdair had ceased to matter. She had work to do. But it wasn't important anymore. Her music, which till then had been her life, receded into the background. The piano's shining lid hiding the ivory keys seemed to be a sign that a chapter had ended.

As she raised her eyes, Alasdair's face seemed to expand and block everything else from her line of vision. She knew that all she wanted was him. He bent to kiss her, sensing the answer to his question. Then her aunt's words of the previous evening came back to her: "Don't become so wrapped up in your music that life passes you by."

Laura shuddered.

Alasdair raised one eyebrow inquiringly.

"I was just thinking," she mused, "how near we came to passing each other by."

"Don't," he said sharply, drawing her back into his arms.

When he released her, Laura became pensive and began fiddling with his tie.

"There's just one thing I don't understand," she said slowly. "The morning of Cristobel's ball I was awake very early, sitting by my bedroom window when you walked out of the house and disappeared. At breakfast someone said you'd gone to the Farquharsons and wouldn't be back for lunch. Your mother assumed you'd gone to see Colin. But Graeme added that it was more likely to be Fiona, judging from the way you'd been dancing attendance on her at the McFadden ball."

Alasdair let out a low whistle. "The old devil. So he did notice."

"He noticed all right," Laura went on. "And his remark plunged me into the depths."

Alasdair gathered her protectively into his arms again.

"You disappeared all day," she whispered shyly, "although you were expected back for tea. The next time I saw you, you were dancing with Fiona and gazing into her eyes."

"That's because Graeme was around," Alasdair laughed.

"But Graeme wasn't at the Farquharsons all day," Laura pointed out. "So why did you have to pretend then?"

"You really should work for Scotland Yard," he laughed. "I was away all day because Colin had telephoned me in Edinburgh about a legal problem, and I'd promised to sort it out for him on Saturday morning. As we also wanted to play golf, we decided to make an early start. Which is what we did. Before breakfast in fact. We finished earlier than expected so had lunch at the club and played golf until quite late. That's why I wasn't back for tea. Colin drove me home about six. I didn't even see Fiona until they all arrived for the ball."

He tweaked her nose. "Now are you satisfied?"

Her eyes shining, Laura drew him toward her and pressed her soft lips against his. She felt his grip on her tighten and, sinking back onto the satin cushions, yielded to his embrace.

"Alasdair," she whispered at last, taking hold of the end of his tie and slowly twining it around her fingers, "why me?"

"The obvious answer," he replied, "is why not?"

"Be serious," she pleaded. "You are surrounded by very attractive women in Scotland, women who fit into your way of life in a way I never could. Why didn't you fall in love with one of them?"

"Because you were so different. You bewitched me."

"But I don't hunt or fish or shoot. I'm not sporty at all."

"That's what I mean," Alasdair answered quietly. "I was never attracted to sporty women. To be perfectly honest, they bore me. And what makes you think I want that way of life? If I did, I'd hardly be here. You can't believe how you stood out among them—like an orchid in a gorse bush. You were elusive and mysterious. And you had that incredible knack of drawing me to you and then slipping away."

"You know why," she interrupted.

"I know now. But I didn't then. I've gone through hell these past few weeks thinking I'd lost you."

"To think," Laura breathed, "that I compared myself to Fiona and decided I could never match up to her."

"Thank heavens you can't!" Alasdair ejaculated. "Fiona's a great girl as a friend, but not as a wife. Not for me at any rate. Horsey women leave me cold. Anyway, why *me?* Why not Ninian or Graeme? You saw much more of Graeme than you ever did of me. You must admit he's very charming. *And* he's the heir. A much better catch than I am. Or there's Colin or one of the numerous Anguses littered all over the place. Why not one of them?"

"I don't know," Laura murmured softly. "There's only ever been you."

"See what I mean." He smiled. "It was a silly question in the first place. There isn't any logical explanation why I knew the moment I set eyes on you that evening that this time it was the real thing."

Alasdair rubbed his face against hers, and she felt the rough stubble graze her cheeks.

"Darling," he breathed, "I have to leave for Edinburgh tomorrow night to start winding things up. I'll do my very best to come back next weekend, but if I can't make it, promise you'll come to Annanbrae for Christmas. It's in less than three weeks, and then we can make it official."

He sat up and thoughtfully stroked his chin. "I should be joining my new law firm sometime in March. . . . Can we have a spring wedding?" He grinned down at her. "Preferably early spring."

Laura didn't even bother to reply. Had Alasdair suggested they marry that very evening, both standing on their heads in the middle of Kensington High Street, she would have joyfully agreed. But Alasdair's next words brought her back to earth with a bump. "And Edwina must come to Annanbrae with you."

Laura's hand flew to her mouth. "Alasdair," she gasped, "Edwina's planned to take me to Vienna for Christmas. She must already have booked rooms at the Bristol and even train and opera tickets, for all I know. What are we going to do? I can't possibly go now." She flung her arms around his neck.

"Darling," he soothed, gently untangling himself, "Edwina seems a perfectly reasonable woman. I'm sure everything can be rearranged. Anyway, I can think of nothing more ghastly than spending Christmas listening to people screeching."

Laura looked at him in surprise.

"Laura," Alasdair groaned, "can you really marry a man who can't distinguish between the London Philharmonic and a Salvation Army band? It's a family failing. Father's tone-deaf, and we've all taken after him. All except Sandy."

Laura turned to him with a radiant smile. "If your mother can take it, so can I," she announced happily. "She and your father seem to have had a blissful marriage in spite of the fact that she's not horsey and he doesn't know a cello from a tin whistle. Which reminds me, I have a father too."

"Perhaps I should meet him before we go any further," Alasdair hesitated.

But Laura cut him short. "Don't worry. There'll be no problem from him. He hardly realizes I'm still around." She snuggled closer to him. "But it doesn't matter anymore," she whispered, drinking in the faint scent of sportsman's soap that clung to his skin. "I'm going to have a *real* family at last."

"My family?"

She nodded her head, and a slow blush crept up her cheeks.

"And ours," she whispered. She lay back in his arms, her shining eyes the color of bluebells in a sunlit wood. "Won't Cristobel be surprised?" Jumping up, she clapped her hands delightedly.

Alasdair caught both her hands in his.

"Darling little Laura," he teased, "how old did you once tell me you were?"

She immediately withdrew her hands. "I shall be twenty the twenty-fourth of March," she answered primly. "Only three months younger than your sister. And she's already expecting a baby."

Alasdair laughed. "Well, we can soon remedy that."

Laura dropped her eyes as her cheeks suddenly flamed. But he laid a finger under her chin and forced her to look at him. "Isn't this where we came in?" he whispered.

Remembering how mortified she had been when he had teased her about her blush as she sat stiffly beside him on the drive to Perth, they broke into peals of such helpless laughter that neither of them heard the drawing room door open. Edwina stood in the doorway, an amused expression on her face.

Alasdair jumped to his feet, hurriedly smoothing his hair and straightening his tie. Edwina affected not to notice.

"Mr. Hamilton." She smiled. "How delightful. I wasn't sure I'd have the pleasure of seeing you when I returned."

Alasdair cleared his throat and looked at his feet. "Well . . . to be perfectly honest, when you left, I wasn't sure either."

"But the situation has somewhat changed since then?" Edwina inquired archly.

His eyes met hers, and a grin spread across his face. "I'm afraid you're going to have to get used to calling me Alasdair, now that I've become your future nephew-in-law."

Edwina's lips twitched as Laura shyly took Alasdair's hand.

"So soon," she teased. "But how splendid. So it wasn't the lack of country air that was ailing you, Laura darling."

She looked in amusement from one to the other.

"We were thinking of going out to dinner to celebrate," Alasdair ventured.

"What a *splendid* idea," Edwina enthused. "Run along and change, Laura. And do wear that blue frock that suits you so well."

"The forget-me-not blue?" Laura asked, grinning across at Alasdair.

She skipped happily across the room. Then she stopped abruptly, her hand on the doorknob. "Edwina," she said hesitantly, "Have you made all the arrangements for Christmas in Vienna?"

"Why do you ask?"

"Nothing, it's only that—"

"You no longer wish to go," Edwina broke in, giving them both a dazzling smile. "I'm so thankful. I must confess I wasn't at all looking forward to that long journey across Europe in the middle of the winter. Changing trains in Paris in the rain. It always rains in Paris when one is changing trains, and there's never a taxi in sight. Then most probably being marooned for days in a wagon-lit outside Salzburg because of an avalanche. It happened to me once before the war. And I can assure you, it was extremely unpleasant. Oh no, darling, I'm most grateful to you for sparing me that. I shall be much happier toasting the New Year in with Effie in my warm, little flat."

"Edwina, you're an *angel!*" Laura cried. Running to her aunt, she threw her arms around the older woman's neck in a highly uncharacteristic gesture. It would be difficult to say which of them was the more surprised. It seemed that Alasdair had unleashed Laura's pent-up emotions from their long imprisonment.

Alasdair cleared his throat.

Edwina, patting her immaculately dressed hair back into place, anticipated his question. "If you'll excuse me, Alasdair, I won't join you both for dinner this evening. I've had rather a busy day. Would you mind awfully celebrating by yourselves?" Her eyes twinkled at Alasdair.

Alasdair's eyes twinkled back at her. Her use of his Christian name for the first time had subtly indicated her approval and acceptance of him as a future member of the family.

"Not at all—*Aunt* Edwina," he replied.

Effie, coming in at that moment with the olives and cheese straws, almost dropped the tray in surprise when, to her astonishment, and for no apparent reason, both Edwina and Alasdair suddenly burst out laughing.

Looking down at the plump blonde baby lying contentedly in Katharine's arms, Maxime sent up a quick prayer of thanks that he had ignored his wife's protests and insisted on having the midwife installed at Le Moulin a week before the expected date of birth.

Their second daughter had arrived almost without warning, like a swift April shower, just as the midsummer twilight was fading into a warm-scented darkness on June 21—her parents' fifteenth wedding anniversary.

"And what are you going to call this one?" Maxime inquired.

"Hebrides," Katharine replied dreamily.

Maxime's brows shot up in astonishment. "Hebrides! Darling, you can't."

"Why not?" Katharine inquired, kissing the baby's warm cheek.

Her husband shrugged his shoulders. "It's like calling a child Pimlico or Chipping Sodbury."

"Little girls are called Lorraine and Nancy," Katharine replied calmly. "And one of the bridesmaids at Philip's wedding was called *Brittany*. So what's the difference?"

Maxime sat down on the bed, smiling indulgently. "There isn't a difference," he conceded. "But Hebrides is an impossible word for the French to pronounce. It'll be massacred. And she'll be laughed at. Anyway, there's a law about names here. You can't call a child what you like. It's got to be on the list of saints."

He ran his finger gently around the baby's tiny face. "That's long enough. Surely you can find *one* you like."

"I like Hebrides," Katharine answered serenely. She smiled appealingly at him. "You'll be able to manage it."

Her husband sat on the bed and took her hand. "I won't, darling," he replied seriously. "They're very strict about names. Can't you add Marie? Make it a double name like Anne-Marie or Marie-Thérèse?" He rutted his brow in thought. "I might get away with Marie-Hebrides at a pinch. Depends on who's on duty at the Town Hall when I register her."

Katharine shook her head stubbornly. Maxime sighed.

"Is Flora a saint's name?" Katharine inquired after a few minutes.

"I think so."

"Then she shall be registered as Flora-Hebrides," her mother announced triumphantly, "after her godmother." She looked mischievously at her husband. "But she'll only be Flora on official papers. Otherwise, she will be called Hebrides."

Maxime knew that he had lost.

There was a tap on the door, and the twins entered. Katharine smiled at them as they tiptoed to the bed, fingering the shawl away from the baby's face so that they could see. They peered silently at her for a few seconds, then, kissing their mother, hurriedly left.

At fourteen they were awkward and shy. And newborn babies weren't their first priority.

"I'll fetch Elisabeth to meet her little sister," Maxime said, rising to his feet as Jehan wandered in.

"Léon's bringing her," Jehan remarked, giving a hurried peep at the bundle in his mother's arms before leaving to join his elder brothers. It was Saturday morning, and the boys had more amusing things to do.

There was another tap on the door, and Léon's blond curly head peeked around. Holding Elisabeth's hand, he crept reverently to the bedside. "Look, Elisabeth," he said in awe. "That's our little sister."

Elisabeth stood on tiptoe as Maxime took the bundle from

Katharine's arms. Removing the baby's braceleted fist from the shawl and holding it in his hand, he squatted on his haunches in front of his elder daughter. "Isn't she sweet?" he asked gently.

Elisabeth looked at the baby, then at her father. Suddenly she leaned forward and viciously dug her teeth into the baby's tiny hand.

"Elisabeth!" Léon gasped, quickly grabbing her as the baby set up a terrifying wail. But Elisabeth swung around and aimed a hard kick at his shins.

He leaped away, rubbing the injured leg, hopping in pain on his one good foot.

"The little beast," Katharine spluttered. "Maxime, smack her."

Elisabeth turned to face her mother defiantly, her mouth tightly shut, her violet eyes flashing anger as Maxime quickly replaced the baby in her mother's arms.

"Elisabeth," her father said sadly, "whatever made you do that? You hurt the baby."

His elder daughter turned her beautiful eyes full on him adoringly, her lower lip trembling. Then leaning against him, she twined her arms tightly around his neck.

"I said, *smack* her," Katharine exploded.

Maxime looked up at his wife, a horrified expression on his face. "Katharine, perhaps . . . ," he faltered.

His wife angrily turned away from him. "Well, take her back to the nursery and tell Nanny to punish her if you can't," Katharine replied icily.

But Elisabeth had already released her stranglehold on her father and run from the room.

"I'll go after her," Léon said, giving a final rub to his leg. He turned in the doorway, smiling his gentle smile. "I don't think she meant it, Maman."

"She meant it all right," Katharine hissed. Sensing her mother's tension, the baby's wails intensified. Katharine rocked the child gently backwards and forwards, crooning softly, her body trembling with anger.

"Léon's right," Maxime soothed. "Elisabeth's bound to feel jealous."

Katharine's eyes widened in astonishment. "Jealous! That wasn't *jealousy*. It was pure, unadulterated viciousness. And she should be severely punished."

"Oh, come . . ."

"Maxime, you're *besotted* with that child, so blinded you can see no wrong in her. How can you let her get away with this?"

"Darling," Maxime pleaded.

"All right," Katharine cut in, "she's jealous of a new baby. But did you see the way she attacked Léon? Léon, of all people, who adores her, always at her beck and call."

Katharine's face hardened as Maxime remained silent. The baby began to cry again.

"Maxime," she cried, a sudden fear gripping her, "do you remember what you said on the evening Elisabeth was born? You asked me if I was afraid of the consequences of calling her after her great-great- and her great-grandmothers, two women whose lives met with disaster."

Maxime did remember. He remembered only too well the fears that had gripped him, not only on that Christmas Eve when their longed-for daughter was born, but also later when Katharine had mentioned the uncanny likeness Flora had remarked upon between Elisabeth and her tragic namesake. Fears that the past might rise up and possess her. It had seemed prophetic.

Elisabeth was born on the same day as her beautiful, unhappy great-great-grandmother. There was no denying that she looked like her. And at three and a half, her unusual prowess as a horsewoman had caused exclamations of surprise and delight from all who saw her handling her pony. Could it be possible that this beloved elder daughter had inherited not only the empress's name and birthday, her beauty, and her prowess as a horsewoman, but also her willful, rebellious nature?

His eyes met Katharine's, and he saw the fear in them. Gathering her into his arms, he gently stroked her hair. "No, darling," he insisted, trying at the same time to convince himself. "That's just fantasy. Elisabeth's a normal, strong-willed little girl—that's all."

"You still think that after what just happened?" Katharine inquired caustically.

"Even after what has happened," he soothed. "You're tired, darling. Let's not start making mountains out of molehills."

Katharine nestled closer to him, her anger subsiding, seeking comfort in his nearness. "I'd like to believe you, Maxime," she whispered. "But I'm afraid Elisabeth's reaction is an omen for the future. . . . And not a happy one."

The baby snuffled and grunted contentedly now. But the sound brought Katharine no reassurance, only an ominous foreboding of what was to come.

PART II
1973

Fifteen

Laura peered intently into the mirror, pulling tentatively at the delicate skin under her right eye.

The years are beginning to tell. She grimaced, discerning the faint tracing of fine lines, like the feathery strokes of an artist's brush, beneath the skin's opaque surface. Propping her elbows among the assortment of glass jars and bottles on her dressing table, she relived the last weekend. Her tenth wedding anniversary. Lying in Alasdair's arms in that country hotel where they had spent their honeymoon, listening to the sea rushing, then whispering as its waves curled along the deserted beach.

"Ten years," she sighed dreamily. "It hardly seems possible. And now I'm thirty."

Rising slowly, she crossed to the casement window, remembering how they had watched the spring moon tint the leaves outside their open window with silver. And Alasdair had told her that she was even more beautiful now than on the day he had married her.

Laura hugged the remembrance of her husband's words to her. Then she shuddered, realizing that she had entered a new decade. Sitting down in a deep armchair, she remembered how happily she had entered the last one that fine March day, her twentieth birthday, with a gentle breeze blowing the early blossoms off the trees in Kensington square as she ran joyfully out of her teens to marry Alasdair.

"Why don't you two go off for the weekend and celebrate

this double anniversary?" Ninian had telephoned the week before. "I'll take Jamie and play uncle."

Laura had hesitated. Ninian was a bachelor, and she wondered how he would cope with her boisterous youngest son for a whole weekend.

"I wonder what's bitten him," Alasdair had replied pensively when Laura told him of his brother's suggestion. He had left his chair by the fire and gone to the telephone.

"Come for dinner tomorrow evening," Laura heard him say. "I think you should know what you're letting yourself in for, before jumping in for a whole weekend."

Ninian had laughed. But when he arrived, they both noticed something different about him. The normally quiet, reserved Ninian had changed. He seemed jubilant.

"You may as well come clean, Ninian," Alasdair teased as soon as dinner was over and they were sitting around the fire in the cosy chintz-covered drawing room. "Nobody in his right mind would want Jamie for a weekend."

"I suppose I want to see what it's like playing house," Ninian replied.

"You haven't decided to take the plunge at last!" Alasdair exclaimed.

Ninian nodded, smiling his slow, sweet smile, so like Flora's.

"Did Sandy give you the idea?" Alasdair probed. "Or shame you into it?"

"Not really," Ninian replied, staring into the fire. "But I intend to introduce her to the family at Sandy's wedding."

In ten days time Sandy, who had now joined Ninian's regiment, was to marry Rose Livesey, the Quaker girl he had so disastrously partnered to her grandmother's ball.

Ninian looked up, his gray eyes soft. "You're the first to know," he said shyly.

"Haven't you told the parents?" Alasdair inquired.

"Not yet," Ninian went on. "Deirdre will meet them next week."

"Deirdre?" Alasdair queried. "Not someone we know?"

Ninian avoided his brother's eyes. "No," he replied slowly.

"And I'm not sure how the parents will take it." He paused as if seeking the right words. "Deirdre comes from Eire and is a Roman Catholic."

Ninian had just been seconded from the regiment in Northern Ireland where Sandy was now stationed on what he called "a stint at the War Box."

Alasdair let out a low whistle.

Ninian raised his eyes to meet his brother's. "I intend to marry Deirdre," he said quietly. "No matter what happens."

"Tell us about her," Laura put in, sensing the tension between the two brothers.

"She's a dancer with the Royal Ballet. A very good one too."

Alasdair let out another low whistle, then laughed self-consciously. "Whoever would have thought it of you?" he joked. "How old is she?"

"Twenty-two. Fifteen years younger than I."

"Age doesn't really matter," Laura broke in hastily. "Not if you really love someone. There are almost twice that many years between your parents. And just think what a happy marriage theirs has been."

Ninian looked at her gratefully but didn't reply. It was obvious that it wasn't Deirdre's age that was bothering him. The Hamiltons had always married Protestants, preferably Scots Protestants. But a Roman Catholic from the Irish Republic!

"What is she like?" Laura asked.

"Very like Mother," Ninian replied, brightening up. "Small and dark, rather fragile."

"Difficult for a ballerina to be hefty," Alasdair said jokingly.

Laura realized that he was embarrassed.

"So you'll lend me my godson for the weekend?" Ninian smiled, turning to Laura. "Deirdre and I would like to take him to the zoo and then do anything else that might amuse him."

"I think it would be a splendid idea," Laura enthused, her heart going out to Ninian. He had waited so long for the right woman and now saw his future happiness fraught with difficulties. "Jamie will love it. And why don't you and Deirdre have dinner with us after you bring him back on Sunday evening?"

Ninian's eyes brightened. He looked inquiringly at Alasdair, not sure how his brother would react.

"Yes, do," Alasdair said awkwardly. "Never actually seen a ballerina off the stage."

It was obvious to Laura that Ninian sensed his brother's embarrassment.

"Got to be at the War Box early in the morning," Ninian said, rising to his feet. "And I suppose it's the same for you, Alasdair. I'll be here at about ten on Saturday morning to pick up Jamie. And . . . thank you for the invitation, Laura."

Alasdair walked pensively back into the drawing room after seeing his brother off. "I wonder if Ninian hasn't got himself into a real can of worms."

Laura, switching off the lamps, looked around in irritation. "Alasdair," she exclaimed, "this is 1973, not the Middle Ages!"

"I agree," Alasdair replied, placing a guard in front of the fire's dying embers. "But Father's almost eighty-five. It might be difficult for him to understand."

Laura sighed as she turned off the last lamp, plunging the room in darkness. She suddenly felt very tired. And the surge of happiness she had felt bubble inside her on hearing Ninian's news abruptly burst.

The weekend had been a tremendous success. Jamie returned dragging the diminutive Deirdre by the hand, obviously as besotted with her as Ninian. She was like an exquisite porcelain figurine, reed-slim, with the smooth, dark hair of the ballerina and a perfectly shaped oval face in which brilliant green eyes sparkled. She barely reached Ninian's armpit. Even Alasdair fell under her spell, and when they left, Laura sensed that Ninian was feeling more relaxed about introducing his future wife to the rest of the family.

"When are you leaving for Annanbrae?" he inquired.

"Iain and Andrew come home for the Easter holidays on Thursday, so we're taking the midday plane on Friday," Alasdair replied. "Should be at Annanbrae in time for tea and the family dinner Mother's giving. Pity old Grace Entwhistle won't be there. She always added color to these occasions."

Lady Entwhistle had died very suddenly, not surprisingly of a massive heart attack, shortly after the New Year's Eve ball she annually gave for her grandchildren. Typically, she had not noticed that her grandchildren were no longer young people but mostly married with young people of their own. Ignoring the passage of time, she had carried on in the same fashion year after year. And her grandchildren had played the game. This year Rose and Sandy's engagement, or betrothal as Lady Entwhistle called it, had been announced. And, at her grandmother's request, Rose had agreed to be married from Eglinton Hall, the Entwhistle family home.

"We might be on the same plane," Ninian said.

He looked fondly down at Deirdre. "Are you ready to face the family?"

She didn't reply, just returned his gaze, her eyes shining like glittering emerald pools.

"Ninian's exaggerating," Laura put in quickly. "They're a delightful family. I'm sure you'll love them."

Deirdre's eyes left Ninian's face and focused briefly on Laura. "But will they love me?" she asked quietly.

For a moment no one spoke.

"I don't see how they could help it," Laura said at last.

They walked across the hall and through the front door in an embarrassed silence.

"Everything is going to be all right," Laura whispered as Ninian held the car door open for Deirdre.

Deirdre smiled gratefully, and the car moved off.

"I only hope you're right," Alasdair sighed, throwing an arm across his wife's shoulders as they mounted the steps to the house.

Reaching the door, Laura paused. "Kiss me," she whispered, reaching up on tiptoe.

Alasdair looked at her in surprise. Then bending down, he brushed his lips against hers.

"No," she protested, twining her fingers into the curls that straggled on his neck. "Not like that. Properly."

Alasdair caught her to him with a laugh. His lips closed on hers in a rough, hard embrace.

Laura nestled against his broad chest. "Don't you want this for Ninian?" she whispered hoarsely.

She felt his arms tighten around her.

"After ten years," she breathed, snuggling up to him as she had done on Edwina's sofa that far-off December afternoon, "it's unbelievable."

Alasdair picked her up and carried her across the threshold.

"After ten years," he remarked, "we don't have to kiss on the doorstep."

He set her down inside the lighted hall and closed the door. Laura walked toward the stairs, but turning on the first step, she looked back at her husband, her eyes twinkling. "Catch me," she cried gaily and began to run up the shallow staircase.

For a fraction of a second Alasdair hesitated. Then taking the stairs two at a time, he caught her in his arms just as she reached their bedroom door.

"Vixen!" he cried.

Laura laughed delightedly and, struggling from his grasp, dodged into the room.

Now, as she sat dreaming of the past two days, she realized that her second honeymoon had been even more wonderful than her first. Remembering Alasdair's tenderness, his caresses, she closed her eyes and relived those precious moments, reveling in her happiness.

Slanting beams of spring sunshine floated in through the open window, bringing with them damp, sweet smells from the garden just beginning to blossom after the darkness of winter.

"Life is so beautiful," she breathed.

Laura felt as if she were waking too. From one beautiful decade to another, which she was convinced would be even more perfect. And, with all her heart, she wished the same happiness for Ninian and Deirdre.

It was Monday morning. There were countless things she should be doing, but, unwilling to let this moment go, she didn't move. She wanted only to bask in her love for Alasdair and the beautiful future stretching ahead.

The telephone's sharp ring brought her back to earth. "Laura?" Graeme's voice came down the line.

"Graeme!" she exclaimed happily. "How lovely to hear you. We're looking forward to the wedding on Saturday. When is Sandy arriving?"

"Laura," Graeme said hesitantly in a strange voice.

Laura could hear him breathing heavily at the other end of the line.

"Is Alasdair at home by any chance?"

"Alasdair?" Laura replied. "No, he's at the office."

"I rang his office," Graeme said dully. "But he wasn't there."

"Oh," Laura went on, "I think he said he had to go to court this morning."

Alasdair was a rising young barrister.

"Do you know when he'll be back in his office?"

"I've no idea."

Laura frowned, wondering why Graeme was being so evasive. "Is there something I can do? If it's about the wedding, I'm more likely to be able to help than Alasdair." She laughed. "I don't imagine you have a legal problem you want to discuss with him at this time."

"No," Graeme answered heavily. "Not exactly."

"Graeme," Laura inquired, "is something wrong?"

He paused again. "I'm afraid so."

Laura sat down abruptly on the edge of the bed. "What is it?" she questioned, apprehension growing within her.

But Graeme did not reply.

"Graeme," she choked, fear strangling her voice, "what's happened?"

Vivid pictures of Robert prostrated with a stroke or Flora cut down by a heart attack tumbled pell-mell through her mind.

"It's Sandy," she heard Graeme say almost inaudibly.

"Sandy?" Laura exclaimed. "What's happened to him?"

Suddenly a piercing pain shot through her, as sharp as a burst of gunfire, and darkness seemed to close in on the room. In the distance the wind began to rise like the sad wailing of gulls. Laura heard Graeme take a deep breath in an effort to control himself. She sat motionless, her body taut and cold.

"He was killed in an ambush last night," Graeme finally managed to get out, his voice devoid of any emotion.

Sixteen

I seldom sit in the drawing room now that I'm on my own," Zag remarked, ushering Katharine and Maxime into Armand's old study. "We seem to have used it only for funeral gatherings in the past few years."

Armand had slipped peacefully away from them one late spring evening, the day after celebrating his ninety-ninth birthday. And Toinette had not survived her brother long. After Armand's death, she seemed to shrivel up and fade away, even losing interest in the constant bickering she and her sister-in-law had specialized in over the years.

Marie-Louise, left alone with Zag who refused to bicker with anyone, had had a massive stroke the following year and died without regaining consciousness. Now the old house echoed somberly to the laughter of bygone days.

"Have you given any thought to the fact that you will one day inherit Castérat?" Zag inquired of his daughter, as he settled into Armand's worn leather armchair.

Katharine looked at her father in surprise. "I can't say it's been one of my major preoccupations. Why do you ask?"

"Because I want your advice on a decision I have been considering for some time."

"You're thinking of marrying again," Katharine teased.

Her father smiled back at her. "Almost right," he countered. "But the bridegroom isn't me."

"Come on, Zag," Maxime chided. "Don't leave us in suspense. What's this all about?"

"It's about the twins. They'll be twenty-four next month. Xavier knows his future, but I was wondering about Louis."

"I thought you knew," Katharine remarked. "When he obtains his law degree in a few months, he's hoping to practice in Toulouse—"

"Where Honorine lives," Zag interrupted.

"I don't see the connection." Katharine frowned.

"I think it is serious between them," Zag replied. "In fact, I know it is."

"Then why haven't they said anything?" Maxime cut in.

"They intend to, but they are waiting until Louis's studies are behind him."

"Zag, what are you hiding from us?" Katharine asked sharply.

"Nothing, darling. But my cousin Cléry came to lunch recently, and, as old men do, we spent our time boasting about our grandchildren. And the conversation turned quite naturally to Louis and Honorine."

"Of course," Katharine put in. "Uncle Cléry is Honorine's grandfather."

"Exactly. And both Cléry and I, as besotted grandfathers, had noticed how fond they are of each other."

"But they're cousins." Katharine frowned.

"They're related," Maxime corrected. "The same as you and I are. You and I share a great-grandmother, and they share a great-great-grandmother. The strain's so diluted as to have almost disappeared."

"I suppose so," Katharine replied doubtfully. "But, Zag, I don't understand. Have they asked you to tell us? If so, I think it's very cavalier of them."

"No, darling," Zag put in hurriedly. "They haven't said a word. But as both Louis and Honorine love Castérat, perhaps more than any of the other cousins, I was wondering whether you would object if I made Louis my heir?"

He paused to let the suggestion sink in. "I've been considering it for some time," he went on when there was no immediate reaction from either Katharine or Maxime, "but I was waiting to see whom Louis would marry. There'd be no point in my offering him Castérat if he fell in love with a city girl who wouldn't be happy there. As things appear to be turning out . . ."

"But Louis is not a Montval," Katharine objected.

"He's half Montval. He could adopt the name and become Montval de Montredon, instead of Montredon de la Livière."

"You seem to have everything cut and dried," Katharine said curtly.

Her father smiled at her and turned to his son-in-law. "I don't know what you think, Maxime. Perhaps you would object to Louis changing his name. If so, I won't pursue the matter any further."

"You've dropped a bombshell, Zag," Maxime answered thoughtfully. "I need to think about it."

"Of course," Zag replied. "I said it was only a proposition."

"It's not a bad one," Maxime admitted. "But we'll need time to digest it. Up to now we had thought of Louis as a lawyer, not a landowner." He looked at his father-in-law. "He has had absolutely no training in estate management."

"Neither had your Great-uncle Armand nor any of our ancestors, for that matter. They relied on their bailiffs," Zag countered. "Baptiste was a wonderful bailiff and gave his son Etienne thorough training. Etienne really runs Castérat. I'm just there as a figurehead. And Etienne is training his son to take over from him."

"I agree," Maxime said thoughtfully. "I didn't have any special training either, but nowadays things are rather different. Xavier has done studies geared toward his future management of Le Moulin. But Louis—"

"Louis could always do a course on business management," Zag suggested. "And law studies are very useful no matter what a person decides to do afterwards."

"I don't see why Louis shouldn't change his name if he wishes," Maxime reflected. "With Xavier inheriting Le Moulin and the two of them always having been so close, it would practically join the two estates into one."

"That's what I thought," Zag put in. "Collective farming is becoming more and more popular."

"Have you mentioned it to Louis?" Maxime inquired.

"I haven't mentioned it to anyone. I wanted to know what you two thought of the idea first."

"I have no objections," Maxime remarked. "What about you, darling?"

"No, I don't think so," Katharine said slowly. "But we can't make any decision before asking Louis."

"If he is in agreement, I had thought of announcing it on his and Xavier's birthday next month." Zag smiled. "And I have a feeling that it might even precipitate a double announcement."

"Inheritance and engagement?" Maxime grinned.

"Could be." Zag grinned back.

He pulled the bell rope dangling from the chimneypiece.

"Shall we raise a tentative toast to the future house of Montval-Montredon?"

Seventeen

The telephone trembled in Laura's hands. "Oh *no*," she moaned.

"Laura," Graeme said anxiously, "I didn't want to have to tell you, but I couldn't get hold of Alasdair . . . Laura? . . . Laura!"

"I'm here," she managed to reply.

"Laura, there's absolutely nothing I can do from this distance. Can't you get hold of Alasdair?"

Laura pulled herself together. "I'll get hold of him somehow," she said hoarsely, her knuckles white as she gripped the receiver.

She paused, struggling to control her voice now that tears were cascading down her cheeks. *Sandy,* her heart kept crying. *Sandy. Dear, darling, crazy Sandy* . . . It wasn't possible.

"How's the family?" she managed to blurt out.

"Mother's being wonderful. But I'm worried about Father. He seems to have shrunk six inches since we received the news—and suddenly become an old man. He's absolutely broken."

Laura pressed a handkerchief to her mouth in an attempt to stifle her sobs. "And R-Rose?" she stammered.

"Rose was at Eglinton preparing for the wedding. She's on her way over. I don't think it's a good idea, but she insisted. Says she'll feel nearer to Sandy at Annanbrae."

"I understand," Laura said bleakly.

The silence was pregnant with their grief.

"Does Ninian kn-know?" she asked.

"I've just telephoned him. He's trying to get permission to go to Ireland and bring Sandy's body back."

He paused again, and Laura sensed that he was fighting for control of his voice. "Looks as if we'll have a funeral on Saturday instead of a wedding."

"Oh, Graeme," Laura cried brokenly.

"I have to go," Graeme said abruptly. "But, Laura, I'm worried about you."

"Don't worry about me," she assured him. "You've got enough on your hands at Annanbrae. I'll get hold of Alasdair somehow."

"Well, see you on Friday as arranged," he ended grimly. "If not before."

"Probably before," Laura choked.

"Oh, good," Graeme responded, relief in his voice. "It would be a great comfort to Mother to have you here."

Laura could feel the terrible strain he was under, coping not only with his own grief but also with Rose's and his parents'. She lay back on the bed and stared at the ceiling. The room, which only a few minutes before had been dancing with sunshine, was now gray and cold. Her certainty that life was on a beautiful course that nothing could change now lay splintered at her feet. One brief telephone call, and her world had crumbled.

She dreaded having to tell Alasdair, dreaded seeing him suffer the shattering pain now searing her heart—a pain which, when she married Alasdair, she was sure she would never feel again.

Laura glanced at her bedside clock. Just ten. There would be no point in trying to reach him before lunch. For ten years they had shared everything, but for the next three hours they would be divided by a terrible chasm of grief. She knew that from this moment onward, nothing would ever be the same. Sandy had taken with him a part of their lives.

As this seeped into her bewildered brain, the floodgates opened. Great gasping sobs wracked her slim body. She knew she was not weeping only for Sandy whose laughter they would never hear again or for Rose whose life now lay in ruins, but in some strange way she was weeping for herself.

The sobbing finally hiccuped to a stop, leaving her limp and exhausted. Lying back on the bed, she knew she should get up, keep herself occupied. But she also knew that however occupied she was, nothing would wipe this tragedy from her mind. Her heart ached for Rose. And she longed to hear Sandy's voice—to wake up and discover it had been only a bad dream.

The telephone rang. Listlessly stretching out her hand, she picked it up.

"Laura?"

"Oh, Ninian," she cried. And the tears overflowed once again. Hearing his voice, she knew she was not going to wake up from this nightmare.

"Yes, I know," he said tightly. "It's *dreadful*. Graeme is worried about you. Are you all right?"

"I'm as all right as you are," she gulped.

He paused. "Would you like to come to town and lunch with me?"

"Oh, Ninian, I don't think so."

"Do come," he urged. "We need each other. We've got to have lunch, so we might as well have it together. I don't want to be alone. And I don't much want to be surrounded by my colleagues either. Meet me at the Savoy Grill at one."

As she walked along the Strand, Laura watched the faces of the people hurrying by. They looked so normal, even happy. How could they go about their lives as if nothing had happened— gazing in shop windows, leaping on and off buses, smiling, chatting?

She looked at them curiously, surprised that they didn't stare back, nudge each other, or whisper as she passed. She *must* look different. But nobody stared curiously at her or even glanced in her direction. It seemed so strange that although the world had stopped for her, had collapsed for the whole Hamilton family, the people scurrying past were completely untouched by the tragedy she was living through. And the thought struck her that perhaps they too were struggling under some heavy burden, some terrible blow. Perhaps their lives had also been shattered, their hearts broken in the last few hours. But there was no outward sign. Life went on.

Ninian rose to meet her as she walked into the restaurant and led her to a quiet table in a corner.

"I left a message for Alasdair to join us if he can," he said as they sat down.

For a few moments neither of them spoke. Then suddenly he leaned forward and touched her hand.

"I know how fond you were of Sandy," he said softly.

Laura looked at him, her lashes glistening. "Weren't we all?" she choked.

"Yes, but sometimes we older brothers had an odd way of showing it," Ninian remarked grimly. "You were always his champion even before you married Alasdair."

Laura smiled down at her plate, idly crumbling a roll between her fingers, not daring to lift her eyes in case the tears would suddenly spill over.

"I don't think he minded," she answered brokenly. "It was only family teasing."

"Perhaps not," Ninian remarked, shaking out his napkin and placing it on his lap as the waiter arrived. "At least, I hope not."

Laura picked up her knife and fork and began pushing the food idly around her plate. "Graeme said you'd be going over to Ireland."

"Yes. On Wednesday. I hope to be at Annanbrae on Thursday evening." His lips tightened. "I imagine the funeral will be on Saturday."

Laura's fork fell with a clatter. "Oh, Ninian," she choked, "their *wedding day*."

"I know," he sighed. "But I'm afraid it can't be earlier. There are all sorts of formalities to be gone through. Friday would have been better, but just in case of a last-minute hitch, we have to make it Saturday. And anyway local people will want to come and pay their respects. They all loved Sandy. It would be cruel to rush it through the minute we arrived." Ninian looked down at the untouched food on his plate. "But leaving it till Monday would be even more cruel."

Finally giving up the pretense of eating, he put down his knife and fork.

"And you?" Laura said at last, finally managing to control her emotions.

"Me?" Ninian queried. He seemed surprised.

"It was to have been a special weekend for you too," she whispered.

"Yes," he sighed. "But I'm afraid for the time being any thought of introducing Deirdre to Annanbrae will have to be shelved."

"Oh, Ninian," Laura cried, "it's so unfair!"

"Life is often unfair," Ninian replied.

"It's strange," Laura reflected, "but when Graeme rang, I was just reveling in the fact that life was so wonderful."

Ninian smiled indulgently as if at a child.

"For Alasdair and me," she went on, "there wasn't a cloud in the sky. Then suddenly, within the space of a few seconds, the world spun around and fell back into place upside down." She broke off and looked at him appealingly. "Ninian," she said hoarsely, "it *is* going to be all right for you and Deirdre, isn't it?"

"I sincerely hope so," he answered grimly. "Someday. But certainly not for the moment."

"Does she know?" Laura asked.

"Yes, I managed to get hold of her."

"And what did she say?"

Ninian pressed his lips tightly together. "She understands. At least she said she did." He wiped his taut lips with his napkin. "But for how long? She's very young."

"Oh, Ninian, she's so right for you. It *must* work out."

Ninian raised his eyes and met hers. "But for this, it most surely would have. Deirdre comes from the Irish Republic. It would be asking too much of the parents to welcome her with open arms at the moment, don't you think?"

Laura nodded dumbly, tears once again welling in her expressive blue eyes.

Ninian reached across and covered her small hand with his, and they sat together in an emotional silence.

"Well, what a surprise!"

Startled, they both looked up to see Alasdair standing above them. Laura could see that he was ill at ease.

"I got your message, Ninian," Alasdair went on. "But I didn't expect to find you holding hands with my wife."

Laura hastily excused herself. She couldn't bear to see the pain that would immediately extinguish the dancing lights in his eyes. He smiled diffidently at her as she left the table.

When she returned, he was slumped in his chair, looking crushed, an untouched plate on the table in front of him. Ninian was stirring his coffee thoughtfully, purposely not looking at his brother.

"I'll take you home," Alasdair said bleakly.

"But you haven't had lunch," she protested.

Then, remembering her own untouched plate, she didn't insist.

"I'll leave Laura to you," Ninian said, rising from the table. "I ought to be getting back."

Alasdair looked at him gratefully. Suddenly, the two brothers seemed much closer.

"Thank you for looking after her, Ninian," he said quietly.

"My pleasure," Ninian replied, bending to kiss Laura's cheek. "Well, see you both at the weekend."

Alasdair nodded blankly as Ninian walked, imposing and erect, among the tables and out into the Strand. He looked across at Laura, then reached over and took her hand, drawing it toward him. "You look whacked, darling," he said tenderly.

She didn't reply. The raw pain she saw in her husband's eyes ricocheted onto her and left her speechless.

"Let's go," Alasdair said quietly.

He tucked her hand under his arm, and the gesture brought with it a semblance of normality.

Puzzled at hearing the click of the receiver followed by total silence from the hall, Maxime rose from the lunch table and hurried into the hall. Katharine sat slumped on the hard wooden chair, the receiver dangling from her hand, staring vacantly into space.

"Katharine, what is it? What did Flora want?"

His wife slowly turned glazed eyes on him. He gasped. They were dark with a mixture of fear and pain.

"Darling," he cried, dropping to one knee beside her and gathering her into his arms, "whatever's happened?"

As if in a trance, Katharine slowly replaced the receiver, her face ashen. "It's Sandy," she whispered hoarsely, passing a hand across her eyes, as if awakening from a terrifying dream.

Maxime frowned. "What's happened to Sandy?"

"He's dead. Last night. Killed by a sniper's bullet."

With a heart-rending cry, she buried her face in her hands, her body trembling uncontrollably.

Maxime knew that she was remembering that other enemy bullet that, twenty years before, had sped lethally across a prison yard to extinguish her first husband's life. Ashley had been a soldier too, not much older than Sandy when it happened.

Gathering Katharine's trembling body into his arms, he made for the stairs, entered their bedroom, and laid her gently on the bed.

"Would you like a cup of tea, darling?" he asked gently, removing her shoes and tucking a quilt around her.

But she appeared not to hear, just stared blankly in front of her. Maxime sat down on the side of the bed and took her trembling hands in his. In spite of the warmth of the early spring day, they were icy cold.

"Sandy," Katharine groaned. "Not Sandy. I can't believe it. Say it's not true, Maxime. Please say it's not true."

She turned her chalky face appealingly toward her husband, unconsciously repeating the words she had uttered when told of Ashley's brutal death.

Maxime shook his head sadly.

"I wish I could, darling," he sighed. "But if Flora rang to tell you, then it must be true."

Katharine removed her hands and clung to his lapel, her eyes searching his face. "But *why*, Maxime, why? Why did God let this happen? Sandy was so young, so full of life. He had everything to live for and . . ." Her lip trembled and her voice broke. "He was going to be married on Saturday."

She buried her face in her hands once again. And this time the tears came, not the dry, gasping sobs that had wracked her body when she had wept for Ashley, but a sudden outpouring of agonized emotion too deep for sound. Her shoulders shook as the silent tears welled up and spilled over.

Maxime gathered her to him once again and held her tight.

"I don't know why, darling," he answered sadly. "I only wish I did. All we can do is pray . . . for strength and peace for Rose and Flora and the whole family. And claim the promise that out of this evil God will bring some good."

Katharine looked up at him, her eyes still glassy with tears. He knew that she was having difficulty accepting this tragedy, that her sensitive nature was rebelling and at the same time reaching out to Flora, putting herself in her friend's place, agonizing with her almost as if by doing so, she could filter off some of Flora's pain and siphon it into her own body. Maxime's heart ached for his wife.

Laura left for Scotland the following day. Alasdair would bring the boys on Thursday. They had been of two minds whether or not to leave them behind. But the children had been looking forward to going to Annanbrae, and they both felt that as Sandy had been the adored young uncle, his nephews would want to be there.

"Anyway," Alasdair decided, gathering Laura in his arms as they lay in bed that night endlessly discussing the day's dramatic events, "I want them with us at this time, don't you?"

In the darkness Laura nodded, longing for his touch yet in some strange way feeling that they would be betraying Sandy by expressing their love for each other while he lay dead across that stretch of sea.

"Oh, Alasdair!" she cried brokenly.

His arms tightened around her, but he also hesitated. His young brother, who had been on the brink of this happiness, had been cut down before he had had the chance to taste it. Yet Alasdair needed the comfort of his wife's arms.

He tentatively put out a hand toward her. She willingly yielded to his embrace, and the pain, the weariness, the hopelessness of the past twelve hours faded. They were cradled on a gentle tide of love, oblivious of everything but each other, and momentarily were at peace.

When Laura landed at the airport the following afternoon, Donald was waiting for her. He took her suitcase and wisely made no comment.

"How is everyone?" she managed to inquire, as he settled her in the car.

Donald hunched his shoulders, and Laura felt for him. He had been born in the lodge by the gate at Annanbrae and had watched them all grow up. He and Janet had never had children, and the Hamilton offspring, to whom Janet had been nanny until Sandy went off to prep school, had become their children.

"And Janet?" Laura asked as the car moved away.

"She's naturally very upset," Donald replied. "Very upset. Master Sandy was her baby in a way."

"I know," Laura said softly.

There the conversation ended. Laura understood Donald's fear that his emotions might get the better of him.

It was early spring. All nature was awakening with glorious splashes of color as if rejoicing to be alive. The sky above the mountains was lit with a curious light, neither silver nor white but something in between. In the low hedges bordering the cottage gardens, birds twittered and fidgeted, flapping their wings as they flew upwards, smudges in the encroaching dusk. From the damp earth rose a sweet, pungent smell. Everything seemed to be bursting into life after the long winter sleep. Laura felt an agonizing jab of pain, remembering why she was here.

The house was strangely quiet when Donald drew up in front of it. Even the dogs seemed subdued, too lethargic to give their usual uproarious welcome. MacDuff, who had succeeded Laird, wandered out from Laird's old hiding place and sauntered aimlessly across the hall. The others stayed in their basket on the half-landing, eyeing Laura mournfully above crossed paws.

As she walked through the doorway, Cristobel came out of the drawing room and, running across the hall, threw herself into Laura's arms. "Laura darling," she cried.

They clung to each other as their tears overflowed.

"How are they?" Laura asked at last.

Cristobel shrugged and tucked her hand in Laura's arm.

"Father's in his study. He's hardly left it all day. *Simply crushed.* You'll hardly recognize him. I don't think he can take it in."

"And your mother?"

"Amazingly brave," Cristobel went on. "I suppose it's her faith that keeps her going, otherwise she'd have become a zombie too, like Father and Rose. She's in the drawing room making lists."

Laura knew what that meant. Since Morag's death, lists had become Lady Flora's bolt-hole in times of stress.

"And Rose? Graeme told me she was coming here."

"She arrived yesterday and hasn't left Sandy's room since. Not a word nor a tear. Just sits dry-eyed on the window seat, staring out at the garden."

Cristobel shuddered as they sat down side by side on the old oak settle in the dim hall. "It's awful. If only she would cry. If only they would *all* cry." She turned and hugged Laura. "I'm *so* glad you're here. I felt dreadful being the only one to shed tears. And I can assure you I've shed buckets since yesterday. I feel it should be me comforting Mother. But it's Mother comforting me!"

A shuddering sob escaped Cristobel's lips, and she threw herself into Laura's arms. "Oh, Laura, poor darling Sandy. I can't believe it." She looked up, her gray eyes brimming. "And we were all so beastly to him."

Laura put her arm around Cristobel's shaking shoulders. "You weren't," she soothed. "Not really."

"But the things we *said* to him," Cristobel sobbed.

A smile flitted briefly across Laura's lips. "What about the things he said to you?"

Cristobel scrubbed a hankie around her tearstained face. "You were always special to him," she gulped. "He was *terribly* fond of you."

Laura didn't reply. Just sat thinking of Sandy, the impossible young boy who had turned into such a charming young man. As tall as Ninian, strikingly handsome with his thick, unruly flame-red hair and laughing eyes. And once again she couldn't believe what had happened. Her mind reasoned that death is always hard to grasp for those left behind to grieve. Always unacceptable. But her heart cried out that Sandy's death was so senseless. How could all that vital energy and enthusiasm for life have been extinguished in a flash by a single sniper's bullet?

"Do you remember how you used to help him with his trumpet practice?" Cristobel said wistfully. "Accompanying him on the piano for hours."

As she heard Cristobel's voice, she knew that with Sandy's death something had died in her life too. In all their lives. None of them would ever again hear Sandy's infectious laugh echoing through the great house or see him bounding into the hall, the dogs yapping hysterically at his heels. The beautiful mosaic that had fallen into place when she married Alasdair now seemed to her to be slowly disintegrating, great gaps showing through the delicate pattern. And Laura knew that not only a decade but an era in her life had come to an end.

"It's strange, but Sandy was the only one of the five of us who was musical." Cristobel paused reflectively. "He was different in so many ways, but you seemed to understand him better than any of us and to have time for him."

Laura reached out a hand to her stricken sister-in-law. "Don't torture yourself," she urged. "Sandy knew you all loved him."

Cristobel nodded bleakly. They sat together in silence, dreading having to face Lady Flora's metallic smile.

"Where's Lindsay?" Laura asked.

"At home," Cristobel replied. "He insisted on my coming immediately."

Lindsay had resigned his commission the year before, following Grandfather Lindsay's death. He and Cristobel now lived on the estate with their three little daughters.

"He'll be arriving with the girls tomorrow," Cristobel went on. "But I think they'll stay at Killistrathan with Lindsay's parents." She sighed and passed her hand wearily across her blotched face. "Annanbrae is no place for children at the moment."

They looked at each other and smiled wanly.

"Annanbrae has always been a paradise for children."

"Perhaps my boys could stay at Killistrathan with their cousins," Laura ventured diffidently.

"Why not?" Cristobel replied. "They'll have a wonderful time fighting together."

Something like a smile flitted across their faces.

"I wonder why they *do* fight so," Cristobel puzzled, relieved to take her mind off the tragic event that had brought them together.

The Fraser and Hamilton cousins had battled nonstop ever since they had met. Flora, named after her maternal grandmother, was only a few months older than Iain. Helen was the same age as Jamie, and little Iona at four was able to give as good as she received when it came to tussles with her boy cousins.

"Different sexes, I suppose." Laura smiled. "They'll probably grow out of it." She looked down at Cristobel's rounded figure. "Maybe you'll have a boy this time and even things out."

For a brief moment the old twinkle came back into Cristobel's eyes. "Jolly well hope so. A fourth daughter would really be a bit much." Cristobel lovingly stroked her abdomen. "It's due mid-August, though after this shock I've been expecting it to arrive any minute."

She turned and squeezed Laura's hand. "Come on, Mother will be pleased to see you. But don't be surprised at her brassy brightness. I'm sure it's a pose. She'll have to break down some time."

"What shall we do, Maxime?" Katharine asked tentatively the following morning when the storm of emotion had passed and she was lying propped on her pillows sipping tea. "Everything's arranged for us to leave on Thursday morning for Annanbrae . . . for Sandy's wedding."

She paused, her lip quivering. Maxime took her hand and held it tightly.

"Emile was to collect the plane tickets when he went into Narbonne this morning," she added sadly.

Katharine had finally overcome her horror of flying. She now knew the fear had been born that December evening when Ashley had kissed her good-bye, for what proved to be the last time, before he parachuted back into occupied France.

"What would you like to do, darling?" Maxime asked gently. "We can still go if you wish."

"I don't know," Katharine demurred.

"Then let's wait for the time being. We can telephone Flora this evening and decide then."

But when Katharine did telephone, it was Laura who took the call. "Flora's sitting with Robert," Laura explained. "He went to bed immediately after dinner."

"Then don't disturb her," Katharine cut in hastily.

"Were you wondering about whether to stick to your original plan and come?" Laura inquired.

Katharine was struck by the young woman's perception.

Perhaps Flora had been right when she said all those years ago that Katharine and Laura were very alike.

"We don't want to intrude—"

"You wouldn't be intruding," Laura interrupted. "But I'm not sure that it would do any good. You were bringing the girls with you for the wedding, weren't you?"

"Yes."

"Alasdair is bringing our boys on Friday, but they won't be staying here. Cristobel has arranged for them all to go to Killistrathan. But I'm sure Lady Fraser wouldn't in the least mind having your girls as well. Iain would be pleased to see Hebrides again. They got on so well together last summer."

But at that moment Flora came down the stairs.

"It's Katharine," Laura mouthed. "She wants to know whether they should still come."

Flora put out her hand and took the receiver. "Katharine," she breathed.

"Oh, Flora," Katharine choked.

"Darling, don't," Flora pleaded. "Or you'll start me off."

Flora took a deep breath. She longed to have Katharine beside her, the one friend with whom she could truly share and be herself. But she suddenly remembered Katharine's visit to Annanbrae after Ashley had left on that last fateful mission. At the memory of her friend's pain, Flora knew that no matter how much she longed to see Katharine, she must not ask her to come. The similarity and the senselessness of Sandy's and Ashley's deaths were too poignant.

"Please, don't come," she said, quickly steeling herself. "It's such a long way, and everything's unreal at the moment."

"But, Flora," Katharine faltered, "if I come, can't I help in some way?"

"No, darling," Flora replied firmly. "There's really very little to do. We are all wandering around in a state of shock and disbelief, wondering what on earth we can do to fill the interminable hours."

"Flora," Katharine whispered brokenly, "I could just be with you. . . . We could weep together." She paused, fighting to gain control of her voice.

Katharine's love and concern flowing across the wires very nearly broke Flora's iron self-control. But with an almost super-human effort, she pulled herself together. "I'd love to see you, darling," she said raggedly. "But at the moment I feel anes-thetized. Come later when the house is no longer a mausoleum. Then we'll have time to talk and be together . . . and remember— *that* is when I shall need you, Katharine."

Flora paused as once again her voice threatened to break. "Poor Rose," she choked. "She *so* needs Jesus. But I can't get near her. Perhaps when William arrives, he will be able to help her. The only sign of life Robert has shown since we received the news was when I told him that William was on his way. They have been friends since before I was born, so they have memories I cannot share. William can perhaps get through to both of them."

"Is William going to take the service?" Katharine asked gently.

"Yes. He was an army chaplain during World War I, so it's very appropriate. And, of course, he's known Sandy all his life."

"Maxime and I are praying for you," Katherine said hoarsely.

"I know, darling," Flora replied, her voice wavering, "and it has made all the difference. There are not many people I can ask—only you and William really understand. Knowing you are praying is the one thing that has enabled me to carry on."

"We feel so helpless," Katharine groaned.

"Just keep praying," Flora cut in softly.

"You know we will," Katharine choked. "And, Flora, if you change your mind—"

"I won't change my mind," Flora said firmly, once again in control of her emotions. "Lavinia is coming with William. It will be like having part of you. When you come, I want to be able to enjoy my little goddaughter. But this is no house for children at the moment. I want their memories of Sandy and of Annanbrae to be full of laughter and joy, which, until we all recover from this dreadful shock, will not be the case."

"God be with you," Katharine whispered and thought she heard a sob as she replaced the receiver.

"I wish Armand were here," Katharine said wistfully, walking back into the drawing room.

Maxime knew what she meant. Their great-uncle had been with them through many a storm. His wisdom and great faith had been a tremendous support, and the gap he had left in both their lives had never been filled.

"Why don't we go to Gure Etchea?" Maxime suggested, afraid that Katharine's meandering thoughts would turn to melancholy.

"I heard Véronique asking Zag if she and the children could go for the Easter holidays," Katharine replied. "Sarlat is a beautiful place to live, but she loves to get the children to the sea whenever there's a school break."

"Splendid," Maxime enthused. "There's plenty of room for all of us, and you and your cousin Véronique have always got on well together. It's a wonderful solution."

"Will you come?" Katharine asked.

"I'll come for a week." He smiled.

"Perhaps Léon would join us," Katharine mused. "He can study there."

"First year of medicine is tough," Maxime commented. "An awful lot of students are eliminated."

"But he works so hard," Katharine argued. "I don't think he needs to worry. After Paris the sea air will do him good as well. And anyway he's the only one of the children who can cope with Elisabeth's tantrums." A cloud crossed her face.

Elisabeth had an iron will and was a law unto herself. She seemed to delight in flaunting every rule and had been in endless trouble at Sévigné, the select girls' school in Narbonne she and Hebrides attended. It was only her father's influence that kept her from being expelled. All she ever wanted to do was fly around the countryside on one of Maxime's thoroughbreds, her long, dark hair streaming behind her as she urged the horse to race even faster.

Her elder brothers tended to ignore her, and her relationship with her sister had not improved since that first day. The gentle Hebrides was frequently reduced to tears by her elder sister's scathing remarks. Katharine still counted for very little in Elisabeth's life, but her passion for Maxime had increased, and he could refuse her nothing.

Remembering this, Katharine's face hardened. Then, reminding herself that from a very early age Elisabeth had done her best to drive a wedge between her and Maxime, she relaxed, determined not to play into her rebellious daughter's hands. She smiled up at Maxime. "I love you, darling," she whispered.

She was rewarded by the adoration she saw mirrored in her husband's eyes.

For Laura the next few days were a living nightmare. Lady Flora had been delighted to see her, but far from being a comfort to her, Laura felt helpless in her presence. Her mother-in-law wandered around the strangely quiet house pretending to be busy— arranging flowers, receiving people who came to call, ringing for tea, and endlessly making lists. Yet always, it seemed, upheld by some force more powerful than herself, a force that enabled her to carry on, remain calm, and bring comfort to those who came to comfort her. Occasionally she could be glimpsed leaving the study where her husband sat hunched and motionless, William by his side, or gliding out of Sandy's room where Rose sat dry-eyed as if in a trance.

Had it not been for Cristobel's presence, Laura would have fled. It was like living in a house full of animated puppets pulled by some invisible string. Realizing that there was little they could do, she and Cristobel spent hours together in the old schoolroom or going for long blustery walks in the park, through the wood, around the lake, anywhere to get out of the nightmare scenario being acted out at Annanbrae.

Laura longed for Alasdair with a longing that had become a physical ache. But when he arrived with the boys late on Thursday afternoon, she too had taken on the atmosphere of the house and seemed frozen.

The boys were subdued but also excited. Death was something that had not really penetrated their young minds. It was difficult for them to suppress the macabre excitement they felt.

When Lady Flora saw Jamie's tousled flame-colored hair as he leaped boisterously out of the car, for a brief moment her composure almost cracked. He was so like Sandy had been as a boy. She gathered the three of them to her, hugging them, not wanting to let them go. When they finally wriggled out of her arms and raced across the hall, she stood looking after them as if she wanted to remain rooted in this moment in time, this memory etched deep in her subconscious.

As soon as tea was over, Lindsay took the boys to Killistrathan to join their cousins. Then came the long wait until dinner, which no one ate. Soon afterward they heard the crunch of tires in the driveway and knew that Ninian had arrived with Sandy's coffin.

Robert opened the door of his study and walked heavily out, looking neither to right nor left. His wife went across and took his arm, but he seemed unaware of her. Hamish shuffled out of the drawing room, his ruddy face woebegone, his moustache drooping lower than ever as Rose, her face almost transparent with grief, walked down the stairs on Graeme's arm.

Laura clutched Alasdair's hand, gripping it tightly as the cars stopped. The great door swung open, and Sandy's coffin draped with the Union Jack, his sword glinting on top, his worn glengarry lying at the hilt, was carried across the hall on the shoulders of six young kilted soldiers from his regiment. Ninian walked behind it, his face drawn with fatigue.

For a few tense seconds no one moved. The only sound came from the ponderous tick of the grandfather clock in a far corner of the hall. Then suddenly Robert lurched forward. His wife quickly caught hold of his arm, but he steadied himself and, leaning heavily on his stick, stood upright and dry-eyed, as his youngest son's coffin was placed reverently on wooden tressels.

Looking up as the soldiers ranged themselves on either side, their heads bowed, Flora recognized Jock's great-grandson,

Sandy's childhood playmate, among them, his face taut with grief.

Laura felt Alasdair's grip tighten on her hand. She wondered how much longer she could stand this deathly silence—this complete control everybody was showing. From behind her came the welcome sound of muffled sobs as the door from the servants' hall silently opened, and the staff stood huddled together in a forlorn group, watching the silent grief.

Suddenly Janet, standing in the doorway with Donald, buried her face in her hands and broke into heartrending sobs. Her husband put his arms around her and drew her away. As they passed him, Ninian looked up and stretched out his hand to them, and the unbearable tension snapped. Hamish took an outsized red-spotted handkerchief from his pocket and blew his nose loudly. Robert turned and, leaning heavily on his wife's arm, shuffled like a sleepwalker back into his study.

Loosening her grip on Graeme's arm, Rose moved forward as if in a dream and laid her hand on top of the coffin. She stood there for a few moments, a faint, unreal smile hovering about her lips, as if she were alone, far away in some never-never land where there are no nightmares and dreams always come true.

"Good-bye, Sandy," she whispered.

Then turning abruptly, she brushed aside Graeme's offer of help and walked swiftly up the stairs.

Alasdair drew Laura to him and half carried her, sobbing quietly into his jacket, back into the drawing room. Lindsay followed with Cristobel. And the two of them sat on either side of the fire, cradling their wives in their arms.

As the men waited helplessly for the weeping to cease, the door opened and Ninian walked in. "Has it been like this all the time?" he inquired, sitting down heavily on the sofa. "This eerie calm?"

"Apparently," Alasdair sighed. "If only they would just let go and break down." He looked at Ninian. "Graeme was right about Father. He looks twenty years older than he did at Christmas."

Ninian nodded mutely. The five of them sat, not knowing what to say.

All day Friday Sandy's coffin remained in the great hall as the villagers who had known and loved him came to pay their last respects, to weep in front of it, and lay little posies of heather or other mountain flowers on the top. Rose appeared from time to time, still with that blank, doll-like expression in her eyes, as if she were not really there but had already gone to join Sandy in a land where there was no more pain. Lady Flora remained upright and gracious, tight little smiles jumping erratically across her lips as they uttered mechanical phrases.

By Saturday morning Laura was feeling so drained with grief and exhaustion that she wondered how she was going to get through the day.

But finally the cars arrived. They all gathered once again in the hall, and Sandy's body was taken for the last time from the house where he had been born and placed on a gun carriage. With the regiment's kilted piper playing the "Lament" at the head of the sad procession, they set off down the long drive under a canopy of fresh, young leaves shining with moisture in the spring sunshine. It was a glorious morning, the second of April. Laura couldn't help thinking what a perfect day it would have been for a wedding.

A group of young men from the estate were waiting in front of the wide open gate. Falling into step on either side of the gun carriage, they accompanied it, with bowed heads, through the village to the door of the old stone church. There the coffin was placed on their sturdy shoulders and carried into the dim interior.

"'I am the resurrection and the life,'" Laura heard William's strong voice proclaim as he walked slowly down the aisle in front of the pallbearers. "'He that believeth in me, though he were dead, yet shall he live.' He shall 'have everlasting life.'"

Laura felt a lump rise in her throat.

Did William *really* mean what he was saying? That Sandy was not dead but alive in another world with another life to live . . . an everlasting life? And that, if she believed in Jesus, one day she would see Sandy again?

At that moment Laura suddenly understood his mother's peace. Like William, Flora believed. Although this brutal parting from her youngest child was agonizing for her, tearing her heart out, Flora knew that it was not the end. Since her son had trusted his life to Christ, he had merely passed through the door that hides the living from that eternal life that had now begun for Sandy. And which, Flora knew, without a shadow of a doubt, would one day begin for her. For Flora, this morning was only a ritual, a ceremonial *au revoir*—"till we meet again."

And Laura longed to believe.

Swallowing hard in an attempt to control her emotion, Laura grasped Alasdair's hand, crushing it tightly in hers. He was standing erect and dry-eyed beside her, but his strained features betrayed his pain. She knew even as she felt his fingers squeeze hers in sympathy that, faced with this sudden tragedy, he too was lost. He too was unsure about what lay beyond death's great mystery.

The service was short and beautiful, the singing tearful but lusty, with Lady Flora's clear soprano rising, full of assurance, above the others. As the strains of "Abide with Me," the Soldier's Hymn, died away, the old clock chimed twelve. It was the hour at which Rose should have been walking, a radiant bride on her father's arm, down that very aisle to meet her bridegroom.

Laura stole a glance at her. As she did so, a sunbeam pierced through the stained-glass window and fell onto the coffin, bouncing off it to highlight the deathly pallor of Rose's face. For a moment Rose's dry eyes wandered briefly to the bier. And Laura thought the girl's composure was going to crack. But gripping the pew in front of her for support, Rose steadied herself and stared stonily ahead as the bearers came to carry the coffin back down the aisle.

The clock striking the last notes of twelve mingled with the tolling bell and the piper's "Lament" when Rose left the pew and followed Sandy's body out of the church.

"Ashes to ashes, dust to dust," William intoned as they crowded around the freshly dug grave. The poignant call of the drummer sounding the "Last Post" trembled on the clear air, and Sandy's body was slowly lowered into the grave. As the bugle's last broken note died away, thirteen young kilted soldiers, their rifles poised over their right shoulder, the barrels pointing skyward, fired three sharp shots—a final salute to Sandy. And the coffin disappeared. For a few seconds, the silence in the churchyard was absolute.

William bent down, his World War I medals glinting on his stole, and threw a handful of earth into the grave. Then, a reminder that death is not the end, the joyful reveille rang out.

Robert lurched forward, to be caught by Ninian. He shrugged his son away. Once again leaning heavily on his stick, he stood erect, looking down into the open grave. In the distance, the plaintive strains of a lone piper playing "The Flowers of the Forest" pierced the deathly stillness. As its mournful cry drew nearer, Rose's composure finally broke. With a last agonized look at the coffin's shiny surface, she gave a terrible shriek, like an animal mortally wounded, and fell weeping into Graeme's arms.

The last strains of the "Lament" died away; the crowd parted; and, headed by the piper playing Sandy's regimental march, the family moved back to the waiting cars.

Laura clung tightly to Alasdair's arm, tears streaming down her face as they followed Lady Flora. Upright and dry-eyed, Flora walked beside her husband, a shuffling, broken old man, back to the house that would never again ring with Sandy's laughter.

Eighteen

In later years when Laura looked back on her life, she realized that her thirtieth birthday and Sandy's death had in some strange way precipitated the series of events that followed. They had both been catalysts. They were a watershed after which life had never been the same. When she replaced the receiver that Monday morning after Graeme's devastating call, her world crumbled. She knew that everything she had so lovingly built up, everything in which she had put her trust, her faith, and her hope were finite. They could all disappear at any time, swept away like a leaf in the wind.

And the old fears began to invade her, coupled with the feeling of rejection that had overwhelmed her when her mother died. At that time, Edwina had done everything in her power to restore her niece's confidence and give her the love and security she sorely needed. But her sisters' absence and her father's apparent indifference had left Laura feeling unloved and abandoned. She had erected a wall and retreated behind it.

The day after Sandy's funeral, Alasdair drove his family away from Annanbrae to Lochincraig, realizing that the best thing to do was to leave his parents to work through their grief alone. And Laura once more began to rebuild that defensive wall, her barrier against pain, determined that never again would she allow her life to be so shattered.

To all outward appearances, the holiday with Lindsay, Cristobel, and their three daughters at Lochincraig helped and refreshed them. Yet that dreadful feeling that something was irrevocably broken, the foreboding that had crept over Laura when she heard of Sandy's death, did not disappear. In the days and weeks after their return home, it seemed to loom larger and more menacing. She saw how easy it was for life to be snuffed out, as swiftly as the flame from a candle. A chilling fear began to erode her happiness.

"I wonder whether it would be a good idea to send Jamie to school with his brothers in September instead of waiting until after Christmas," Alasdair remarked casually one evening in May. They were sitting together in their garden after dinner.

Laura turned to him, an iron band tightening inside her chest. "But why?" she cried.

"Well," Alasdair went on, "he's ready for it. Always asking when he's going to join Iain and Andrew."

"But he's only *seven*," Laura protested.

"He'll be eight in January," Alasdair reminded her.

"Yes, but he's only seven *now*."

Alasdair turned to her with his amused smile. "Do I hear the mother hen clucking?" he teased.

Laura rose angrily to her feet. "Call it what you like," she snapped. "I *still* think he's too young."

"All right, all right," Alasdair appeased her, catching at her hand as she flounced past him. "It was only a suggestion."

But for Laura, the peace of the spring evening had gone. Pulling away from him, she stamped into the house, not even sure why she was angry. Her husband had made a perfectly reasonable suggestion. And it *was* only a suggestion. Yet she'd reacted as though he'd wanted to put their son in an orphanage.

Crossing the drawing room, she sat down at the piano. But running her hands over the keys only set her nerves jangling, her fingers refusing to obey her brain. After a few futile attempts, she closed the lid and, with a sigh, walked over to the curved bay window.

Alasdair had picked up the evening paper and was squinting at it in the dim light. She saw him put it down and clasp his hands reflectively behind his head. Her heart softened, and she almost ran to him and twined her arms around his neck. But that tight feeling returned to her chest, and instead she moved toward the stairs. Lying on her bed in the darkness, she heard the sounds of the May night whispering up to her from the garden below. She could smell the lilacs and the lavender. But this evening they brought her no comfort.

When Alasdair came to bed, her eyes were closed. She heard him moving quietly about the room, and the slight creak as he climbed in beside her, the click as he switched off the bedside lamp, the gentle heave as he leaned on one elbow and bent over to kiss her cheek. But she remained tense and unresponsive. He turned over, and within a few minutes his regular breathing told her that he was asleep.

Slipping out of bed, she wandered across to the window and leaned on the sill, drinking in the sweet, damp air. A waning harvest moon hung low in the sky, lapping the garden with its opal light. She could just make out the faint outline of the white wooden chairs on the terrace below, the steps leading down to the smooth lawn, the dim silhouette of the overhanging roof, and the shadow of a wheelbarrow propped against the side of the house. All the familiar sights of her home where until a few weeks ago she had felt so secure. And she couldn't understand this sudden misery engulfing her.

Alasdair had brought her here as his bride. It was here that their three sons had been born. She loved the house because it was their home—her protection against the outside world. Yet inexplicably that protective shell had cracked and fallen off, leaving her exposed and vulnerable. She imagined the house without Jamie and suddenly felt empty and useless, her role in life usurped by a school matron. She heard again Alasdair's teasing voice: "Do I detect the clucking of a mother hen?" She knew that he was right.

Laura had experienced a feeling of desolation when Iain left for prep school. But Andrew and Jamie were still at home and needed her. When Andrew had joined his brother the following year, Jamie's lively presence had filled the empty space. But now it was Jamie's turn. She could not bear to part with the last of her babies.

Her mind wandered to Annanbrae, and she wondered

whether Flora was now thinking back to the locust years—those years when Sandy, her baby, had only come home for the holidays, those years when he hadn't been growing up beside her, running to her with his cuts and bruises or to have his tears wiped when the world had turned against him.

With these bleak thoughts, the reality of Sandy's death hit her again. And laying her head on her arms, she wept.

Out of her weeping words from her childhood, learned by rote and long since forgotten, floated back into her consciousness. "Our lives are like a blade of grass, here today and gone tomorrow." In that instant Laura realized that nothing was completely safe. She had once again come face to face with death in all its finality. And once again she felt helpless and afraid.

Her father's death from a sudden heart attack three years earlier, when she was secure in her marriage and her love for Alasdair, had not really disrupted her life. It had merely left a momentary sadness.

But Sandy's death was different. It had not been "after a long illness courageously borne," as the newspaper had described her mother's passing. Sandy had been young, on the threshold of life. He had also been part of this new life she had forged, where everything was as solid as a rock, and nothing ever changed. Yet, when she least expected it, that rock had splintered, and she found herself thrashing about in deep waters. She began to ponder about life, about death, and to ask herself the meaning of it all. Raising a tearstained face to the night sky, she wondered if she would see Sandy smiling down at her. But there was only a preening peacock strutting across the heavens, its tail studded with a thousand glittering stars.

Alasdair stirred and raised himself on the pillows, blinking in the darkness. He got out of bed and padded over to her. "Darling," he said anxiously, putting his arms around her shaking body and leading her back to bed, "whatever's the matter?"

Tucking the blankets tenderly around her, he lay down beside her, gently stroking her hair. She longed to turn and snuggle against him. But the darkness with its black fantastic shapes closed in on her, and she was afraid—afraid that this rock on which her foundations were built, on which her life and happiness depended, might also one day disintegrate and leave her drowning. She stiffened and drew away, burying her head in the pillow, unable to explain because she did not understand herself, unconsciously refusing any contact that could render her vulnerable again.

Neither of them broached the subject of Jamie's departure again. It seemed as if they were both skating around the issue. But the question resolved itself the following weekend.

"Dad," Jamie said moodily, "why do I have to wait till after Christmas to go to school with Iain and Andrew?" He kicked a discarded paper cup lying on the grimy platform as they walked away from the train that was taking his brothers back to school after the half-term holiday.

"You can't go now," his father answered mildly. "It's the middle of the term."

"Well," Jamie plunged in belligerently, finding another discarded cup and giving it the full force of his anger, "why can't I go *next term*? I'm *sick* of that stupid day school and that twit Miss Fanshawe."

Alasdair smiled at Laura across their youngest son's head.

"'Now let us pretend we're all little fishes having a lovely swim in a great big pond,'" Jamie mimicked, taking mincing steps. "'Jamie, I've already told you, haven't I, dear, we don't pull little girls' plaits and make them cry. And we *mustn't* shut Amelia in the shoe cupboard; it isn't kind. *No*, Jamie, *please* put that cricket bat *down*. Eustace didn't mean to make a face at you.'"

Laura couldn't help laughing. Her youngest son's imitation of the twittering Miss Fanshawe who ran the small private school he attended was perfect.

Jamie turned, his arms akimbo, glaring belligerently at his parents. "Honestly, Dad," he spat, "she's *pathetic*."

Alasdair tweaked his son's ear as he hailed a taxi. "Your turn will come soon enough." He smiled, handing them both in.

"Dad!" Jamie protested as his father slammed the door.

But the taxi had already moved away. Jamie sat moodily back against the seat, and now with no cups on which to vent his anger, began kicking at the cab's upholstery.

"You really want to go to school with your brothers, don't you?" Laura remarked diffidently, putting a restraining hand on his jerking leg.

"You bet!" he exclaimed, his eyes shining. "Oh, Mum, *can* I?"

"We'll see," she answered guardedly, her heart lurching.

Alasdair didn't mention the subject that evening. It was Laura who brought it up. "It seems that the question of when Jamie leaves for St. Bede's has resolved itself," she said quietly as they sat together in the drawing room, listening to the summer rain patter against the window.

Alasdair glanced at her over the top of his newspaper. "It's up to you, darling," he replied. "If you want arrangements to stay as they are, then he'll go after Christmas."

"Not entirely." Laura smiled. "If he continues to misbehave at Windsmoor House, I very much doubt whether Miss Fanshawe will take him back in September." She sighed. "So we really have no choice."

"Darling," Alasdair soothed, putting down his paper and crossing to her side.

But she rose hurriedly. "The last few days have been rather tiring," she muttered. "I think I'll go up to bed."

He looked at her curiously but said nothing.

"I expect everything will seem different after the holidays," she stumbled on, seeing the look on her husband's face and feeling guilty.

She paused in the doorway and smiled diffidently at Alasdair. "I'm looking forward to it," she said softly. "Do you think Ninian will come?"

"I don't know," he answered thoughtfully. "I hope so. It would be nice if he could bring Deirdre. But I wonder if it isn't too early."

Laura didn't reply. The old ache returned when she thought

of Ninian who had waited so long for the right woman and now was not sure she would ever be his.

"I'll ask him and Deirdre to dinner next week," she promised, trying to make up to Alasdair for her coldness. "I expect they need cheering up."

Alasdair looked at her intently. "You look as if you do too," he answered slowly.

Nineteen

B ut the holiday at Annanbrae turned out quite differently
from what Laura had expected.

When their car drew up, Flora was waiting for them in the
great hall. The terrible desolation that had enveloped the house
in April had gone, and life seemed to have returned to normal.

Flora greeted them as she had always done, but Laura
noticed that her eyes misted over as she gathered her youngest
grandson to her and held him as though she never wanted to let
him go. Jamie looked more like Sandy than ever.

"Is Helen here?" Jamie asked excitedly, referring to
Cristobel's second daughter, as he wriggled from his grandmother's grasp.

"No," Lady Flora replied, regaining her composure. "The
last time you were here together, you kept teasing her and making her cry."

"That was at Christmas," Jamie piped, grinning up at her.
"We quite like the girls now. Can they come, Grannie?"

Flora smiled down at him and ruffled Jamie's already hay-
wire hair.

"I don't see why not," she replied gently. "Perhaps with the
baby due very soon, it would be helpful for Cristobel if they were
here. How stupid of me not to have thought of it before. I'll telephone Lochincraig immediately."

"Is Hebrides coming?" Iain asked shyly.

"She was here in June with her parents and Elisabeth," Flora replied. "The school holidays start so much earlier in France."

Iain's face showed disappointment.

"I really must invite her at the same time as you next summer," Flora continued. "I'd forgotten how well you two got on together last year."

Pausing to give Jamie another long look, she turned and walked into the hall.

When Laura saw her father-in-law, she had a shock. Robert seemed to have shrunk. His clothes hung on his once massive frame as if supported by coat hangers. But, whatever their private grief, neither Flora nor her husband allowed it to show or in any way to cast a shadow over the holiday.

Early one morning, about ten days after their arrival, Robert had a massive stroke that left him paralyzed and speechless. The doctors were pessimistic but said that if he survived the first few days, there was a great likelihood that he would partially recover and live. Yet as he lay in the vast bed in which he and his father and grandfather before him and all his children had been born, a pathetic shadow of the man he once had been, Laura wondered whether he really wanted to live. He seemed to have grown tired of the life that had once been so full.

Flora scarcely left her husband's side but sat holding his hand, talking softly to him. And through sunken eyes, that never left her face, he seemed to communicate with her. The rest of the family tiptoed in and out of the bedroom, but the couple appeared to be so content in each other's company that their presence seemed almost an intrusion.

On the first day Flora agonized over whether to inform Cristobel. She knew the strong links that bound her to her father. But she also knew that to travel with the birth imminent would be unwise, and she could not be sure that Cristobel, under the stress of emotion, would act wisely. Graeme suggested telephoning Lindsay and letting him decide. Lindsay promised to break the news to his wife as gently as possible.

On the third day Graeme persuaded his mother to leave the sickroom and join the family for tea in the drawing room. It had been raining since dawn, but as the tray was brought in, a pale yellow sun struggled to break through. Flora decided to have tea on the little table in the west turret where they could look out over the damp garden and watch a rainbow just beginning to throw long scarves of lilac, pink, and sapphire across the deepening turquoise sky.

As they were finishing, the telephone rang.

"It is for you, milady," the maid announced.

"I'll take it," Alasdair said, suspecting that Flora would seize the opportunity to return to the sickroom.

But he returned a few minutes later, a puzzled frown on his brow. "It's Lindsay," he announced. "He won't give me a message. Insists on speaking to you, Mother."

Flora rose with her usual vague smile and glided across the drawing room. Laura noticed that her slight figure had become almost wraithlike in the last few months. Her heart went out to this mother-in-law who had been more like a mother.

Within a few minutes Flora returned.

They all looked up expectantly.

"Lindsay telephoned to announce the arrival half an hour ago of Robert Alexander Hamilton Lindsay-Fraser," she faltered. "Eight pounds, ten ounces. Red hair. Mother and son both doing well."

Lady Flora took a deep breath in an attempt to gain control of her voice. "Cristobel sends her love," she choked. Her voice finally broke.

Laura looked across at her, and their eyes met. In that split second something fused between them, something that had been hanging in abeyance for years. The tears of joy that had been gathering behind Laura's eyelids cascaded down her cheeks. And as Flora held her gaze, something broke inside her too. The iron grip she had imposed upon herself snapped, and tears began to trickle slowly down her cheeks.

"Mother," Laura cried, calling Flora by the name she had longed to use ever since she had married Alasdair. But it had always stuck in her throat. Leaping from her chair, she ran toward the older woman, a tremendous surge of joy at being able to once again pronounce the word that had frozen on her lips the day her own mother died.

Flora held out her arms, and Laura embraced her, weeping uncontrollably as her mother-in-law led her from the room.

Graeme and Alasdair sat in silence for a few minutes. This unexpected show of emotion on their mother's part had unnerved them, and they each searched for some phrase that would restore normality.

"Perhaps someone should go and tell the girls they've got a baby brother," Alasdair ventured at last.

"Oh, leave it for the time being," Graeme answered. "I've had enough emotion for one afternoon, haven't you?"

Alasdair agreed, his eyes on the tip of his shoes.

"I wouldn't mind another cup of tea," Graeme went on. "Ring for Kirsty and ask her to bring some more scones as well."

Alasdair walked over and pulled the long tasseled rope dangling at the side of the fireplace.

"The baby'll keep," Graeme stated, settling himself back in his chair. "Janet's got them all under control playing in the old schoolroom. Let's save this piece of news till they start fighting."

As their weeping gradually subsided, Lady Flora gently released Laura.

"I *must* go and tell Robert," she declared, dabbing her eyes with a sodden hankie. She paused. "Robert Alexander Hamilton," she whispered.

Hearing it, Laura choked again.

"Go back into the drawing room," Flora urged. "I saw some fresh tea being taken in."

She glanced down at the old-fashioned fob watch, an engagement present from Robert. "Good gracious!" she exclaimed. "I've been away for almost an hour. Robert will wonder what has happened to me."

When she entered the sickroom, her husband was lying as

she had left him, except that his eyes were now closed. They always seemed to be closed, as if he had already said good-bye to the world. Sensing her presence, he slowly opened his eyes.

"Darling," she said softly, sitting down in the chair at his bedside and taking his dry, blue-veined hand in hers.

Robert's gaze moved toward her face until it met her eyes. She noticed that the dancing green and gold lights that Alasdair and Sandy, and now Jamie, had inherited were dull and glazed. Only the hazel shell remained.

"Darling," she whispered again, holding his paper-thin hand caressingly against her cheek. "The most wonderful news. Lindsay has just telephoned to say that Robert Alexander Hamilton arrived this afternoon."

For a moment the old light flickered in Robert's eyes. But Flora also saw fear there. They had become so much a part of each other that, even without words, she understood his meaning. Gently laying his hand on the sheet, Flora covered it with hers.

"He's a fine boy," she said softly. "And he and Cristobel are both very well."

Immediately the fear left his eyes.

"Everybody is very happy," Flora whispered.

She had the impression that his head, with its shock of hair now almost white but still with a few rebellious streaks of red, nodded his approval.

Then, as if a great weight had been lifted from him, for the first time since his stroke, Robert visibly relaxed. The arrival of Cristobel's son seemed to give him hope for the future, the continuity of life—this grandson whose eyes had just opened to the light of day.

Flora sat by his side, her hand cradling his. The evening sun struggled in through the mullioned windows, sending pale beams dancing across the foot of the bed, pinpointing the loved objects in the large, old-fashioned room. The light lingered waveringly on the silver-backed hairbrushes on the mahogany dressing table, and it seemed to Flora as if she and Robert were saying good-bye— good-bye to a life slowly ebbing away, taking her husband through the door that divides us from the world to come.

Robert had been waiting to hear of the safe arrival of Cristo-bel's baby. Now it was as if diaphanous veils were wafting over him, hiding him from her sight, carrying him away to a place where she could not follow. The soft rose-tinted light of a late summer's day slowly began to fade. And Flora knew that this was the end.

She did not call the nurse. She did not call their children. She wanted this to be a farewell between herself and Robert—the man she had married against all good advice, who had given her love and devotion more than any woman could wish for.

She bent forward. His eyes were not as bright as they had been a few minutes before. She squeezed his hand. But there was no longer the faint feathery pressure of his response.

"Robert," she murmured softly, leaning over him. "Robert, my darling."

With a great effort he raised his drooping lids.

"Robert," she whispered brokenly. "Oh, Robert, I love you so much."

For a fraction of a second she thought he was going to rise on his pillows. But it was only a gesture. He opened his mouth, but no words came. His eyes looked at her pleadingly, willing her to understand what he was trying so desperately to tell her.

"I know," she said softly. "I know, Robert. You love me too."

Relief crept across his face. With a final effort he opened his mouth, and a soft fluttering sound, so unlike his usual booming tones, filtered through the bloodless lips. "Flora," he managed to whisper, his voice scarcely more than a ripple in his throat. "My . . . Flora."

She gripped his hand more tightly in both of hers as tears meandered down her cheeks. Almost imperceptibly his head moved from side to side, and she knew he was trying to say "don't cry."

Flora took a corner of the linen sheet and wiped her eyes. Then, smiling through her tears, she laid her smooth cheek against his cold, withered one.

"I won't cry, Robert," she whispered brokenly. "I promise. There's nothing to cry about. You've given me such happiness all these years."

Hearing her words, he appeared to relax. They lay side by side, his cheek touching hers.

The door opened quietly, and Alasdair stood there. Seeing his parents together, their eyes closed, a look of ecstasy on his mother's face, he tiptoed away.

As the long summer twilight faded, Flora felt Robert's hand slacken in hers. The bedclothes that had scarcely moved with his shallow breathing suddenly became still. And her husband quietly slipped away.

Twenty

I s there any news of Ninian?" Lady Flora asked later that
evening. They were all sitting around the drawing room fire
feeling slightly unreal, trying to make plans and arrangements
and not achieving much.

"I telephoned when Father had the stroke," Graeme replied,
"and the War Box said they would contact him. He should be
arriving in London about now. I daresay he'll be here tomorrow."

"I see," Lady Flora acknowledged.

They all fell silent again. No one except Flora seemed able
to take in the fact that Robert, the rock on whom they all
depended, upon whose broad shoulders this vast house had
rested for as long as any of them could remember, was no longer
with them. And in their shock they silently looked to Flora, seeking refuge in the aura of peace radiating from her.

"Mother," Graeme said gently, "you should try to get some
rest."

"Yes, dear," she replied automatically. Suddenly she realized
that for the first time since she had come to Annanbrae as a bride,
she would not be able to sleep in her own bedroom. Robert's
body was now lying lifeless on the great bed they had shared for
almost forty years.

"I—think I'll sleep in your father's dressing room," she
added quietly.

Alasdair frowned. "Is that wise? Wouldn't it be better if you
went to another part of the house?"

"No, Alasdair," his mother replied with unusual firmness. "I will sleep there with all your father's things around me. It will make everything seem less unreal and help me to get used to this new situation." She looked across at her eldest son. "This is your house now, Graeme."

"Oh, Mother," he protested.

"No, Graeme, it is. And I don't wish to be a burden to you in any way. I want the necessary arrangements for you to take over to be made as soon as possible. Then, of course, I shall move out."

Graeme walked across and sat down on the arm of Flora's chair. "Mother," he said gently, putting an arm around her shoulders, "it may be my house, but I'm going to have enough to do running the estate on my own now that Father's gone. I can't run the house as well. I want you to stay here. I need you to stay. If I were married, it would be different."

"You may wish to marry one day," his mother said quietly. "Marrying late seems to be a Hamilton family trait. Your father waited till he was in his mid-forties. And Ninian doesn't seem to be in any hurry."

"Perhaps," Graeme answered patiently. "If and when that happens, we'll rethink the whole situation. But for the time being, let's stay as we are. There have been enough upheavals in this family in the last few months."

Lady Flora looked as though she were about to argue but suddenly changed her mind. "Thank you, darling," she whispered. "If that is what you wish."

"It is," Graeme said firmly.

He looked at Hamish, who had bumbled over from the Fort as soon as he heard the news and was now sitting slightly apart, stunned and bewildered, his watery blue eyes staring glassily in front of him. His hands hung loosely between his knees like two great paws.

Laura's eyes followed Graeme's gaze, and she hurt for Hamish who looked so alone. She, more than any of them, knew what he was feeling—a sense of isolation even in the midst of this close-knit group that was his family, yet not his family.

Hamish and Robert had always been close. Now everything

had abruptly fallen apart, and it was Hamish's eldest nephew who was about to take over the place where he had been born and grown up, where he had doubtless dreamed his dreams— some of which must have come true, but many of which would never be fulfilled. And Laura understood his loneliness.

Robert had been his last link with his childhood. Now Hamish was cut off and alone. Perhaps the same thought had been going through Graeme's mind. He got up and stood with one foot on the fender, looking down at Hamish's face, usually so florid, but tonight drained of all color. "It's your home too, Uncle," he said gently.

Hamish looked up at him balefully but didn't reply.

"Why don't you shut up the Fort and come and live here?" Graeme suggested. "Back to your roots. Your help in running the estate would be invaluable."

Laura knew that Graeme was being kind. Hamish had no idea how to run the estate, and she knew that Hamish knew it too.

"Thank you, Graeme," he replied gruffly. "Thank you, m'boy. Very civil of you. Very civil indeed."

"Jeannie must be just about on her last legs," Graeme went on, seeing that he had not convinced his uncle. "How long has she been with you? Certainly before any of us was born."

"Since '34 when I retired from the army," Hamish answered dully.

"Then it's time she retired," Graeme insisted.

"Yes, well, dunno about that," Hamish mumbled. "We'll see."

"Why don't you both pack up and come over here?" Graeme coaxed. "Jeannie can always give Cook a hand in the kitchen." He grinned mischievously. "Or spend the rest of her days haunting the galleries, like Morag did until she faded into the woodwork."

"Graeme," Lady Flora reproached.

Her eldest son smiled affectionately at her. "Come on, Uncle," he insisted. "I know Mother would be pleased to have your company."

Hamish flushed and dropped his eyes. Laura suddenly realized that not only had he lived vicariously through his brother's family, but that he had also been in love with his brother's wife. Probably still was. Smiling sadly to herself at the thought of those long years of unrequited devotion to Flora, she wondered if Graeme had also guessed Hamish's secret.

"Wouldn't you, Mother?" Graeme ended.

Flora looked at Hamish, who was now blushing furiously. "Of course, Hamish," she answered warmly. "And perhaps that is what Robert would have wanted—that we join ranks so that the dreadful loss in our lives doesn't hurt so much."

She smiled her sweet smile, now ringed with an immense sadness. "One of the last things Robert said to me before he died was . . . 'don't cry.'"

"Did Father regain his speech?" Alasdair asked in surprise.

"No, darling, not really. But we were so close, words were superfluous between us."

Alasdair leaned across and squeezed his mother's hand.

"Well now, that's settled," Graeme put in quickly.

Laura sensed that the atmosphere was becoming too charged with emotion for him.

"Move in as soon as you like, Uncle. Your old room in the east turret is still empty. Why don't you sleep there tonight?"

Hamish grunted, not trusting himself to speak. Fumbling in his overflowing pockets, he dug out a large khaki handkerchief and blew his nose fiercely with his usual honking sounds.

"I'll be saying good night to you all," he said gruffly, creaking slowly to his feet. "Come along, Archie."

The spaniel had been lying beside him, his head resting on his crossed paws, his sad brown eyes gazing mournfully at his master. The dog now lumbered to its feet and followed Hamish as he shuffled across the room, a bent, broken old man.

"Now, Mother," Graeme said firmly, holding out his hand to Flora, "I think you should try to get some sleep too. The next few days are going to be exhausting."

"I'll see you to your room," Laura said, getting up from her chair.

"It's not necessary, Laura dear," Flora replied gently. "I'm perfectly all right."

"I know you are, but I'd like to."

Taking her mother-in-law's arm in a totally uncharacteristic gesture, she steered Flora across the gracious drawing room.

"I wonder why Laura did that?" Graeme commented, returning to the fire after opening the drawing room door for them.

"I suppose she wanted to help Mother," Alasdair replied, without mentioning that he too had been surprised. "She's very fond of her. And women are often more sensitive than we are. Laura certainly is. Perhaps she thought it was better not to leave Mother alone."

"Perhaps," Graeme agreed. "Blowed if I understand women." He grinned at Alasdair. "After ten years of marriage, do you?"

"I thought I did," Alasdair puzzled, "but these last few months Laura has shown some strange behavior. Come to think of it, she's not been herself since Sandy's death." He smiled ruefully at his brother. "To answer your question—no, I don't think I do."

They both laughed, relieved that the tension had diffused after the emotional evening.

As Laura and Flora reached the door of Robert's dressing room, Flora sighed. "What a day this has been. Robert is born. And Robert dies."

Her hand involuntarily gripped the heavy brass knob. "I'm so glad Robert died when he did, Laura. He would have hated to be an invalid."

Her eyes filled with tears that she made no attempt to brush away. "And I'm so glad you're here, darling. It's such a blessing to have a daughter by one's side at a time like this."

Quickly kissing Laura's cheek, she said good night and entered the very masculine room papered with sepia photographs of Robert as a boy at school and as a young subaltern in full-dress uniform. As her eyes roamed over the numerous silver trophies crowded on the tops of cupboards, her thoughts strayed to Katharine, and she longed to have her friend beside her now.

"I thought I understood how she was feeling when Ashley died," she murmured brokenly. "I even tried to comfort her by telling her so."

Flora sat down in her husband's old leather armchair and dropped her head into her hands.

How could I have been so presumptuous? No one can understand what it's like to lose half of oneself until going through it. My poor dear Katharine. You were both so young and had so little time together.

From the depths of her being a heartrending sob slipped to the surface.

As the twelfth stroke echoed through the empty galleries, Flora looked up, and her eyes fixed on the heavy studded door separating her from her husband's lifeless body. It was already another day. With the last booming stroke, yesterday had vanished. A page had turned. And a new life had begun. A life without Robert. Finally the full significance of what had happened struck her.

"Robert," she cried brokenly.

Her slight body shook with sobs.

"Oh . . . Robert!" she exclaimed in an agonized cry. "How can I live without you?"

And cradling her head in her arms, she wept as if her heart would break.

Laura tapped hesitantly at Lady Flora's door. It was the day after Robert's funeral, and Flora had retired to bed early.

"May I come in and talk to you?" she asked diffidently.

"Darling, of course," Flora answered warmly, ushering her inside. "How sweet of you to come."

She bent to put a match to the logs lying ready in the grate and then stood warming her hands at the blaze as the dry wood sputtered into a hissing orange flame. Pulling an armchair up to the fireside, she motioned Laura to take the one opposite.

"Sit down, darling. Would you like some tea?"

Laura shook her head. "No, I just wanted to be alone with you for a while."

On the night Robert had died, Flora had mentioned that

Ninian seemed to be in no hurry to marry. Her remark had sparked a thought in Laura's mind, and she had accompanied her mother-in-law to her room that night, intending to broach the subject. But as they stood outside Robert's door, she saw the pain in Flora's eyes and felt that it was not the time.

Ninian had been obliged to return to London that morning, and Laura had been surprised that he had not said a word about his engagement to Deirdre during his short stay.

She had been shocked by Ninian's changed appearance. He had looked drawn and tired, and she was convinced that it was not just the shock of his father's death. So, taking her courage in both hands, she decided to approach Lady Flora.

"It must have been hard for Cristobel not to be here," Laura remarked, playing for time. "She and Father were very close."

"Yes." Flora smiled sadly. "But now she has another Robert in her life. And one who, at the moment, can't do without her." Flora's eyes strayed to the photograph in an old-fashioned silver frame on her desk—her husband as a young man.

The week had been emotionally exhausting for them all, but Laura realized how much more so it had been for Flora. As they sat together in a companionable silence, staring into the red-gold flames leaping against the logs, Laura wondered whether her mother-in-law would ever recover. She stole a glance at her. Flora's eyes were now closed and her face drawn with fatigue. But there was an aura of peace surrounding her that seemed to fill the quiet room.

Again Laura marveled at Flora's almost superhuman courage in the face of this double tragedy. Could it be this God whom Flora believed in so wholeheartedly? Was God giving her this strength, this power to overcome and remain tranquil, almost joyous, when her whole world lay in ruins?

Laura really wanted to know.

At that moment Flora opened her eyes. Seeing Laura's puzzled frown, she smiled and raised her eyebrows inquiringly.

"I don't understand you," Laura faltered. "What has happened to you in the past four months is the worst thing that could happen to any woman and yet . . ." She shrugged help-lessly. "You seem happy."

Flora's smile deepened. "Not happy, Laura," she answered quietly. "Happiness depends on happenings, things that *happen* to us. But you're right. In spite of everything I have joy, which is quite different."

Laura shook her head in bewilderment.

"A joy only Jesus can give," Flora explained. "It doesn't depend on outside circumstances; it constantly wells up from deep within us. And at times like this it seems to overflow. I wish I could explain it, darling. But I can't. It's just another precious gift God gives us when we surrender all to Him and accept His plan for our lives."

She smiled again, a smile of immense sweetness.

"I long for that for each one of you, my children," she said softly. "It's what I pray for every day."

Laura couldn't take Flora's words in. If this God really had a plan for Flora's life, why did He let such terrible things happen to her? It didn't seem fair. Flora referred to Him as her loving Father, but what loving father would torture his child this way? No, it was all too far-fetched. And yet . . . She remembered Sandy's funeral and how broken they had all been. All except Flora, who had this certainty that death was not the end. Doubt began to creep in and erode her anger. Perhaps, after all, there was something in what Flora said.

She looked up and saw her mother-in-law's beautiful eyes upon her. Not for the first time Laura had a strange feeling that Flora was looking straight through her, seeing into her very soul. Quickly looking away, Laura was suddenly embarrassed. She cast about desperately for something to say. "You love your children very dearly, don't you?" she said hurriedly, grasping at the orig-inal reason for her being there.

Flora looked at her in surprise. "Of course, Laura. As you do."

Laura wondered what Flora would think if she told her of her present obsession with Jamie, her terrible fear of letting him go.

"Does their happiness mean more to you than anything else?" she probed.

"I believe so, darling. Why do you ask?"

"I was thinking of Ninian," Laura continued, now launched and not really knowing where the words would lead her, or even whether Ninian would thank her for what she was doing. "You mentioned earlier that neither he nor Graeme seemed to be in any hurry to marry."

Lady Flora raised puzzled eyebrows.

"If Ninian isn't married, it's because he wants to spare you. Or he wanted to spare both of you."

"Laura," Flora said bewilderedly, "what are you hiding from me?"

"I'm not hiding anything," Laura answered quietly. "But Ninian is. The Sunday Sandy was killed, Ninian came to dinner with us and brought his fiancée. He intended to introduce her to you at the wedding." She paused. "As things turned out, he didn't feel it was possible."

"Perhaps not that weekend," Flora said slowly. Her brow rutted in a puzzled frown. "But why hasn't he brought her since? Why hasn't he said anything?"

"Ninian met Deirdre through mutual friends when he was stationed in Northern Ireland," Laura confided. "She's an Irish Catholic. From Dublin."

For a moment there was an electric silence between them. Then Lady Flora looked up, her face gray. "Why didn't he tell us?" she asked hollowly, her voice scarcely more than a whisper.

"Would you have accepted her?" Laura asked tightly. "In theory she's on the other side—the side that killed Sandy."

"Laura," Flora cried brokenly, "perhaps a year ago, perhaps even six months ago I would have been reticent. But now . . . of course I will accept her." She gave a short sharp cry. "Poor Ninian. What he must have been suffering!"

She shook her head in bewilderment. "And . . . how little he knows me," she ended sadly.

"Would Father have accepted her?" Laura pursued.

Flora sighed deeply. "I don't know," she reflected. "Yes, after what happened, I think he would have."

She sighed again, twisting that same scrap of handkerchief around and around in her fingers.

"As one gets older, one realizes the futility of strife, people brought up to hate each other merely because they've been born on different sides of a man-made border. Oh, Laura, just think. It could have been Sandy. He could so easily have met and fallen in love with a girl from Dublin . . . instead of Rose." Flora's voice threatened to break. "Imagine how I would have felt now if that had happened, and we had opposed the marriage."

Her breath came in a sob, and Laura understood what she meant.

"Oh no, Laura," Flora went on in a rush. "None of us knows what tomorrow may bring. I want Ninian to be happy. Of course I'll accept his Deirdre . . . and love her. If Ninian loves her, then there must be something very lovable about her."

"She *is* lovable." Laura smiled. "She's also a very lovely person."

Flora smiled back sadly. "Isn't it wonderful, Laura," she murmured, "that when God closes one door, He always opens another?"

Laura looked at her in puzzlement. Her mother-in-law must be talking about losing Rose as a daughter-in-law and gaining Deirdre. But she didn't see what God had to do with it.

"I am no longer Naomi—having lost husband and son," Flora murmured to herself. "God has brought Deirdre to be my Ruth."

Laura began to wonder if the traumatic events of the past few months had affected Flora. Who was this Ruth? Flora seemed to consider God a person, someone who actually had a part in her everyday life and intervened in her favor. She frowned bewilderedly.

Apart from their conversation on the way home from church that far-off Sunday morning when Flora had spoken of a personal God, Laura had never heard anyone talk like that. And as on that Sunday morning, she wanted to know more. But glancing at Flora, she saw the tired lines around her eyes and the dark circles beneath them, and the questions died on her lips.

"Alasdair will wonder what has happened to me," she said lamely, rising to her feet.

Flora got to her feet and slipped her arm through Laura's.

"Thank you, darling, for telling me about Ninian." She smiled, tears shining on her lashes. "I'll telephone him first thing in the morning and let him know how delighted I am by his news."

Reaching the door, Flora caught Laura to her and held her tightly in a warm, unexpected embrace.

Twenty-one

"What a lovely summer this has been," Katharine murmured happily, settling herself more comfortably in her seat as the car swung through the wide-open gates of Gure Etchea and started out on the long journey back to Le Moulin.

There was a grunt from the backseat.

"You don't agree?" Katharine remarked, half turning toward Elisabeth hunched beside Hebrides. But Elisabeth didn't reply.

"I do, Maman," Hebrides piped up.

Her elder sister cast a disgusted glance in her direction. "You *would*," she remarked scathingly. She returned to staring moodily at the passing countryside.

Katharine sighed. Her elder daughter hadn't changed. Along with bitter antagonism toward her sister, Elisabeth now had added a blanket disagreement with everything the rest of the family enjoyed. The only person who could spark the slightest interest in her was Maxime.

Léon, at the wheel, put a hand consolingly on his mother's knee. "You know Lizzie," he comforted.

"Don't call me Lizzie," his sister spat.

"Why not?" Hebrides asked. "Papa does."

"That's *why*," Elisabeth answered coldly. "And take that disgusting mongrel of yours off my skirt."

Hebrides hastily scooped up the nondescript dog snoozing on the backseat between them and moved defensively toward the other side of the roomy car.

Léon looked down at his mother, an amused expression on his face. He wrinkled his nose at her, and she smiled.

"It was lovely that you were able to join us, darling," she said, looking gratefully up at him. Léon, her gentle son, always managed to diffuse the explosive moments Elisabeth delighted in creating. "You will be able to stay for the family gathering at Castérat?"

Léon's brow creased. He had passed his first year's examinations as a medical student that summer and was now anxious to get back to his studies.

"It's only a few days till the first of September," Katharine wheedled.

"Well, just till the reunion. Then I really must leave. What about the others?"

"The twins are arriving back from America on the 31st," Katharine explained. "They've had a splendid time, though when it came to it, poor Louis didn't want to go at all."

"Because of Honorine?"

"Yes. Their engagement was officially announced only two weeks before he and Xavier were due to leave. But all the arrangements for their visit had been made so long in advance it would have been difficult to cancel them."

"I expect Honorine's been in such a fluster preparing for her wedding she won't even have noticed that the bridegroom's not around." Léon grinned.

"In the end he thoroughly enjoyed it." Katharine smiled. "Hope and her husband have been so kind, taking them everywhere. They've visited Philip in Washington. I had a card from Philip, and he said he was delighted to meet his European cousins."

"Are we really cousins?" Léon inquired.

"No, but Philip and Ben are William's grandsons. And since you've all adopted William as a surrogate grandfather, Philip and Ben have become unofficial cousins."

"What about Jehan?" Léon inquired, changing the subject. "Will he be coming to the annual gathering?"

"I don't think so, darling. His regiment is on maneuvers. Such a pity. Otherwise we'd all have been there together."

There was an exaggeratedly deep sigh from the backseat. "Not *another* family reunion," Elisabeth groaned. "Haven't we had enough this summer? Doing the rounds in Scotland. Now all those dreary aunts and uncles who should have been buried years ago droning on about the good old days and how they won the Battle of Waterloo. Not to mention our odious cousins—"

"I don't think they're odious," Hebrides protested. "I love the annual gathering at Castérat. Uncle Cléry is great fun. And we had a lovely time at Annanbrae."

"Annanbrae!" Elisabeth snorted. "Freezing picnics and disgusting food."

"They weren't freezing," Hebrides said angrily. "And it was fun swimming in those gorgeous lakes—"

"Icebergs, you mean," Elisabeth snapped. "You're totally without feeling. A holiday in an igloo would please *you.*"

Léon winked at Hebrides in the mirror. "Taken another one of your nasty pills, Lizzie?" he teased.

Elisabeth's smoldering blue eyes met his amused china blue ones. "I told you not to call me Lizzie," she exploded, aiming a vicious kick at the back of his seat.

"Elisabeth," Katharine said exasperatedly as her daughter slumped back in her corner, "does *anything* please you?"

"Yes," she retorted. "Being with Papa. When he's not there, nothing's fun. I don't know why he had to go to Paris last week. Since he left, it's been boring."

"You know very well Papa had to go on business," Katharine said tersely. "He should have arrived home this morning, so by this evening you'll have your Papa again."

Léon, detecting an acid note in Katharine's voice, looked anxiously down at his mother. "Don't take any notice of her," he said quietly. "She's at the difficult age. I expect you went through it with us when we were in our teens."

"I don't think so," Katharine reflected.

"We were tucked away at Sorèze, so you didn't notice," Léon continued. "Or we were probably so pleased to get away from the place that during the holidays we were on our best behavior."

"Was it so awful?" Katharine questioned.

Noreen Riols

Léon grimaced. "It certainly wasn't a picnic. Probably more difficult for me than the others. The twins were brilliant, and you know what stress Sorèze places on academic achievement. And Jehan, though bone idle, worked that immense charm of his to get around everyone. While I was left limping behind—in more ways than one."

Katharine glanced down at Léon's right foot clamped firmly on the accelerator. She thought about her son's earlier handicap, the calipers he had once worn, the surgical boot, his limping gait. Closing her eyes, she once again thanked God for the surgeon's skill.

Léon grinned down at his mother. "But we survived. Perhaps boarding school would be the answer for Elisabeth."

His sister shot up in her seat like a rocket. "I'm *not* going to boarding school," she flared, her eyes blazing. "It's bad enough being shoved off every day to that Sévigné dump."

Katharine sighed resignedly.

"What *do* you want to do, Elisabeth?" Léon asked quietly.

Elisabeth flopped back, her eyes shining. "Ride Nimrod," she announced. Nimrod was the thoroughbred Arab gelding Maxime had given her for her fourteenth birthday.

"But you can't do that all day," Léon protested.

"I can. I can ride him for hours and hours and hours." She lay back against the seat, and her beautiful eyes had a faraway look in them. "And be with Papa."

As she spoke, her voice lowered and took on the beautiful contralto tone it was later to develop. Katharine caught her breath. She could almost believe it was Maxime's mother, Elisabeth's namesake and grandmother, speaking. Maxime's mother had been very like her grandmother, the beautiful tragic empress, and Katharine's heart constricted with fear.

Léon glanced conspiratorially at his mother. "We seem to be back on the same old merry-go-round," he said wryly. He again placed his hand reassuringly on Katharine's knee. "Better drop the subject."

But his action only partially dispelled the irritation Katharine felt toward her elder daughter. Elisabeth's obsession with her father and antagonism toward the rest of the family, especially her sister, rather than lessening as her mother had hoped, seemed only to have increased over the years. Now it seemed almost to be veering out of control.

Katharine's lips tightened in a hard line. She once again determined that Elisabeth would not succeed in driving a wedge between her and Maxime—a wedge of which Maxime, besotted by his elder daughter, seemed unaware.

Maxime was waiting on the steps as the car drew up with its weary passengers. Before anyone else had time to alight, the back door of the car flew open, and Elisabeth shot out. "Papa," she shrieked, throwing herself into his arms.

It was the first time she had shown any sign of life since her father's departure from Gure Etchea the previous week.

Katharine climbed out, as Maxime, with Elisabeth still clinging to his neck, turned to greet her. He gently disentangled his daughter, but she possessively caught hold of his hand as he walked down the steps.

"Tired?" he inquired solicitously taking his wife's arm as, with a crowd of dogs racing around them, they walked into the cool, dark hall.

"Everyone's feeling weary," Katharine replied. "Let's have an early dinner."

"But I want Papa to go riding with me," Elisabeth protested.

"Not this evening, Elisabeth," her mother said firmly. "Papa and I have things to discuss."

Elisabeth shot a venomous look in her mother's direction and sulkily let go of Maxime's hand. As Katharine and Maxime entered their room, a violent altercation broke out between Elisabeth and her sister, followed by loud sobs from Hebrides.

"Leave them to sort out their own problems," Maxime advised, urging her into a chair.

"Elisabeth is so aggressive . . . and unpleasant," Katharine protested. "Since you left Gure Etchea, she's been odious, not only with Hebrides, but with everyone. Even Léon. And you know how sweet he is with her and how difficult it is to ruffle his good humor."

"It's her age," Maxime soothed, echoing Léon's words. "She'll get over it."

Katharine glanced at her husband. He seemed unconcerned. She sighed, hoping he was right.

"Tell me what's been happening." She yawned, kicking off her shoes.

"Nothing very much. A pile of letters, of course. Oh, and Flora telephoned twice."

Katharine raised her eyebrows.

"She told Eugène it wasn't urgent and could wait till you returned."

Eugène had replaced the faithful Alphonse when the elderly butler had finally retired.

"We really *must* ask Zag to have a telephone installed at Gure Etchea," Maxime went on. "I understand that as long as Armand was alive, out of delicacy we didn't. But it's almost six years since he died, and it really is inconvenient being without one. Anything could happen, and we just wouldn't know."

"But it's so peaceful without one." Katharine smiled. "I don't imagine Flora rang with dramatic news. It was probably to let us know that Cristobel's baby has arrived. It was due sometime in August. Or perhaps Flora is able to come to Louis and Honorine's wedding after all."

Katharine frowned. "It's getting very near—the fifteenth of October is barely six weeks away! When their engagement was announced in June, I thought we had plenty of time . . . but the summer has flown past. I'll have to think about getting the invitations out very soon."

She smiled at her husband. "It's strange to think that we'll soon have a married son . . . and perhaps grandchildren before long." She looked up at him, her eyes wide. "Oh, Maxime," she groaned, "we're growing *old*."

Maxime rose and, taking her hands, placed a kiss in each

upturned palm. "To me, darling," he said softly, "you'll never be old."

Katharine leaned back in her chair, eyes closed, savoring this moment, her irritation with Elisabeth momentarily banished from her mind.

It was only after dinner that Katharine telephoned Annanbrae. She and Maxime had decided to have an early night. Propped comfortably on her pillows, Katharine picked up the telephone and dialed the number.

"Flora," Maxime heard her exclaim, "we got back only this evening. Tell me quickly—what is it? A boy or a girl? A boy! Oh, how wonderful! When did he arrive? The fifteenth. Already twelve days old, and we didn't know. What must Cristobel think of us. I'll telephone her immediately."

There was a pause. Maxime, sauntering out of his dressing room, saw Katharine's face blanch and the telephone tremble in her hands.

"No," he heard her groan. "Oh, Flora . . ."

"What is it?" he mouthed, hastening to her side.

Katharine slowly replaced the receiver. "Maxime," she croaked, "it's Robert."

"What about Robert?"

"He . . . died a few hours after Cristobel's baby was born." She grasped her husband's hand. "He's dead and buried, Maxime. And we knew nothing about it!"

Maxime sat down on the bed and drew her into his arms. "Flora should have asked Eugène to get in touch with us," he declared. "He could have sent a telegram."

"She didn't want him to. She said there was nothing we could do."

"We could have gone to the funeral."

"I can't believe it, Maxime. Robert dead! It was obvious when we were there that he had been terribly affected by Sandy's death. But he seemed to be recovering and regaining his old strength . . . and he and Flora were so close. They've always been close, but there was something special about their relationship this summer."

She turned her anguished face toward him, tears streaking down her cheeks. "Maxime, how is she going to bear it? Losing Sandy and Robert within just a few months."

Maxime gently stroked her hair. "Would you like to go to Annanbrae now?" he asked gently. She shivered against him. "Or would you like us both to go?"

"I—I don't know. I don't know what to do."

"I'll ring Flora and suggest it," he soothed.

Gently laying Katharine back against the mound of pillows, he picked up the receiver.

As if from a long way off, she heard her husband talking to Flora, but the words didn't penetrate her brain. Everything was a blur. All she could think of was Robert dead and buried and her best friend widowed while she had been sunbathing on the beach.

Maxime held the receiver out to her. "Flora would like to talk to you."

A look of panic shot into Katharine's eyes.

"It's all right." Maxime smiled. "Flora is very calm, and she wants to comfort you."

"Flora comfort me?" Katharine gasped as he placed the receiver in her hand.

"Darling," Flora said quietly, "Eugène offered to get hold of you, but I told him not to. I didn't want you to come racing over to the funeral. What good could it have done? Robert died very peacefully holding my hand, and I thank God that he didn't linger as a helpless invalid. He lived just long enough after the stroke to hear about the birth of Robert Alexander Hamilton Lindsay-Fraser. I didn't tell you the baby's name, did I? And he died at peace knowing that both Cristobel and the baby were well."

"But, Flora—"

"We had almost forty blissfully happy years," Flora went on calmly. "William stressed that wonderfully when he spoke at the funeral. God has blessed me richly, Katharine, and He does arrange things beautifully. William was one of Robert's oldest friends, and he and Lavinia happened to be staying at the Farquharsons when Robert died."

Flora took a deep breath. "And now I am to receive another blessing. Ninian is bringing his fiancée to meet the family next weekend."

Katharine did not know what to reply.

"William's prayers have upheld and sustained me during the past few weeks. And I know that you and Maxime also will pray for me, for all of us," she ended softly. "And that is the most important thing."

"Can you come and stay with us?" Katharine said hesitantly.

"Later, darling. But I want Hebrides to come back to visit with me very soon. Iain was so disappointed she wasn't here in August. Now that she is old enough to travel alone, I really want to get to know my goddaughter better. Don't cry, darling. Just remember us all in your prayers . . . and especially Ninian. Isn't it wonderful news? I can't wait to welcome Deirdre."

Katharine rubbed away her tears as she replaced the receiver. "There doesn't seem to be anything we can do," she sniffed. "Flora is incredible."

"We can pray for her," Maxime said quietly. "Shall we do that now?"

Katharine looked up at her husband, her eyes shining with unshed tears as she placed her hand in his.

Twenty-two

Deirdre arrived at Annanbrae to met her prospective family at the beginning of September, just two weeks after Robert's funeral. Her beauty, her simplicity, and her obvious devotion to Ninian charmed and conquered everyone.

She and Ninian were married in London at St. James' Spanish Place toward the end of November. Throughout the short ceremony, Hamish glared fiercely in front of him, angrily flapping at whiffs of incense, which he said got up his nose and made him sneeze, stating loudly that he did not hold with poppery and muttering about "all this bobbing up and down and people waving things around, mumbling in Latin." Lady Flora, her eyes riveted lovingly on Ninian, stood erect at Hamish's side, taking not the slightest notice of his antics.

Deirdre, as a bride, looked more beautiful than ever. Laura thought what a pity it was that she had not had the traditional white wedding with pages, bridesmaids, guards of honor, and all the other trappings. But Deirdre had shown a wisdom and a sensitivity far beyond her years in choosing this simple family ceremony that could not in any way bring back painful memories of the fashionable nuptials arranged for Rose and Sandy.

"Shall we have tea?" Lady Flora inquired.

The little wedding party was walking up the carpeted stairs into the foyer of the Ritz after waving good-bye to the happy couple. Ninian and Deirdre would have a short honeymoon in

Switzerland before Ninian took up his new appointment as military attaché in Berne early in December.

"Not for us." Cristobel smiled, grabbing Laura around the waist. "Let's have it in my room. I haven't seen anything of you for ages. And I've got a suggestion to make."

Laura looked at her questioningly, but Cristobel only dimpled, putting a finger to her lips as the lift mounted to her floor.

"Will you all come to Lochincraig for Christmas?" Cristobel asked, settling comfortably into an armchair as tea was brought in. "Now that our children seem to be on speaking terms, we may as well make the most of it. It may not last!"

Her eyes twinkled as she handed Laura a cup. "I'm going to persuade Mother and Co. to come as well," she went on. "It would be too painful for them to stay at Annanbrae after the year we've had."

She sighed as she lifted the lid off a silver salver. "All those wonderful Christmases we had at Annanbrae. The gigantic tree in the hall. The carol singers on Christmas Eve. Scrumptious things to eat and presents and fairy lights and games." Cristobel giggled. "And the charades. Do you remember when Uncle Hamish was the fairy queen?"

They both burst out laughing.

"I want to make it like that for my children," Cristobel continued dreamily, munching contentedly on a hot buttered scone. "Something they'll always remember."

Cristobel turned her enormous gray eyes appealingly on Laura. "*Do* say you'll come," she coaxed. "We all need to be together. And you and I can spend hours sitting around chatting like we used to do in the school holidays."

"And the children?" Laura asked.

"Oh, it's bound to snow," Cristobel replied airily. "Alasdair and Lindsay can take them skiing."

So a few weeks later they went to Lochincraig, returning home only just in time to get the boys off to school for the new term. And Christmas was as they remembered it at Annanbrae—a time of happiness and excitement and starry-eyed children.

Jamie had joined his brothers at St. Bede's in September. But it had been autumn—a glorious autumn with a lot of work to be done in the garden and golf on weekends with Alasdair. Laura had been busy helping Deirdre and Ninian with plans for the wedding, and once it was over, there had been all the preparations for Christmas. So the full force of her youngest son's departure had not struck her. But when she waved the three of them good-bye, as the school train steamed out of the station that dreary January afternoon, and returned to an empty, silent house, a feeling of hollowness descended on her.

"Boys get off all right?" Alasdair asked on his return home that evening. "Sorry I wasn't able to get to the station, but something turned up as I was about to leave that had to be dealt with immediately. By the time I'd finished, it was too late."

He followed Laura into the drawing room, rubbing his cold hands together. "I wanted to take you out to tea afterwards," he went on, holding his hands out to the blaze. "Thought you might be feeling rather low."

He looked at Laura, but she didn't reply. Something inside her seemed to have frozen over as she watched the train draw away from the platform and disappear into the distance, leaving her alone and isolated, shut off from her husband even.

"I'm rather tired," she announced when dinner was over. "I think I'll go to bed."

Alasdair smiled at her over the top of the briefs he was leafing through. "You do that," he answered gently, getting up to open the door for her. "The holidays must have been exhausting for you. Now I hope you'll be able to take things easy."

Entering their room, Laura walked over to her dressing table and stood gazing down at the large oval photograph of her three sons. As their happy faces laughed up at her, she crumpled onto the stool and wept.

The long, dark January days dragged by, and Laura's mood did not change. She had heard that the second term was always difficult, not only for the boys but for their mothers as well. The newness had worn off for them both, and they were each returning to a life that had become routine and no longer tinged with excitement. And the summer holidays seemed very far away.

But she expected that once the first week had passed and their compulsory ink-stained letters, written after church on Sunday morning, had arrived, she would settle down—like the other mothers she knew whose children were away at school.

But she didn't.

The garden was sleeping, the house impeccably tidy. And Alasdair was very busy. Laura felt abandoned and useless, her mission in life snatched from her. She knew she had to find something to occupy the long, lonely hours. But she didn't know what. Alasdair and the boys had filled her life completely, had been all she ever wanted. Now both seemed to have distanced themselves from her. As she wandered around the empty rooms and watched the January frost turn into dreary February downpours, she felt listless and desolate.

One evening as they sat together in the uncanny silence that now always seemed to lie between them, Laura took her courage in both hands. She knew that what she was about to suggest would upset her husband. But she had reached such a point of desperation that she felt she could no longer go on as she was.

"Alasdair?" she said tentatively.

He looked up from his papers, his pen poised in the air.

"Do you think you could put those things aside for a minute?" she asked irritably, and immediately hated herself.

With a sigh her husband laid down his pen and piled the files onto the small table beside him. "Well?" He smiled.

"I'd like to move," she blurted out.

Suddenly she had all his attention.

"It seems silly for us to live out here, practically in the country, now that the boys have gone," she went on hurriedly. "I thought we could move to London. It would save you hours of traveling."

"I don't mind the traveling," he objected.

"But I mind it for you," she said, forcing herself to smile. "And anyway I find the days long now that Jamie has gone."

Alasdair crossed one leg over the other and reached in his pocket for his pipe. "So that's it," he said slowly.

"What do you mean, 'that's it'?" she retorted angrily.

"Nothing." He looked directly at her as he pressed down the tobacco. "Go on."

Laura was on the verge of tears. "You don't seem to understand," she cried.

"I'm trying to," Alasdair replied calmly as he placed a match to the bowl and began puffing. He looked up at her through the smoke. "I thought you were happy here."

"I was," she said defiantly, "as long as I had something to do, as long as there was a reason for my being here. But now . . ."

"There are lots of things for you to do," he answered levelly, leaning back in his armchair and staring up at the ceiling through a haze of smoke.

Laura picked up a cushion and banged it furiously. "Oh, I know what you mean. The Mothers' Union, the village fête, coffee mornings." She gave the cushion another angry bash. "But, Alasdair, that's just not me. I'm not gregarious. I'm not terribly sociable—you know that. I don't want to spend the rest of my life on women's committees, presiding over the teapot at local charity fairs."

Almost beside herself, she threw the cushion to the end of the sofa and gazed sullenly into the fire.

"All right," Alasdair said at last, uncrossing his legs and looking directly at her. "What do you want to do?"

Laura carefully studied her feet. "I thought we might move to London. When the boys leave St. Bede's, it would be easier for them to come home for weekends."

Alasdair had wanted his sons to follow the family tradition and go to Gordonstoun. But Laura had pleaded with him not to send them so far away. Finally, he had given in, and they were all down for Westminster.

"And I could see more of Edwina," she hurried on. "She's

not getting any younger, and since my father died, she has no one but me."

"You seem to be forgetting Philippa and Mary," Alasdair put in drily.

"Mary's in Vancouver," Laura protested.

"But Philippa isn't," Alasdair pointed out. "She's living in Lowndes Square, practically on Edwina's doorstep. And when her daughter Polly gets married in April, she'll be living in London too. So Edwina will not only have a niece but also a great-niece living around the corner. And anyway Edwina's never been averse to coming out here to visit you. On the contrary, she always seems to enjoy it."

Laura knew that she had lost that round. "Hugo's in London at the Foreign Office now," she persisted. "But for how long? He and Philippa could go off to the other end of the world at any time."

Alasdair gripped his pipe hard between his teeth. He had been aware of the tension mounting in Laura since Sandy's death. He had noticed her preoccupation, her apparent indifference to him since Jamie had left. But he had believed it to be merely the result of the traumatic year they had all lived through and that it would pass. Now he realized that it had not, and he faced a crisis he had not envisaged.

He sighed. He had believed that this house would be their permanent home—one where they would build memories like he had of Annanbrae, where their children would grow up and their grandchildren come to visit. But judging from Laura's present state of mind, his hopes for the future had gone up in smoke.

He leaned forward to take her hand, but she drew away.

"I'd like to take up my music again," she said tensely, not looking at him.

"You can take it up here, can't you?"

"No, I mean go back to the Academy."

Alasdair frowned. "You're not thinking of becoming a professional pianist?" he asked sharply.

Laura laughed briefly. "Of course not. It's far too late for that even if I wanted to. But if I do take it up, I want to do it properly—not have lessons from the music mistress at the local convent."

Alasdair said nothing. He glanced at Laura, but she was sitting hunched in a corner of the sofa fiddling with a tassel on a cushion, avoiding his eyes. He could see from the damp patches on her face that she was crying. And he knew that she mattered more to him than the home they had lovingly created, more than anything in the world. In order to keep her and recapture that wonderful closeness that had existed between them for over ten years, he was ready to sacrifice anything.

"Very well, Laura," he said slowly. "If that's what you *really* want, let's find somewhere to live in London."

Knocking his pipe out against the edge of the grate, he crossed to sit beside her. "What about the boys?" he asked gently. "The holidays?"

"We hardly ever spend our holidays here," she reminded him. "Now that your mother's alone, we'll probably go to Scotland more often. And since the boys have developed this passion for their girl cousins, there's always Lochincraig. We don't really need this house." Her lips tightened. "They'll hardly be in it anymore. Once they've gone, they've gone."

Alasdair sighed, feeling her draw away from him again.

"All right, darling," he said quietly. "You win. Once the Easter holidays are over, we'll start house-hunting and move before the autumn. Then you can enroll for all the courses you want."

He threw an arm around her shoulder. "Any idea whereabouts in London you want to live?"

He felt her tension evaporate, and she turned to him, her blue eyes shining like many-faceted sapphires in which golden flecks of firelight danced. "Oh, Alasdair, thank you."

He tentatively drew her closer. "Happy?" he asked softly.

She nodded, her eyes closed. "I had thought of Chelsea," she murmured. "It would be near Edwina."

Alasdair smiled, brushing his lips through her soft hair. "And near Sloane Square tube station, which connects with Westminster," he teased.

Laura snuggled close to him. "Yes," she murmured happily. "And your office."

He tilted her head backwards and smiled into her eyes. "Mother hen," he teased. "Don't think you fool me."

"I don't want to," she whispered as his mouth closed over hers.

She sighed contentedly as she lay in her husband's arms, happy once again, convinced that she had found the solution.

"What about those case sheets you were studying for tomorrow?" she asked.

Alasdair's arms closed more tightly around her.

"Blow the case sheets," he said quietly, gathering her up and carrying her toward the door. "They can wait."

Soon after the boys returned to school in September, they moved to London. Throughout that spring and summer Laura had been her old self again, happy and at one with Alasdair. And once they were settled in the tall house in leafy Chelsea Square and Laura had enrolled at the Academy, she convinced herself that she had been right to insist on the change.

The boys did not appear to be in the least affected by the upheaval. The fact that their garden now consisted of a small patch the size of a pocket handkerchief didn't appear to bother them one iota. And even Alasdair seemed relieved no longer to have his working life dictated by a train timetable.

If, initially, there had been more to this move than was apparent, Laura was not aware of it. But as she became more and more absorbed in her music, gradually the close link between her and Alasdair again loosened. And her piano became her god.

Alasdair noticed it but said nothing. His devotion to Laura was absolute. She was his whole life, and he was prepared to sacrifice anything to keep her by his side. So he ignored the mounting signs of their growing apart, throwing himself into his work. Until suddenly, as he watched her thirty-fifth birthday come and go, he realized that, although nothing had been said, the woman he had loved for so many years, and still loved deeply, was someone he no longer knew.

The shy, young girl who had blossomed into womanhood as they became one no longer responded, no longer gave herself willingly to his embrace. Without anything being said, without any outward sign of the subtle change in their relationship, she had distanced herself from him—as if a key had been turned on her emotions, locking them tightly out of reach, so that her lovemaking became mechanical, a duty to be performed and dispensed with as quickly as possible.

Alasdair sadly acknowledged the cynical truth that often in a marriage there is one who loves and one who allows herself to be loved . . . because that was what was happening in his own marriage.

PART III
1978

Twenty-three

Laura looked up from the piano as the postman mounted the steps to the house. Hearing the plop of letters, she removed the pencil from between her teeth and, placing it on the music stand, walked into the hall.

Three envelopes lay on the mat. Stooping to pick them up, she turned them over in her hand and saw that two were bills for Alasdair, but the third bore a Toronto postmark. It was from her sister Mary.

She eagerly tore it open. She hadn't seen Mary and Edward since her father's funeral. Although they promised with every Christmas card to visit England the following year, somehow it never happened. Laura sometimes wondered whether, had it not been for birthdays and Christmas, their links would not have been severed altogether. But it was only February. Her birthday wasn't till the end of March. Why was Mary writing now? She tore it open and began to read.

The reason for my letter is to introduce Josh Faraday, who is leaving to study for a few months in Europe. He's a very talented pianist and has won a prize enabling him to have lessons with someone famous in London. I'm afraid I can't remember whom. Would you be awfully kind and give him a meal occasionally and perhaps be his bolt-hole if he gets homesick? I don't think he will. I've known him since he was a small boy, and he's an outgoing fellow. But Lois, his mother, who's a great friend of mine, is rather concerned about him,

as this will be the first time he's been out of the States for any
length of time on his own.

I forgot to mention, he's American, not Canadian—comes
from Niagara Falls right on the Canadian border. I met Lois
some years ago on the Maid *of the* Mists, *a boat taking*
tourists on the Ontario River to visit the falls. You must come
to Canada one day, Laura, and see those waterfalls. They're
breathtaking. Lois and I discovered we were both interested in
the history of Canadian and North American Indians, and we
have been friends ever since. Toronto is only an hour's drive
from the border, and we often pop back and forth to visit each
other. Now where was I? Oh yes. You'll like Josh, and he'll fit
in easily with your family of boys.

Laura frowned. *How typical,* she thought. Mary and Edward
had no children of their own, so her sister didn't understand that
her nephews, not being in the same age group, would have little
in common with this young man, especially since they had all
three inherited Alasdair's tone-deafness.

She turned to the last page and finished reading.

Knowing of your interest in the piano—how's it going by
the way?—I thought this wouldn't be too much to ask.
Anyway, I've given him your telephone number and told him
not to hesitate to contact you. Bless you!

Laura sighed. Music had already had an effect on her relationship with Alasdair, who could not understand her passion for
it. The last thing she wanted was someone else pounding on the
keyboard.

She glanced back to the second page. "Josh," she repeated.
"What a strange name. Short for something, I suppose. Why on
earth do North Americans have to shorten everything?" She wondered whether her scholarly brother-in-law was now called Ed—
and winced at the thought.

"Oh, well," she said shrugging, "perhaps he won't telephone."
Putting the letter in a drawer of her small desk, she went

back to the piano, never for one moment imagining that those few hastily scribbled pages would prove to be a catalyst in her life, leaving her, bewildered and afraid, her emotions in shreds, at a perilous crossroad.

"I had a letter from Mary," she remarked to Alasdair over dinner that evening.

Although outwardly nothing had changed in their relationship, there was an underlying tension between them. They no longer shared as freely as they had once done. And when the boys were not at home, subjects of conversation were sometimes thin. So Laura was glad to have some news to animate their evening meal.

"She's given our address to the son of a friend of hers who's coming to London for a few months."

She purposely omitted mentioning that he was a musician.

"Mary didn't say when. But I imagine it must be soon, or, knowing her, she would have waited and added the request that we offer him a bolt-hole as a P.S. to my birthday card."

Alasdair carefully wiped his lips with his napkin. "And will you?" he asked.

Something in his tone irritated Laura. "If he telephones and asks to come and see us, I can't do anything else," she replied testily.

"I suppose not. Only hope he doesn't ring this weekend. I thought we might get out of London for a game of golf."

Golf seemed to be the one thing Laura and Alasdair enjoyed doing together these days. Recently she had begun to wonder about their relationship and to be afraid. She still loved him. Or believed she did. But since they had moved to London, things had changed between them. She opened her mouth, wanting to slip back into their old, easy intimacy, to say something that would bring those green and gold lights dancing into his eyes.

She wanted to see that crooked smile that had always made her heart beat faster, but which seldom touched his lips nowadays.

But no words came. She realized that a gaping chasm had opened up between her and her husband, and she wondered almost dispassionately if, with time, it would lessen . . . or grow even wider.

"You did warn the boys that we wouldn't be home until teatime?" Alasdair inquired as he tossed their golf clubs into the car the following Saturday morning.

All three boys were now at school in London but often came home on Saturday afternoon for the weekend.

He slammed down the boot and, climbing into the driver's seat, smiled diffidently at her. She smiled back and placed her hand lightly upon his knee, telling herself that she had been imagining the tension.

It was a perfect winter day, dry and blustery with a mild west wind blowing, and Laura determined to enjoy their outing.

When they returned, relaxed and happy, the three boys were hanging admiringly around a tall, young man seated at the piano, running his hands up and down the keyboard.

"I'm Josh," he said shyly, rising to greet her. "I hope you don't mind my dropping by like this. I did call and Iain said to come on out."

"No, of course not," Laura replied, slightly confused. Then she remembered. "Josh Faraday, isn't it? I'm sorry we weren't here when you arrived."

A smile broke across his lean, taut features. "No problem. The boys and I have had a great time."

"He doesn't play the same stuff as you, Mum," Jamie piped up, wiggling his hips and grimacing. "He plays rock."

Laura looked slightly taken aback, and all four boys laughed.

"Just to get acquainted," Josh explained. "I *do* play other things."

At that moment Alasdair, having put the car away, walked into the room.

Jamie pushed Josh across the drawing room toward his father. "No need to let yourself be dragged off to concerts anymore, Dad," he trumpeted. "You can snore at home instead. Mum's got a resident pianist now. Come on, Josh, play that tiddle-dee-dee-dee bit. You know, the Gary Glitter song you were playing when Mum walked in."

Josh looked uncertainly at Laura.

"Go ahead," she said smiling. "I'm going upstairs to change."

"I'll come with you," Alasdair said hastily as Josh swung around on the piano stool and crashed down on the keyboard in a series of discordant notes.

"Do come back whenever you wish," Laura heard herself saying when they bade Josh good-bye after dinner.

"Yes," Jamie chirruped, cantering up and down the steps, "tomorrow."

Josh smiled and ruffled his red hair. "I gotta work," he laughed. "You guys don't seem to realize that."

"Well, promise to come back next weekend," Andrew coaxed.

Josh looked across at Laura.

"I did say whenever you wish." She smiled.

"Thank you, Mrs. Hamilton," Josh answered. "I appreciate that."

Laura clasped his outstretched hand, surprised at herself for having given the invitation and suddenly realizing that she meant it.

"I hope you don't mind," she apologized, glancing anxiously at Alasdair as they walked back into the house.

"Why should I mind? He seems a nice enough fellow. And the boys appear to enjoy having him around."

From that moment on, Josh Faraday became part of their family. The weekend of her birthday, he arrived, almost invisible behind an enormous pink camellia, singing "Happy Birthday" as he walked through the door.

The boys began shushing, flapping their hands like agitated penguins.

"Oh, Josh," Iain groaned. "It was supposed to be a *surprise*."

"Say, you guys, I'm sorry."

He looked so crestfallen they all rushed to reassure him.

"How old are you?" Jamie piped, as Laura took a deep breath to blow out the ten pink candles on her cake.

"You don't ask a lady her age," Alasdair reproved him.

"Thirty-five." Laura smiled. Her eyes suddenly widened. "No, I'm not. I was thirty-five yesterday. Today I'm thirty-six." She covered her face in mock confusion. "Oh, how ghastly!"

"Whew," Josh whistled. "You could almost be my mom."

"How old are you?" Jamie pursued.

"I'll be twenty-two in the fall."

"What's the fall?" Jamie chirruped.

"Don't you know anything?" Andrew hissed. "It's American for autumn."

"I thought it was the same language as ours," Jamie harped on.

"It is sometimes." Josh smiled.

"When in the fall?" Jamie persisted.

His brothers sighed, casting their eyes to the ceiling.

"That's enough, Jamie," Alasdair said sharply.

"October 31," Josh whispered.

"Ooh, Halloween," Jamie mooed. "Ghosties!"

He spread his arms and dangled his fingers, looking like an animated coat hanger as he tiptoed heavily around the room, emitting weird sounds.

And that was how it had all begun.

Josh fitted so easily into their family life, arriving on the doorstep whenever he was free, downcast, or hungry. At first he came only at weekends, but as he got to know them better, he would often drop in during the week and sit improvising at the piano or chat with Laura about his home, his family, and his hopes for the future, or follow her into the kitchen, lifting off saucepan lids and sniffing appreciatively.

The boys always made a tremendous fuss over him. He was like a big brother. And to Laura, to begin with, he was like another son.

It was all so innocent. Then subtly, imperceptibly, things had changed.

Twenty-four

D arling," Katharine exclaimed, "young girls nowadays all have careers! We've simply got to find something for Elisabeth to do." She sighed. "Though I can't imagine what. She didn't do a scrap of work at school."

"And she won't do any if we force her into something that doesn't interest her," Maxime replied.

"But what *does* interest her? Other than racing wildly around the countryside on that horse of hers?" She looked at her husband, her eyes pleading. "Maxime, I can't *cope* with Elisabeth. I never have been able to. But I'm her mother, and I feel responsible."

There was a discreet cough in the doorway. "Monsieur is wanted on the telephone," Eugène announced.

"Who is it, Eugène?" Maxime inquired, frowning impatiently.

"Monsieur Xavier, sir."

"I'll take it," Katharine said, quickly getting up from the sofa, pleased at the diversion. Elisabeth had become a bone of contention between them lately.

As she left the room, Maxime picked up the evening paper and glanced at the headlines. He smiled to himself as he heard the murmur of her voice in the hall. Xavier's telephone call had come at just the right time and would, he hoped, diffuse the tension he had sensed mounting in his wife.

"Xavier would like a word with you, darling." Katharine smiled, coming back into the drawing room.

Sitting down again, she picked up the piece of tapestry she had been working on all winter and began putting the finishing touches to a golden chrysanthemum. The strains of a Beethoven symphony pulsated around the room as her needle plunged rhythmically in and out of the canvas. Glancing through the long windows opening onto the park, Katharine smiled happily. The sky was rose-pink with the fading sunset, and she savored the lengthening days and the promise of summer to come.

The tinkling chimes of the small gold clock on the chimneypiece mingled with the whisper of muted violins. Katharine put down her needle, a slight frown creasing her brow, wondering what Xavier could possibly have to say to his father that could be taking so long. He had already exchanged his news with her at great length, and she couldn't imagine what there could be left to say.

"You were such a chatterbox," she teased, picking up the coffeepot when Maxime finally returned, "that I'm afraid it's cold. Ring for some more before you sit down. Whatever were you and Xavier talking about? I thought he'd already given me all the news."

Maxime smiled absently. He seemed preoccupied.

"Maxime?" Katharine frowned, an anxious note in her voice.

"Oh, nothing dramatic," he hurriedly reassured her.

"Then what?"

"Xavier's engaged," Maxime said slowly, sitting down on the sofa beside her. "He wants us to go to Paris to meet his fiancée and her father."

"But, Maxime, why didn't he tell me?" Katharine exclaimed.

"Don't get upset." He hesitated. "Xavier wanted to tell you but . . . he preferred to tell me first."

"I don't understand," Katharine cut in. "What are you hiding from me?"

A telltale muscle began to work furiously in Maxime's

cheek, which did nothing to reassure Katharine. It was always a sign that he was anxious about something. "I'm not hiding anything. . . . But Xavier is afraid you might be upset. That's why he didn't want to tell you on the telephone. He meant to, but . . . he said the words stuck in his throat."

He paused and avoided his wife's eyes. "His fiancée is German."

Katharine relaxed against the cushions. "I can't see why I should be upset."

"Because of Ashley," Maxime answered quietly.

Katharine rose quickly to her feet. "I'll telephone Xavier immediately."

Maxime waited tensely, but almost immediately he heard her footsteps returning.

"There was no reply," she announced. "Poor Xavier. It was sweet of him to be concerned but . . . that was all so long ago!" She sighed. "Thirty-five years, half a lifetime away."

Maxime drew her to him, and she nestled her head against his shoulder.

"What's her name?" she asked.

"Michaela."

"Michaela what?"

"I'm afraid I didn't ask."

"Maxime," Katharine chided, "she might be one of your relations."

"My relations are Austrian," Maxime corrected her. "And that's also a very long time ago."

"Not on the empress's side." Katharine dimpled. "They were German."

She paused and a puzzled frown rutted her brow. "But why doesn't Xavier bring her here?"

"Her father lives in Berlin, and he's coming to Paris next week especially to meet us."

"And her mother?"

"They're divorced. She now lives in Bangkok."

Katharine's frown deepened. "Isn't it all very sudden? Xavier hasn't mentioned her before."

"It is rather. He apparently met her at a New Year's dinner party at the Courcelles. And it was love at first sight."

He smiled reassuringly at his wife. "Xavier will be thirty at the end of the month. He *should* know what he is doing. And he doesn't appear to have been so smitten before."

"Do you know when they are thinking of marrying?"

"Xavier didn't say. Later this year, I imagine. After all, Louis has been married for over five years and has two children."

"And still no son and heir."

Maxime tweaked her nose playfully. "Aren't you happy with your two little granddaughters?"

Katharine looked up at him, her eyes shining. Then she snuggled contentedly back in his arms.

"Let's decide about next week," Maxime went on. "Michaela's father will be in Paris on Friday evening. Xavier would like you to arrange lunch or dinner at the Rue de la Faisanderie on Saturday, as her father has to leave the following morning."

"We can go up on Friday."

"Don't you want to go before?" Maxime queried.

"Not really. Hebrides is having a difficult year at school, and I don't want to leave her and Elisabeth alone for too long. You know how beastly Elisabeth is to her sister."

She sat up abruptly, her previous tension returning. "Maxime," she repeated, "we've *got* to find something for Elisabeth to do."

Maxime drew her tenderly back into his arms. "You worry too much about Elisabeth," he soothed. "Leave her alone. She'll be all right."

Katharine turned her eyes full on him. "Do you *really* think so? She looks more like her great-great-grandmother every day. And—I know you'll think me stupid—but I have an uncanny feeling that they share the same tragic destiny."

Maxime laughed and held her tightly. "I do think you're stupid," he whispered affectionately.

But her words, and her fears, were to prove strangely prophetic.

One warm May afternoon Laura was sitting at the piano struggling with Liszt's original version of "Liebestraum" when Josh strolled in, humming the refrain.

"Ma'am," he told her, "you sure are a glutton for punishment. I sweated blood over that last year when I was working for the concours."

And sitting down beside her on the stool, he took over.

As the last note faded away in a melancholic whisper, Josh took her hands and placed them on the keyboard. For a brief instant she was startled. His touch had sent a tingling thrill zigzagging through her body, and suddenly Laura was afraid.

Josh laughed. "Don't look so scared. Your turn now. Play it with me if you like."

But Laura rose abruptly. Walking to the window, she saw once again that gaping chasm and aching loneliness from which her marriage had rescued her.

"What's the matter?" Josh frowned. "Have I goofed?"

Laura turned and forced a smile. "No, Josh, of course not," she said trying to sound casual. "It's just that you're too good for me."

He began to protest, but she cut him short. "Play it again while I put the kettle on. It will help me for my own practicing."

She turned in the doorway and smiled at him. But he had already swung around on the stool, the cascade of notes echoing around the room as his supple fingers careened up and down the keyboard. Laura glanced at herself in the hall mirror as she passed, half expecting to see someone different gazing back at her, some visible change in her appearance. But apart from a slightly heightened color, the face reflected was exactly as it had always been. She felt reassured.

"How ridiculous," she muttered. "Whatever came over me?"

Things had improved enormously between her and Alasdair during the past few weeks, almost as if Josh's arrival had been the needed catalyst to open up the lines of communication. In fact

Josh had been good for them all. Picking up the tea tray, she told herself that Josh was what the family had come to consider him—a fourth son.

"You have an unusual name," Laura remarked as they sat sipping tea. "Is it short for Joshua?"

"No." He grimaced. "St. John. Ghastly, isn't it?"

He pronounced it "gastely."

"I don't think it's ghastly," Laura replied. "I think it's rather nice. I like it better than Josh."

"You wouldn't if you were a kid at school in North America," Josh said grimly. "Dunno what came over my mom. Euphoric with her first, I guess. The ones who came after were luckier."

"What are their names?" Laura inquired.

"My brother's Dan."

Laura shuddered at this North American mania for cutting the tail off everything.

"And my sister's Mary Ellen. Good old-fashioned names. My dad realized I was going to have a time of it at school saddled with a handle like St. John, so he nicknamed me Josh. And Josh I've been ever since."

"Even when you're billed?"

"Even when I'm billed."

"I think it's a pity," Laura protested. "St. John is quite theatrical. It would look good on a programme."

Josh laughed. "Talking of programmes, I've got your tickets for my concert next week. Almost June—I can't believe it. Then in July I go on tour in Europe with the orchestra for the best part of two months." He laughed again. "The Grand Tour before I go back home."

Laura abruptly put down her cup. The strange fear had suddenly returned. Angrily she tried to shake herself free, but it refused to go away.

"How lovely," she echoed faintly. "I do hope the concert is on a Saturday. The boys would love to come."

"I think it's a Thursday. But you'll come, won't you?"

He looked at her appealingly, and her stomach turned over.

"Of c-course, Josh," she stammered. "We'll both come."

Josh popped the last biscuit into his mouth and stood up. "I gotta go. Have a lesson at 5:30."

"Shall we see you this weekend?" she heard herself asking.

"Probably." He smiled. "I'll let you know."

And with a wave he was gone.

She remained on the steps, looking after his lanky frame until it disappeared around the corner of the square. Then she walked slowly back into the hall, unable to understand what was happening to her.

The telephone rang. Lifting the receiver, she heard Alasdair's voice. He repeated her name when she didn't reply.

"Alasdair," she managed to gasp.

"Darling," he questioned, "whatever's the matter?"

"N-Nothing," she stammered. "I was thinking of something else. The telephone startled me."

"Were you practicing?"

Nowadays the mention of the piano did not bring a note of tension into his voice, and she relaxed.

"Yes," she lied. "And you interrupted the sonata."

He laughed.

"Darling," she said on impulse, "would you like to take me out to dinner this evening?"

Alasdair hesitated. "As a matter of fact, I rang to say I might be late."

"It doesn't matter," she cut in breathlessly. "I can meet you somewhere. I-I just feel like going out. Do say yes."

"Yes," he laughed. "Book a table wherever you like. Half past eight should be all right."

"Lovely," she breathed.

To Alasdair she sounded like a young girl again—the young girl he had married.

"You're a stupid idiot, Laura Hamilton," she scolded herself, firmly replacing the receiver. "With a far too vivid imagination."

❧

"The concert was a huge success," Laura told the boys on the following Saturday afternoon. "Such a pity you couldn't come."

"Was it rock?" Jamie chirped.

"Not exactly." Laura smiled. "But Josh was superb. He had a five-minute standing ovation."

"What's a standing ovation?" Jamie asked.

"When everyone in the audience gets up and claps," his father explained.

"Did *you?*" Jamie asked.

"Had to." Alasdair grimaced. "I was dragged to my feet by . . . guess who?" He grinned at Laura.

"Actually," he confided, "I'm not surprised it lasted five minutes with the racket your mother was making, shrieking 'encore, encore' and jumping about like a firecracker. I thought at one point she was going to fall into the pit."

"What's the pit?" Jamie piped.

"Oh no," Iain groaned. "Go and look it up in the dictionary."

Jamie really didn't care a hoot what the pit was or a standing ovation either, but he had gotten into this maddening habit of questioning everything.

Laura smiled at Alasdair as the boys ambled off.

"Doesn't he remind you of Sandy?" she remarked.

Alasdair returned her smile. "Is Josh coming this weekend?" he inquired, leaning back in his chair.

"I don't know," Laura answered thoughtfully. "I think he said he'd be busy with rehearsals for his European tour."

"Be strange next year without him," he commented.

Abruptly, a wave of anguish swept through Laura. "I'd better see about dinner," she said tightly, rising unsteadily to her feet.

Alasdair frowned and reached for her hand. "Laura, are you all right?"

But at that moment the front door opened, and she heard his step. Then his face appeared briefly around the drawing room door, and she quickly withdrew her hand. The memory of Josh's hand on hers was too vivid.

"Hi, you guys," Josh called, as the boys thundered down the stairs to greet him.

Alasdair put his arm around her shoulders and held her close. "What is it, darling?" he asked tenderly, sensing that something was wrong.

Laura looked up at him, her beautiful blue eyes wide with fear. Shaking her head, she began to weep.

He led her back to the sofa and sat down beside her, cradling her in his arms. After a while her tears stopped, and she gazed bleakly in front of her.

"Can't you tell me what's the matter?" he pleaded.

"I . . . don't know," she whispered, her emotions in confusion.

She saw anxiety begin to grow in his eyes, as if he sensed the protective covering that had always bound them close slipping. He seemed to be aware that something threatened their happiness, but he couldn't fathom what.

As they sat there, mute and lonely, each trying to work their way through their private fears, the door burst open, and Jamie fell in. He stopped abruptly when he saw them. "Oh, hallo," he chirped. "Why are you two sitting like statues? Isn't it time for dinner? I'm *starving*."

Laura slipped out of her husband's arms and attempted to smile. "It won't be long—"

But Alasdair cut her short. "Tell the others to make themselves tidy," he announced. "We're going out to dinner."

"Yippee!" Jamie shrieked.

With a deafening crash, he slammed the door and yelled the news so that the entire neighborhood could hear. Then he roared back up the stairs.

Twenty-five

I t's a great pity the three of us won't be able to meet, as arranged, before you introduce us to your fiancée and her father," Maxime said, a sharp edge to his voice.

"Papa, I'm *so* sorry," Xavier's contrite voice came down the line. "You know I'd meant to come to lunch with you and Maman. But Michaela has her exams in two weeks' time, and her professor has offered to give her some extra tutoring today at half past one. She couldn't possibly say it wasn't convenient. So I've offered to go to the airport for her. Her father's plane arrives at 2:40."

"I see," Maxime replied. "Well, I suppose it can't be helped."

There was a pause, and from the drawing room Katharine could sense the tension winging across the line.

"I could let him make his own way," Xavier ventured uncertainly. "After all, he knows Paris well enough. He used to live here."

"During the war perhaps?" Maxime cut in tartly, and he immediately regretted his ill-humor.

"No, Papa. Before the war when he was a student. His mother's French."

Xavier paused, and Maxime could feel his son's discomfort.

"The problem is, Michaela promised to meet her father, and if no one's at the airport, he won't know what's happening. There'd be no point in his ringing his flat, where Michaela lives, because she'd be working at the school—"

"Never mind, we quite understand," Maxime interrupted,

sorry that he had added to his son's dilemma. "By the way, you didn't tell us what Michaela is studying."

"She's at ESIT, the Ecole Supérieure d'Interprètes et Traducteurs, just down the road from you at the Porte Dauphine. Training to become a conference interpreter."

"How strange," Maxime reflected. "Your grandmother suggested that as a postwar career for your mother. But I turned up and spoiled all their plans."

He laughed, and Xavier, relieved that his father's unaccustomed testiness had evaporated, laughed with him.

"How are all these high-powered studies going to fit in with being a farmer's wife?"

"Very easily. I hope I won't be taking over Le Moulin from you for years yet. In the meantime Michaela and I will be living in Paris. She'll work freelance or for one of the numerous international organizations here."

"Of course," Maxime agreed. "Yours is another generation, and women now have their own careers. It just takes a bit of getting used to, that's all. Your mother's always on Elisabeth about finding something to do, but apart from becoming the first woman jockey, I don't see what."

He laughed again, and any lingering tension between them vanished. "So, Xavier," Maxime ended, "we'll look forward to seeing you this evening and meeting this high-powered fiancée of yours."

"You'll like her," Xavier assured him. "And if I can possibly pop around beforehand, I will. It depends if the plane's on time and what the traffic's like on the way back into Paris."

"Don't give it another thought, Xavier," Maxime said warmly. "We'll see you all at eight."

"It's my fault," Katharine apologized as he walked into the drawing room and sat down beside her. "We should have done as you suggested and come earlier."

"Don't worry, darling," her husband soothed. "By the look of things, we've got the rest of our lives to get to know Michaela."

He clicked his tongue in annoyance. "Would you believe

it?" he exclaimed exasperatedly. "I've again forgotten to ask her family name!"

Katharine dressed with extra special care that evening.

"You look lovely, darling," Maxime told her admiringly.

She glanced up at him and smiled. "Can't let the side down in the face of the enemy." She dimpled, pinning to her dress the diamond and sapphire coronet brooch Maxime had given her as a souvenir of his mother all those years ago. "Into battle!" she exclaimed, her eyes dancing with amusement as she rose and took her husband's arm.

Overcome by a sudden rush of love for her but afraid to smear her carefully applied lipstick, Maxime twined his fingers tightly in hers.

They had just reached the drawing room when the doorbell rang. Manon padded along to answer it, and a few seconds later Katharine heard her eldest son's voice warmly greeting the maid who had known him since his birth. Footsteps sounded on the stairs, and a sudden panic seized her. She looked anxiously at Maxime.

He smiled reassuringly as the door opened, and Xavier appeared, ushering a blonde young woman, almost as tall as he, before him. Behind them came an extremely tall man with dark hair heavily laced with gray.

"This is Michaela," their son announced proudly.

Michaela was wearing a simply cut pale gray dress. As Katharine went forward to greet her future daughter-in-law, she was struck by her eyes. They were the same color as her dress. Unusual eyes. Light gray, rimmed with silver. Katharine's brows drew together in a slight frown. She had seen those eyes before, but the memory was hazy and eluded her.

"May I introduce my parents," she heard Xavier say as he turned to Michaela's father.

Katharine looked up, and her puzzled frown vanished. She

caught her breath in a sudden gasp, the smile of welcome dying on her lips. As the color slowly drained from her cheeks, she knew where she had seen those amazing gray eyes before. Standing before her, his head inclined in a slight bow, but those unforgettable silver-gray eyes boring right through her . . . was Theo!

"What an evening," Katharine said weakly, as the door closed behind their departing guests. She seemed to deflate and suddenly become very small.

"You look whacked," Maxime said. Sweeping her into his arms, he carried her up the stairs and placed her gently on their bed.

"You've been so strange all evening, darling," he went on, concern in his voice as he pulled off her shoes and drew a quilt around her. "Like a wooden doll. You were perfectly all right before they arrived; then you suddenly froze. Whatever happened? Don't you like Michaela?"

"It wasn't Michaela, Maxime," she said slowly. "It was her father."

"What about her father?" Maxime inquired. "I found him a pretty cold fish."

Katharine smiled weakly. "He's not cold, Maxime. I think he was as embarrassed as I was."

Maxime's brow rutted in bewilderment. "Darling," he pleaded, "I'm afraid I'm lost. Can you stop talking in riddles and tell me what this is all about?"

Katharine lay back against the pillows. "Michaela's father is the German officer who wanted to marry me," she said almost inaudibly.

Her husband let out a deep breath. "So that was it. At least it explains your strange behavior. I thought you must be ill."

"No. Just shocked. Oh, Maxime, if only Xavier had told us Michaela's last name, I'd have been prepared. But meeting Theo again after over thirty years—especially as the last time was traumatic for us both—brought all the memories rushing back." Her eyes filled with tears. "I hurt him very much."

"Well, he seems to have gotten over it." Maxime smiled. "Otherwise Michaela wouldn't be here."

He suddenly broke off, and that telltale muscle began working in his cheek. "Katharine," he asked hesitantly, "has this evening brought back memories you were trying to forget?"

For a few seconds she did not understand what her husband's words implied. Mistaking her silence, Maxime leaned forward and took her heart-shaped face in his hands, looking straight into her eyes. "You don't still love him, do you?" he asked hoarsely.

Katharine's eyes opened wide with astonishment.

"Do you, Katharine?" he insisted when she didn't reply.

Suddenly the full force of his words hit her. "Maxime," she cried, grasping his lapels and pulling his face close to hers, "Maxime, darling, how could you even think such a thing? Of course I don't love Theo. I love you. But . . . seeing him again in the room where we parted with such angry, bitter words uncovered the remorse I must have kept hidden all these years."

Her lip trembled as the memories surged again. "Theo couldn't understand why I wouldn't marry him and go back to help him rebuild Germany. But, Maxime, I couldn't. I couldn't make my life with the people who had killed Ashley."

Maxime held her close, relief flowing out of him. "Of course you couldn't," he soothed.

"Theo didn't understand," Katharine said brokenly. "He was hurt and bewildered. And I said some wounding things that I afterwards regretted."

"It's in the past, darling," Maxime breathed into her chestnut curls. "It's over. And I'm sure that he has no hard feelings. Not after so many years."

"Oh, Maxime, if only I could be sure. I know Theo went on hurting for a very long time." She paused as if uncertain how to continue. "I didn't tell you at the time," she began hesitantly, "but do you remember our coming to Paris just after Léon was born?"

Maxime frowned.

"We arranged to meet for tea at W. H. Smith's on the Rue de Rivoli. While I was waiting for you, I picked up a book that had just been published. It was the one Theo was writing when I knew him in 1946."

Maxime shook his head in bewilderment. "Darling, why are you torturing yourself like this?"

"I'm not torturing myself," Katharine said hoarsely. "I'm trying to explain. Theo had dedicated it to me, Maxime. He *hadn't* forgotten. He called me his unfulfilled dream."

Maxime sighed. "That was a long time ago. Since then a lot of water has flowed under the bridge. Theo has married, had two children."

He gathered her back into his arms again. "Don't worry, my darling, Bonn is a long way from Narbonne. We're not going to bump into each other all the time. Once the wedding is over, we may never see him again."

"Michaela talked about the wedding," Katharine said hazily, as if everything was unreal. "She wants to be married in Berlin."

"But I thought her father lived in Bonn."

"He does. And she was brought up there." Katharine pursed her lips thoughtfully. "Perhaps it has unhappy memories. Her parents' divorce—"

"Did she mention her mother?"

"Yes. Apparently she remarried five years ago. An Austrian diplomat. That's why she lives in Bangkok. They've been there for the past two years, but Michaela said they'll come back to Europe in September, and she'd like the wedding to be in October."

"In Berlin?"

"Yes. At her grandmother's home. Zag told me Theo's family had a beautiful estate at Königsberg on the Polish border, but it was annexed by the Russians at the end of the war. So the family home is now in Berlin. Sybilla, Theo's elder sister lives there with her mother, who is now over ninety. Michaela appears to be devoted to them both."

"You seem to have winkled out the whole family history," Maxime teased.

Katharine shrugged. "I concentrated on Michaela after dinner and let you three men talk among yourselves . . . to avoid having anything more than polite conversation with her father."

She leaned back in her chair, her eyes fixed on the beveled ceiling. "Michaela's like me in a way," she went on thoughtfully. "She lost her roots in her teens when her parents divorced and is clinging to her extended family for security."

"So the wedding will be in Berlin in October," Maxime put in hastily, afraid that Katharine might lapse into painful reminiscing.

His wife looked up at him with a sad smile. "If there *is* still a wedding."

"What on earth do you mean?"

She gave a deep sigh. "This evening was a disaster, Maxime. And I *so* wanted it to be a happy occasion for Xavier."

"It wasn't a disaster. I was the only one who noticed you weren't yourself. You fooled all the others. And if you and your future daughter-in-law got as far as discussing wedding arrangements, you can hardly say that the atmosphere was strained. Xavier and Michaela seemed perfectly happy when they left." Maxime smiled down at her. "I like her, don't you?"

"Yes," Katharine replied absently. "I do. They make a very handsome couple."

But the past was surging up and blinding her vision. She hoped and prayed that her husband was right—that ghosts from that distant past would not now rise to insinuate themselves into her son's happiness, as former ghosts had insinuated themselves into hers. She sighed and closed her eyes. Tomorrow she and Maxime would go back to Le Moulin. Theo need never again play any part in her life.

But that was where she was wrong. That one evening had set in motion a chain of events she would be powerless to stop.

"Isn't this perfect?" Alasdair remarked, glancing down at Laura lying in the deck chair beside him.

They were relaxing by the Serpentine on a glorious summer day, lazily watching the ducks float past. Although they both had books in their hands, neither was even pretending to read, just enjoying the peaceful hum of bees and the soporific lap of the water.

It was early August. Iain and Andrew had left on a climbing expedition in Switzerland with a party from school, and Jamie had rushed up to Lochincraig to be with Helen. Cristobel had added Roddy to the family three years earlier and was now expecting her sixth child. So Laura had been loathe to send Jamie. But Cristobel had insisted, and, from what she had heard, the cousins were all having a wonderful time. Helen was the tomboy of the family, and she and Jamie suited each other perfectly.

"This time next week we'll be at Annanbrae," Alasdair murmured sleepily. "Looking forward to it?"

"You know I always do." Laura smiled.

Alasdair yawned, laid his book facedown on his chest, and, tipping his hat over his eyes, dozed off.

Laura sat gazing over the expanse of the lake. Josh had gone on tour almost a month before. She had imagined that once he left her world, which appeared to have been turned on its end in the past few months, it would right itself. But that hadn't happened. Instead she felt an ache and a loneliness she had never known before—a sense of desolation quite unlike the emptiness left behind when the boys returned to school after the holidays, and the house echoed their absence. Then it was momentary, and it soon passed. But this hollow despair was different. As the weeks slipped by, it didn't go away. It became worse.

Lying in the sunshine, she turned over in her mind the events of the summer, trying to analyze them, slot them into neat compartments. She tried to reason with herself and pretend that Josh hadn't happened.

A young girl in a flowered dress sauntered by, a transistor slung over her shoulder. From it flowed the last haunting bars of "Liebestraum," which Josh had played for her on that late May afternoon. Hearing it, she remembered the touch of his lean hands as they took hers and placed them on the keyboard. And Laura knew that she no longer loved Josh as a son.

She glanced at Alasdair peacefully sleeping at her side, only the tip of his nose and his slightly open mouth visible beneath his tilted hat. To her anguish came the thought that this time she could not turn to him for comfort.

A half-stifled cry escaped her lips. Alasdair stirred and, pushing back his hat, looked at her inquiringly.

"It's becoming chilly," she said, getting up and smoothing down her frock. "Let's go."

"If you say so." He smiled, rising stiffly from his seat. He took her arm, falling into step beside her as they walked across the springy turf. Suddenly she felt she had to get away from her husband, go someplace where she could be alone and think. She loved Alasdair, but she seemed helpless in the face of this rising tide of emotion threatening to submerge her.

"Do you mind if I go to Scotland ahead of you?" she asked as they left the park.

Alasdair looked at her strangely. "If you wish," he answered slowly. "But why the rush? We'll be going in a week."

"I know," Laura went on hurriedly. "But since Cristobel won't be there this year, it might be nice for your mother."

Alasdair's grip tightened on her arm. "Of course," he agreed. "When would you like to go?"

"Perhaps Monday morning?" She looked up at him, her eyes soft and strange. "Edwina's coming to lunch tomorrow; otherwise I could have left in the morning."

Alasdair dropped her arm and stopped in his tracks. "What's the matter, Laura?" he asked sharply. "Why this sudden rush? Are you trying to get away from me?"

"Don't be silly," she muttered, avoiding his gaze.

"If I may say so," he replied coldly, "I think you're the one who's being silly."

Edwina noticed the tension between Alasdair and Laura at lunch the following day. She sensed that something was desperately wrong; yet, like Alasdair, she couldn't fathom what. But she had the feeling that her niece's total absorption in her music had something to do with it.

"Why don't you go with Laura to Annanbrae tomorrow?" Alasdair remarked as he carved the joint.

"Is Laura leaving tomorrow?" Edwina queried. "I thought you were going together on Saturday."

"We were," Alasdair replied tightly. "But Laura wants to get away." He savagely plunged his fork into a slice of beef.

"Alasdair," Laura protested, "I thought perhaps your mother—"

"Yes, I know," he cut in testily. "But I really don't see what difference a few days will make." He shrugged, his eyes fixed on his plate. "However, you've made up your mind, and I've got your reservation for the morning train. But perhaps Edwina would like to accompany you." He looked inquiringly at her.

"It's rather short notice, Alasdair," Edwina demurred.

Once again Edwina wished she had a faith she could share with this niece who was so dear to her, some words to bring her peace and comfort. Perhaps a tête-a-tête with Alasdair would reveal the problem. He was down to earth and sensible, and she had no doubt that he was devoted to Laura. Maybe with a little gentle probing, she could get to the root of the trouble. She laid down her knife and fork and smiled at Alasdair. "Will you come and have dinner with me tomorrow evening?"

"Perhaps not tomorrow," he answered. "I'll take advantage of being alone to clear up some backlog at the office. It may enable me to get away a day or two earlier." He paused and looked pointedly at his wife. "That is, if Laura would like me to," he ended, a note of sarcasm in his voice.

"Darling," Laura pleaded, "you know I would."

"Just needed to be reassured," he answered grimly.

"I'll leave it to you then, Alasdair," Edwina broke in. "Any evening you feel like company, do telephone me. I'd be delighted to have you."

Their eyes met briefly, and Alasdair saw the unspoken question in Edwina's. Dropping his own, he felt suddenly helpless and vulnerable, as if he were about to finally lose his footing and crash over the edge of the chasm that he now knew had never closed between him and Laura ever since Sandy's death.

He did not understand what had happened to them at that traumatic time. He had been aware of the chasm and the danger, but his love for his wife had blinded him to the fact that they could one day actually plunge into that yawning blackness.

Until today he had imagined that he alone was aware of their precarious situation. But seeing the look in Edwina's eyes, Alasdair realized that the tension in their marriage had been apparent to others as well.

The following morning Laura left for Annanbrae in an atmosphere of strained politeness. The communication between them appeared to have completely broken down, and the wonderful unity that had crept back into their marriage during the past few months had completely disappeared.

When the train drew away, and Laura saw Alasdair's tall figure walking from the platform, she sat back in her seat, her mind in a turmoil. She felt as if a steel band were being screwed onto her forehead, forcing out every happy memory and leaving only intense pain. Staring out the window at the railway lines meeting, joining, separating, dancing before her eyes, she saw them gradually give way to a tangled web of sordid streets. The fine weather had changed overnight, and heavy rain fell on the slimy black pavement spreading endlessly like a vast wet macintosh.

Suddenly Flora's deep faith, her utter trust in an unseen God, came to Laura's mind. Staring blankly at the derelict factories, the tattered billboards, and the depressing rows of ill-kept gray streets straggling in every direction, Laura wondered if, in the midst of all this, God really did have a loving plan for each person's life.

Since she married Alasdair and until Sandy's death, she had never given the question a thought. Her future had risen before her like a gently sloping heather-covered mountain, its heights disappearing into soft shell-pink mists of snow-capped beauty. But now it seemed to have turned into an endless black tunnel. Huddling into a corner of the empty compartment, she shut her eyes and tried to wrap herself in nothingness—safe in some haven where the past few months were obliterated, and life was orderly and crystal-clear again.

By the time the train drew into Perth station, a dreadful lassitude had swamped her. But Donald's homely face and welcoming smile, the drive through the early evening countryside ablaze with glorious flashes of rust and mauve and gold, and Flora's delight at seeing her momentarily dispelled the gloom.

When she walked into the room she had shared with Alasdair for so many years and saw the photograph of the nineteen-year-old Laura who had captivated him, she felt warm and secure and safe again.

The old house wove its spell, and peace gradually enveloped her: Annanbrae, that place where clouds never cast a dark shadow for long but were always pink-tipped, floating serenely in a blue sky, where the grass was always green, the sun's rays more caressing, where nothing ever changed. And life glided by in an endless summer afternoon with the promise of scones and honey and velvety raspberries for tea.

Laura peered into the small mirror on Alasdair's highboy and saw a white, drawn face with dark circles under the eyes staring back at her. Her eyes wandered from her reflection to the portrait of the smiling young girl. And she resolved to become that girl once again. She even convinced herself that she had been right to leave before Alasdair—that when he arrived with the boys on the weekend, all the hurt and the misunderstandings would have been wiped away by the magical touch of Annanbrae.

Twenty-six

On Friday afternoon as Laura sat at the piano trying to play "Liebestraum" the way Josh had played it, Flora came into the drawing room and stood in the doorway listening. Feeling her presence, Laura turned around.

"It's *amazing* how much you've improved, darling," Flora enthused. "Your playing has a depth and a maturity it lacked a few years ago."

She sat down on the stool beside Laura and ran her fingers lightly over the keys. "Music's a wonderful solace, isn't it?" she murmured.

Laura didn't reply. She knew that beneath Flora's vague exterior was a painfully sharp perceptiveness, and she wasn't sure she wanted to be laid open to such scrutiny.

"Did I tell you that I shall be moving to the Fort very soon?" Flora went on innocently.

Laura turned to her in astonishment.

Hamish had died early in the new year while watching a boxing match on television. One minute he had been sitting bolt upright angrily pounding his stick on the floor and hurling abuse at the referee. The next all had been still.

"You leave Annanbrae!" Laura gasped incredulously. "And for the Fort! It must be in a dreadful state. It's been shut up since Father's death."

"Oh, the Fort only needs a little arranging," Flora replied airily, keeping the real bait dangling. "It could be a very pleasant place to live. I was on my way over there when I heard you playing. Why don't you come with me?"

Flora smiled sweetly, and rising from the piano stool, held out her hand to Laura. "Annanbrae will soon have another mistress," she ended archly.

Speechless, Laura followed her mother-in-law out onto the terrace and across the lawn, Flora still with her faint amused smile, as if she were enjoying a secret joke. Neither of them spoke, but it wasn't an awkward silence. As they sauntered out of the dancing sunlight into the darkened woods and around the lake, Laura had a feeling that this moment hadn't happened by chance.

"Here we are," Flora announced, pushing open the creaking front door. She wrinkled her nose in distaste. "Smells musty, doesn't it?"

Crossing to the drawing room, she flung open the windows.

"Ugh." She grimaced as she looked out onto the garden, which was threatening to rise up and totally submerge the house. "Malcolm is going to have a wonderful time trying to make something of this."

Flora dragged a dust cover off a large sofa under the window and, sitting down, patted the seat beside her.

"Come and look at this view, Laura. Ignore the weeds. Isn't it wonderful? It's always been one of my favorites. And it catches the late afternoon sun on the mountains, turning them the most beautiful shade of pink." She laid her head against the faded damask sofa. "I'm going to love living here."

Flora looked mischievously at her daughter-in-law. "Aren't you going to ask me why?"

Laura relaxed and smiled. "Well, why?"

A little smile played around Flora's lips. "Haven't you noticed a change in Graeme?"

Laura had noticed very little. "Not really," she answered. "Why? What's happened?"

"Like Robert," Flora answered dreamily, "he's at last fallen in love. And I couldn't be more pleased. It seems that in His time God works everything for good."

Laura was embarrassed, yet at the same time intrigued. It hadn't occurred to her that God ever worked at all. He was just a mystical figure way up there who did nothing in particular either for good or evil. Yet here was Flora again talking about God in that intimate way.

"Out of the tragedy of Sandy's death," Flora went on, "He has brought something beautiful."

"But what?" Laura demanded. "Who has Graeme fallen in love with?"

"Rose," Flora replied softly.

"Rose!" Laura gasped.

"Yes." Flora smiled. "She's been nursing in Hong Kong since Sandy died, but she finally came home. Graeme met her again at a New Year's Eve dinner party in Edinburgh. Since then he's had many an unexplained trip to the capital—especially on weekends." Her eyes twinkled. "He was always the secretive one of the family."

She smiled at Laura.

"Do you remember at Sandy's funeral it was in Graeme's arms that Rose finally broke down and wept? Apparently it stirred something deep in him, and from that moment he has never been interested in any other woman. He brought Rose to Annanbrae last weekend, and their engagement will be officially announced in a few days. I think they intend to marry in October. After all, Graeme is already forty-four, and Rose is thirty-two. They don't want a big wedding. Just a quiet family ceremony in Edinburgh so as not to bring back any memories."

She looked at Laura, smiling her vague, sweet smile.

"Isn't it wonderful, Laura darling, that Rose will be my daughter-in-law after all? It's especially wonderful to see them together. They look so right."

Laura suddenly burst into tears. "I'm sorry," she gulped, her deep blue eyes swimming. "But it's so unexpected. And so wonderful to think of their happiness."

Flora slowly turned her gaze to Laura's tearstained face. "And you, Laura," she asked softly, "are you happy?"

Startled, Laura looked up through her tears. "Of course," she stammered. "Why do you ask?"

Flora got up and, walking over to the window, stood leaning against the sill, gazing out across the lake. "Life isn't always easy," she said, as if talking to herself. "And marriage isn't always easy either."

"Why do you say that?" Laura asked suspiciously.

"Just an old woman's musings, my dear. I remember a very difficult period I went through in my marriage. And I imagine it must happen in most, especially when a woman marries young. At such a time one either survives and carries on or . . . goes under. And if one goes under, I am sure one lives to regret it."

"Mother," Laura cut in breathlessly, "what do you mean? You and Father were blissfully happy."

"We were," Flora said, coming back to sit beside her. "Right to the end. But there was a crisis in our marriage, though I don't think Robert ever knew about it. If he did, he didn't say so. But it was very traumatic for me. And at one point I really did not know which road I would take."

"Go on," Laura said tightly.

"It was during the war. The house had been turned into a military hospital and convalescent home for Allied officers, and I was alone here with the children, who were all very young. I missed Robert terribly, and I fell in love with a young Polish officer who was convalescing at Annanbrae."

"Mother," Laura gasped, "I can't believe it. You and Father were devoted to each other."

"We were," Flora agreed. "And I still loved Robert. That was what was so dreadful. I thought at one point I was losing my reason." Her eyes wandered back to the distant mountains. "It was music that brought us together."

Laura stiffened.

"Jaraslaw was a brilliant pianist, beginning to make a name for himself internationally. When Poland was invaded, he was in Paris and immediately came to England to join the Royal Air Force. He was badly wounded, almost lost a leg, and after a great many operations came to Annanbrae for a long convalescence."

Flora smiled dreamily.

"I think it was his limp that made me notice him. And the fact that he was always alone. He used to walk endlessly around the lawn, at first on crutches and later leaning heavily on a stick. I used to see him from the nursery window where I spent most of my days with the children."

She paused and Laura held her breath. When after a few minutes Flora had not broken the silence, Laura felt she would burst if she did not hear the end of the story. "Please go on," she whispered.

Flora looked at her as if returning from another world. "He used to spend hours playing Chopin on the drawing room piano. After a while I couldn't resist creeping in to listen."

"I always admired your technique when you played Chopin," Laura murmured, without opening her eyes. "Did he teach you?"

"Yes," Flora replied. "He sat beside me on the stool and played with me. I'd never had anyone interpret the music to me the way Jaraslaw did. They do say only Poles can really play Chopin as it's meant to be played."

Flora lay back against the soft cushions, a faraway look in her eyes. "It was inevitable, I suppose. He was lonely, and so was I."

"What was he like?" Laura asked.

"He was much younger than Robert, about my age, I believe, though he may have been younger." She laughed. "It's strange how little we knew about each other. Yet there was this irresistible attraction, this magnetism between us, like something beyond ourselves drawing us toward each other."

Flora sighed.

"We both resisted it. And, looking back, I think perhaps it wasn't even love. Though, at the time, we thought it was."

Laura leaned her head against the back of the sofa and closed her eyes, feeling as if she were watching the past few months of her life enacted on a screen. Flora's story so closely resembled her own—even to the ambiguity of loving two men at the same time.

"None of the other officers was musical," Flora went on quietly. "Jaraslaw was musically isolated, and so was I. And he met

253

that need no one else had been able to. Robert was tone-deaf, and all the children had taken after him."

She paused, and her silver-gray eyes misted over. "All except Sandy," she whispered brokenly.

As the implication of Flora's words struck Laura, she slowly sat up, her eyes wide with astonishment. "You can't mean . . . You're not saying that Sandy wasn't . . ."

"Wasn't Robert's son?" Flora finished for her. She broke into a tinkling laugh. "Oh *no*, my darling, Sandy was every inch Robert's son. He was the child of our reconciliation, though Robert didn't realize there was a reconciliation."

Flora smiled to herself.

"Men are strange creatures, aren't they? They don't sense things the way we do. And mercifully don't notice things either. Robert never knew about Jaraslaw. Or if he suspected, he never said anything. Jaraslaw returned to Poland the summer the war ended, and soon after that Robert arrived home from the Middle East."

She looked at Laura, pain hidden in the depths of her eyes.

"It was hard, Laura. So hard. I was *torn* and really did not know what to do. I didn't think I could go on living without Jaraslaw. Even the children seemed to fade into the background when I thought what it would mean to be without him."

"Were you . . ." Laura hesitated. "Were you . . ."

"Lovers? No, we weren't. I don't know why. It would have been so easy. But something stopped us. Some code that doesn't seem to exist today."

Flora's eyes wandered once again to the still waters of the lake. "I think if we had been lovers, I would have walked out of Annanbrae the day Jaraslaw left. I wouldn't have been able to face Robert when he came home."

"Do you still think of him?" Laura whispered.

"Yes," Flora replied evenly. "I don't think I shall ever forget him. But it is without pain now. It has been for many years. It was like a dream. Had it come true, it likely would have ended in a nightmare."

She turned to face her daughter-in-law.

"Just think, darling, had I followed Jaraslaw, I'd have lost everything that gave meaning to my life, gone to live in a foreign country where I didn't speak the language, perhaps been ostracized and unable to adapt. My roots and everything I'd ever known would have been torn away. And, in time, I'd have ached for my children and tortured myself because of what I'd done to Robert and to them. Looking back, I think that what seemed beautiful at the time would have turned into something sordid had we let our emotions overwhelm us."

Flora gave an almost imperceptible shudder. "No, darling, I am so thankful that, even in my moments of wildest despair, something held me back."

"Was it very dreadful?" Laura asked, purposely avoiding her mother-in-law's eyes.

"Yes," Flora replied. "It was. I was about your age, and the road ahead looked very bleak."

"How did you survive?"

For a moment Flora remained silent, gazing out the window at something far away that Laura could not see. "Because," she said at last, her voice low and soft, "I believed that God had a purpose for my life. And I trusted Him to carry me through the difficult times."

Laura picked up a faded cushion and began playing idly with the tassel. "You speak as if God were a human being," she said, without looking up.

"He came to earth as a divine/human being," Flora answered, her eyes still looking into the distance. "And He is a person . . . who has our lives in His hands—someone we can trust."

Laura laid the cushion carefully back in place. "I wish I had your trust," she said bleakly.

"You can have, my dear. Look what He has brought out of the evil of Sandy's death. Look what He has done for Rose." She turned toward her daughter-in-law. "And in a way God gave me a gift in Sandy—so very much Robert's son, yet blessed with my love and Jaraslaw's love of music. That in itself after four tone-deaf children was a wonderful compensation."

Flora smiled to herself. "Dear Sandy," she said huskily. "Jamie reminds me of him more and more."

Laura impulsively placed her hand on her mother-in-law's, and they sat together in silence, remembering. "And Jaraslaw—did you ever see him again?"

"Only once. About ten years later. Robert had taken me to Venice for my fortieth birthday. It had been like a second honeymoon." She slowly twisted a large diamond ring on her finger. "Robert bought me this ring that day we spent in London on the way back. To mark the occasion. He was always so thoughtful and generous."

She looked directly at Laura. "Like Alasdair."

"Did you meet Jaraslaw in Venice?" Laura prompted, ignoring Flora's last remark.

"Yes," Flora murmured. "On our last day we were having tea at the Danieli, and he came in and sat down almost next to us. With his beautiful Hungarian wife."

"What did it feel like?" Laura questioned. "Meeting him again?"

Flora shrugged her shoulders expressively. "Like meeting an old friend with whom one has lost touch. He introduced me to his wife. She was absolutely exquisite. A violinist. Much younger than him. I introduced him to Robert. We spent a pleasant half-hour chatting, and then we had to leave to catch our train."

"So he didn't go back to Poland?" Laura inquired.

"No," Flora answered thoughtfully. "I don't believe so. I think he said they were living in Paris . . . or was it Vienna? I really can't remember."

She suddenly laughed. "Isn't it strange, Laura? I once thought I couldn't live without him. Now I can't even remember where he does live."

Flora paused, and a frown creased her brow. "I wonder why I'm telling you all this. The only other person who knows is Katharine." She shrugged. "Perhaps that's why. In many ways, you're very alike. And for both of you Annanbrae has always been a bolt-hole, a place to scurry to in times of pain."

Flora pursed her lips thoughtfully.

"Katharine came here after she parted from Theo, a young German Luftwaffe officer she had fallen in love with. They both realized their love was doomed. In 1947 Englishwomen didn't marry Germans—certainly not widows who had lost their husbands during the war."

She shook her head sadly.

"Like me, Katharine realized that after the initial euphoria had worn off, their marriage would have been a disaster. She would have found it difficult, if not impossible, to settle in the ruins of postwar Germany away from everything that gave meaning to her life. But, like I was when Jaraslaw left, she was hurting very badly."

Flora squeezed her daughter-in-law's hand affectionately. "Nothing lasts, Laura. Not even the worst pain. When Ashley died, Katharine thought her life was over. The idea that she could ever love again, much less marry and be happy with another man, was inconceivable. Yet, after the trauma of her parting with Theo, God brought Maxime into her life. And He brought Robert home from the war back into mine, just at the moment when I needed him most. Long before I met Jaraslaw again, I had found a new love with Robert. Strange though it may seem, I'm convinced that our love, Robert's and mine, deepened and became more beautiful through my idyll with Jaraslaw."

Flora smiled mistily, her gray eyes brimming with unshed tears. "Meeting Jaraslaw again made me realize how much I loved Robert—that he was the man I couldn't live without. Sandy was the living proof."

They remained silent, watching the sun dapple the lake.

"There's nothing special about me, Laura," Flora said at last. "What I did, with God's help, any woman can do . . . if she really wants to."

Flora paused expectantly, but Laura didn't turn around. She knew perfectly well that what her mother-in-law had meant was "what I can do, you can do." But her tact, her delicacy, perhaps her love for Alasdair had prevented her from intruding into their personal dilemma.

"That's where you're wrong," Laura remarked at last. "There is something special about you. Something very special."

"I've been very blessed," Flora said softly. "I always seem to have been surrounded by beautiful things and beautiful people. You and Deirdre. And now Rose whom I thought I'd lost forever. God is so good."

"Mother," Laura asked hesitantly, "is it because you go to church that you have this inner strength? I often go with you when I'm here, but it hasn't meant very much."

"Going to church didn't give me the peace I now have," Flora answered. "It was meeting Jesus as a person, a living God, someone I could talk to and call upon in times of need—not a beautiful figure in a stained-glass window."

"But how did it happen?" Laura insisted.

Flora lay back against the sofa cushions. "When I knew that Jaraslaw had to leave, the pain was unbearable. One night I called out to God and said, 'If You're real, if You exist, then show Yourself to me.'"

Laura stared at her, her eyes wide with amazement.

"He did. It only lasted a few seconds, but I saw Jesus. He looked at me with such love and compassion in His eyes and held out His hands to show me the marks of the nails. It was as if He said, 'I suffered for you because I love you.'"

Flora smiled to herself.

"Perhaps you'll think I'm just a silly, old woman, and a lot of people will find some rational explanation. But when it happened, a wonderful peace flooded through me. And with it came a deep certainty that He would help me and carry me through these deep waters."

"And what happened then?"

"Jaraslaw left the next day. I won't say it was easy. It was very hard. But, as when Sandy was killed, there was this certainty deep inside me that I wasn't alone, that Jesus was holding me and wouldn't let me fall into that pit of black despair. Robert was demobilized and arrived home soon afterwards. I told you I still loved Robert. When he returned, and we were a family once again, life slowly began to return to normal. And I knew I had made the right decision. The only possible decision."

"And did the church help?"

Flora laughed shortly. "The church never knew. I don't

know what their reaction would have been if they had. But, yes, going to church did help. I now went to worship the God I had come to love, instead of out of habit. And it made *all* the difference."

Laura glanced surreptitiously at her mother-in-law and saw that her eyes were shining. "Jesus had shown me that the human spirit with its changing moods is not unlike the sea—sometimes sparkling like a June morning, sometimes dull and sullen like a gray January day. But when a person has God's Spirit living inside, although life and outside circumstances can change dramatically, like the sea, deep down all is calm."

"I wish I could have your experience," Laura said wistfully.

"You can. What happened to me can happen to anyone— has happened to many people. Just call on Jesus and ask Him to come into your life and give you His peace . . . and He will come. I promise you."

Laura studied her hands. There was silence in the dusty, cobwebbed room as each waited for the other to speak. The sun glided behind a gray cloud, and a dark shadow fell across the window.

"Good gracious!" Flora exclaimed, glancing down at her gold fob watch. "It's almost teatime, and we haven't even *looked* at the rest of the house."

She rose from the sofa and held out her hand to Laura.

"Darling," she apologized, "can you forgive a sentimental old woman for droning on? I *really* brought you here to ask your advice about color schemes. You have such exquisite taste."

Glancing into the dining room as they passed through the hall, Flora shuddered. "I *must* have this room stripped and fumigated first of all! It's monstrous. Hamish always refused to change the paper. I think he must have liked the smell of last year's mutton." She quickly closed the creaking door.

"Come, dear," she went on gaily. "We've just got time to do a quick tour, and you can tell me what you think."

Later as they walked back down the stairs, Flora took Laura's arm. "You're a very precious daughter-in-law," she murmured. "I've felt close to you since the first time Cristobel brought you to Annanbrae. I'm *so* glad you married one of my sons and have made him so very happy."

She squeezed Laura's arm, resting lightly in hers.

Laura looked at the older woman intently and knew that she had been right not to be deceived by Flora's apparent vagueness. She realized that Flora had been aware of her own inner turmoil and, by confiding in her, had tried to defuse some of the pain she sensed Laura was feeling—and show her that she understood.

She squeezed Flora's arm in return.

As they walked out of the house into the late summer sunshine and the great oak door slammed behind them, Laura felt that its closing had concluded a chapter in her life. With the words "what I have done, with God's help, any woman can do" echoing in her head, she determined to turn her back resolutely on the past few months.

Twenty-seven

As the two women strolled back across the lawn toward the house, Laura saw a car round the bend of the drive and swerve toward the front door.

"Mother," she exclaimed, shading her eyes, "I think that's Alasdair!"

Slipping her arm from Flora's, she ran swiftly across the lawn and up the terrace steps. Bursting into the drawing room, she heard barking and howling from the half-landing and answering shrieks of delight from her sons. She crossed the room and stood in the doorway watching the scene in the hall.

Andrew looked up from the floor where he was kneeling, gently stroking the growling MacDuff, who had waddled from his turret to see what all the excitement was about.

"Mum," he cried excitedly, leaping to his feet as Iain disentangled himself from the other dogs' enthusiastic licks and galloped toward her. Laura held out her arms, hugging them in delight. Then, releasing them, she turned toward her husband standing awkwardly to one side. Slowly removing Joe's large paws from his waist, Alasdair smiled diffidently at her. He seemed ill at ease, as if he didn't know how he would be received.

"Darling," Laura breathed, walking over to him and holding up her face for his kiss. "How lovely to see you all."

The green and gold lights began to dance in Alasdair's eyes. Taking her slight body in his arms, he pressed her to him.

"What happened?" she asked, stepping back from his warm

embrace and looking up at him. "We weren't expecting you till tomorrow evening."

"The school rang yesterday to say that there had been a mess-up with plane bookings, and Iain and Andrew would be arriving at five o'clock," Alasdair explained, putting a protective arm around her shoulders as they followed the boys and the yapping dogs into the drawing room. "So I decided to leave early this morning and give you a pleasant surprise." He looked down at her. "I hope it is a pleasant surprise."

"Of course it is," she whispered.

Flora, arriving at a more leisurely pace, walked into the room. "Alasdair, what a pity I didn't know you were coming today. It would have saved Donald a trip to the airport."

Alasdair raised his eyebrows inquiringly as he crossed the room to embrace his mother.

"Hebrides's plane arrived about an hour ago. You could have picked her up on the way."

She smiled conspiratorially at Iain, who had suddenly turned red. But he stared fixedly at the floor, shuffling his feet uncomfortably as his color heightened. Alasdair frowned slightly at his eldest son's discomfort. But before he had time to comment, a car slid to a standstill outside the front door.

"She's here!" Flora cried. "Donald's done it in record time."

At her words Iain bolted.

Running lightly across the room, Flora returned with her arm around a fair-haired, freckle-faced girl.

"Now we can all have tea together," she said happily, as Sheana entered and set the tray on a small table in the turret. "Sit next to me, darling. I want to hear all the news from Le Moulin. And, Iain, you sit beside Hebrides. I know you—" She looked around her. "Where *is* Iain? Isn't he coming to tea?"

Now it was Hebrides's turn to blush.

Laura noticed the blush, but remembering how inseparable Hebrides and her eldest son had been last summer, she didn't comment as Andrew slipped from the room to warn his brother.

"Can't you guess where they've both gone?" Alasdair grinned. "Down to the kitchen to be spoiled. We stopped for an early lunch outside Edinburgh, so I imagine they're starving. And," he added, lifting the lid from a silver salver, "I doubt whether scones will be enough to keep them going till dinner."

He looked at Hebrides with an amused smile. "I don't imagine airline food filled you up either. Why don't you go downstairs and join them?"

Still blushing, Hebrides rose and hurriedly left the room.

"Do I sense romance in the air?" Alasdair laughed.

"Oh, Alasdair, don't be ridiculous," Laura remonstrated tartly. "Iain's only *fifteen*."

"He's almost sixteen," Alasdair reminded her. "And if what my spies tell me is true, you had your eye on me when you were twelve."

"You didn't by any chance bump into Graeme in Edinburgh?" Flora asked, sensing the sudden tension between her son and his wife.

Alasdair took a large bite into a scone. "No, we avoided Edinburgh. It's always crowded in August with the Festival coming up. Why? What's he doing there?"

"Shall we tell him, Laura?" Flora smiled mischievously. "Or shall we keep him dangling?"

Alasdair looked from one to the other, then let out a low whistle when his mother told him the good news. "The cagey old devil!" he exclaimed.

Picking up his cup, he stared thoughtfully at his mother over the rim. "And you?"

"I'm moving into the Fort. Laura and I were on our way back from there when you arrived. I wanted her advice about colors and furnishings."

"So finally you've managed to get rid of all your offspring," Alasdair said gently.

"And mother hen that I am, I may even have all of them around me for the wedding. Graeme is going to telephone Ninian and Deirdre as soon as he and Rose have decided on the date."

Ninian had been appointed to the embassy in Washington the previous year.

"It would be lovely if they could all come," she went on

wistfully. "It seems such a long time since I saw Michael and little Anna."

Alasdair grinned at Laura. "Any news of Jamie?" he inquired.

"None at all," Laura replied. "He and Helen are apparently inseparable."

"Then that leaves only Andrew on the shelf," Alasdair teased. He turned to his mother. "Why don't you ring Cristobel and suggest that all the little Frasers come here? When's the baby due, by the way?"

"Not until the end of September," Flora answered thoughtfully. "But what a good idea to have all the children here together. Cristobel prefers to stay quietly at Lochincraig this year. She's not getting any younger. And it *is* her sixth."

"Double our output," Alasdair laughed.

"I'll help you clear the car," Laura said, abruptly getting up. Her husband looked at her intently. "It's not necessary."

"I know it's not," she replied quietly. "But I'd like to."

As they entered the large high-ceilinged room with their bags, Laura walked over to the highboy and stood looking at the smiling young girl in the photograph.

Alasdair came up behind her and, twining his arms around her neck, pressed his face close to hers. "You haven't changed a bit," he said softly.

"Oh, Alasdair," she cried plaintively, reaching up a hand to his.

Their eyes met in the oval mirror.

"Happy?" he asked, turning her around and taking her in his arms.

Hiding her face against his broad shoulder, she sighed contentedly. They told themselves they had imagined their strained farewell. It was fatigue. The end of a long summer. Now that they were back inside these solid gray walls, everything would be as before.

She lay back in his arms, her fingers tracing the contour of his face. But abruptly it disappeared, and Josh's lean sensitive features rose in its place, his dark eyes seeming to bore through her. Laura stiffened, then turned away.

She felt Alasdair stiffen also. He placed his hands on her shoulders and turned her to face him. But she dropped her eyes. As she did so, his hands fell listlessly to his side. With a sigh he walked across the room toward the open window and stood looking over the garden, the silence between them ominous.

"Alasdair," she pleaded, sensing his bewilderment. But her voice sounded forced, and he didn't turn around.

"I'm not the girl in the photo anymore," she said brokenly, putting her hands to her face in a helpless gesture. "But I will be . . . I promise you. Just give me time."

He turned and stood facing her, the lines of his face taut, the laughter gone from his eyes. "What is it, Laura?" he asked quietly.

She looked at him, and his face reflected her own pain. But no words came. With a strangled sob, she ran from the room.

The young people's animated conversation at dinner masked the tension between Laura and Alasdair. But before coffee was served, she pleaded a headache and retired to bed. As she reached her bedroom door, Flora came up beside her.

"May I come and sit with you?" she asked as Laura put her hand on the heavy brass knob.

Laura saw the compassion and understanding in Flora's expressive gray eyes. She hesitated, longing for the relief she knew confession would bring, longing to be reassured that she wasn't losing her reason and that all the things that meant so much to her were not about to be shattered, that life would one day return to normal, and she would no longer be strangled by fear and despair.

She smiled and half opened the door. Then she remembered that Alasdair was Flora's son. "Not tonight, Mother," she answered tightly, lowering her eyes, afraid that Flora would see the fear in them. "I'm very tired. I just want to sleep."

Flora embraced her warmly, then turned away. And the moment when Laura could have obtained relief passed.

As she entered the darkened room that held so many memories, a shaft of moonlight beamed on the highboy, throwing a ghostly silver gleam onto her smiling portrait. Laura caught her breath. Then, running swiftly across the room, she tugged the curtains across the window, shutting out the vision of the girl she once had been.

Twenty-eight

Just before lunch the following day Graeme arrived with his fiancée. Laura had not seen Rose since Sandy's funeral, and she was shocked when this poised young woman stepped out of the car. Standing close to Sandy at their engagement reception earlier, Rose had appeared much smaller and plumper, more bubbly. Her dark hair had been short and bobbed. Now she wore it like a ballerina, smoothed back into a soft roll at the nape of her neck, accentuating her high cheekbones and delicate bone structure. Slim and erect at Graeme's side, she was the same Rose, yet subtly different. Her former infectious gaiety was replaced by a serenity.

As she came forward to greet the family gathered on the drive, her deep brown eyes seemed almost too large for her finely chiseled face. They were luminous with happiness. But in their depths was the afterglow of intense suffering.

To everyone's surprise and delight, Lindsay drove up with his family just before tea.

"Cristobel!" Laura cried excitedly, as Lindsay helped his wife, cumbersome with the impending birth, out of the car. "We never expected to see you this summer."

Cristobel hugged her. "Couldn't resist it after hearing the wonderful news last night," she chirped. "Graeme, you dark horse, why didn't you *tell* us?"

She stood on tiptoe to kiss him as Jamie crept up behind his mother and caught her around the waist in a smothering bear-hug.

"I'm *so* happy for you," Cristobel breathed, her eyes shining. "And for Rose." She let go of her brother and looked around. "Where *is* Rose? I must see her immediately."

Rose was standing in the doorway slightly apart from the family reunion. But as Cristobel called her name, she walked gracefully forward to be clasped to her future sister-in-law's heavily pregnant figure.

The rest of the weekend was spent making plans for the wedding scheduled for October 2 in Edinburgh. Flora was in her element making lists for a small reception in a fortnight's time, so that everyone could share their wonderful news.

Rose watched the excitement and planning going on around her with a certain detachment. Seeing her, Laura remembered the time, which now seemed so distant, when she and Alasdair had been engaged, and a lump rose in her throat.

But it was difficult to be melancholy for long. The old house had taken on its former atmosphere, filled with people and laughter. In spite of herself, Laura was caught up in the happy swirl of events. And although she occasionally found Flora's eyes resting thoughtfully on her, there was so much happening around them, they had little chance to be alone—for which Laura told herself she was grateful.

Even her relationship with Alasdair seemed to settle once again into an easy friendliness, the tension momentarily banished. He was happy to be on holiday with his sons and his nephews, with Lindsay and Graeme and the older nieces. When they all went off on grouse shoots, Laura stayed behind with Cristobel.

"I suppose you're hoping for a boy," Laura remarked one afternoon as she and Cristobel lazed on the terrace.

"Not really," Cristobel answered. "I don't mind either way."

"But don't you want to even it up and have three of each?" Laura pursued.

"After Rob and Roddy," Cristobel said with a yawn, "I'd be

quite happy with another girl. Even Helen is easier to cope with than those two. I don't know how you manage with *three* boys."

"Are girls so different?" Laura inquired.

"Very," Cristobel said grimly. "At least mine are. It was quite a shock when Robert and then Roderick appeared. They're gorgeous, but little horrors!"

They lapsed into silence, closing their eyes and lying back with the sun beaming down on their upturned faces.

"You should have a little girl, Laura," Cristobel murmured sleepily. "Have you never thought about it?"

"Alasdair always wanted a daughter," she said quietly. "We were going to call her Elspeth." There was a wistful note in her voice. But suddenly her mood changed, and she shrugged. "It just never happened."

The sagging deck chair groaned as Cristobel repositioned her heavy body to face her sister-in-law. "It's not too late," she insisted. "After all, you're three months younger than I am."

She lay back again, her sentence trailing off in midair. Laura felt her limbs stiffen and a cold sweat trickle slowly down her back. She shivered and sat up. The sun was still shining, but she suddenly felt cold.

"I'll ring for tea," she said, abruptly rising. "It must be almost time. Anyway I'm ready for a cup, aren't you? And then I must find Mother. I promised to walk over to the Fort with her. They've begun painting the drawing room, and we need to decide on the color for the bedrooms. Time's running out. It will soon be October."

But the only response from Cristobel was a gentle purring from her half-open mouth. The end of her nine months was in sight. The inevitable fatigue combined with the last warm rays of the northern summer sun had done their soothing work. She was fast asleep.

That year the weather was unusually warm for August. Between the long, lazy days spent idling and chatting with Cristobel and sessions with Flora and the workmen poring over catalogues and color schemes, punctuated by trips into Perth to buy materials for the new furnishings, the holiday passed quickly.

Rose and Graeme were so obviously happy that they wove a web of joy around everyone else. And Flora was more sparkling than Laura had seen her since Robert's death, as she organized her new home and prepared for the approaching wedding. Laura and Alasdair met each evening in an atmosphere both affectionate and relaxed. And Laura regained her sense of peace and well-being.

Contrary to forebodings, Cristobel did not have her baby in her old home. When, in early September, Alasdair packed his family into the car for the return journey, she was still trotting happily around Annanbrae under Lindsay's watchful eye.

"We'll be on our way in a couple of days," Lindsay remarked, as Alasdair slammed down the lid of the laden boot.

"Hope you make it," Alasdair laughed.

"Oh, we will," Lindsay replied. "Cristobel's like her mother. Looks frail as a daisy but is really as strong as a horse."

He threw an arm affectionately around his wife who had waddled out to say good-bye.

"You let us know the minute the baby arrives," Laura reminded her.

"Promise," Cristobel replied, one hand caressing her distended abdomen. "And, Laura, don't forget what I said."

Laura frowned as Cristobel gave her a knowing look, one hand still pointedly on her stomach. "Think about it."

"Come on, boys," Alasdair called, putting a stop to further conversation. "We should be off."

He looked around him as Andrew and Jamie sauntered toward the car.

"Where's Iain?" he inquired.

"I know," Andrew mumbled. "I'll go and get him."

"*I* know too," Jamie chortled. "He's behind a rose bush holding hands with Hebrides."

Andrew shot him a venomous look and raced back into the hall. But, totally unperturbed, Jamie cupped his hands around his mouth and hollered, "Come on, loverboy, kiss her quick. The party's over."

Helen collapsed in a fit of giggles, and Jamie, encouraged, prepared to make another ear-splitting announcement. But Laura caught him roughly by the arm. "Get into the car," she hissed.

Jamie grinned wickedly at her and hopped onto the back-seat just as Andrew and a red-faced Iain ran down the steps of the house. There was no sign of Hebrides.

"Say good-bye to everyone and let's get moving," Alasdair said, giving Iain an amused, quizzical look.

Alasdair walked around the car and climbed in beside his wife. With Jamie hanging out the back window yelling recommendations to his cousins, they moved off down the drive.

"Whatever did Cristobel mean?" Alasdair inquired, as they swung through the open gates. "What did she want you to think about?"

"Nothing," Laura replied curtly.

Alasdair looked at her strangely. Then pressing his foot on the accelerator, he drove along the country road with a reckless abandon totally uncharacteristic of him. Out of the corner of her eye, Laura saw his lips compressed into the hard line she had noticed on that first afternoon in their bedroom.

"Dad, where are we having lunch?" Jamie piped, breaking the uneasy silence.

"Good heavens, Jamie," Alasdair replied irritably, "you've only just had breakfast."

"Okay, okay," Jamie chirped. "Only asking."

Laura noticed her husband's hands slacken on the steering wheel as he reduced speed. "Where would you like to stop for lunch?" he asked, looking down at her with a half smile.

"Let the boys choose," she replied, tentatively touching his hand as she smiled back.

And, as they sped along past quilted fields and low stone walls with drifts of wildflowers peeping out of their crevices, she once again convinced herself that everything was going to be all right. The holiday had renewed and refreshed her, had allowed her to see things in perspective. The past few months had merely been a bad dream from which she was now fully awake.

Leaning back in her seat Laura relaxed.

Flora walked swiftly down the long gallery, pausing to listen outside the end bedroom door. From inside came the unmistakable sound of weeping. Knocking softly, she entered, without waiting for an answer.

Hebrides was sprawled across the bed, her blonde hair disheveled on the pillow into which she was crying bitterly.

"Darling," Flora cried, swiftly crossing the room and taking the distraught girl in her arms. Hebrides leaned against her godmother, her shoulders heaving with uncontrollable sobs.

"Is it Iain?" Flora asked gently.

Hebrides looked up, her eyes starry with tears, her pretty face smudged and red. She rubbed a hand across her eyes. "And . . . Jamie!" She almost spat out the last word. "I *hate* him."

Flora hugged her closely. "Jamie's a silly little boy. He doesn't mean any harm."

"He's horrible," Hebrides sobbed. "Always spying on Iain and me and then . . ." The tears spurted and flowed in a heavy torrent down her cheeks. "Did you *hear* him? Did you hear what he said?"

"Yes," Flora soothed. "But nobody ever takes any notice of anything Jamie says. He's always teasing."

"Helen does," Hebrides gulped. "They were in it together."

"Helen's just a big tomboy," Flora comforted.

But Hebrides continued to sob.

"You're very fond of Iain, aren't you?"

Hebrides gulped again. "I love him," she faltered, raising her brimming eyes to meet Flora's. "But nobody will understand. They'll say we're children and don't know our own minds. But we do, Aunt Flora. We *do*."

"I understand," Flora said quietly. "And you're not children."

She held Hebrides away from her and looked fondly at her. "Your mother was not very much older than you when she married for the first time. And neither was I. And Laura fell in love with Alasdair when she was very young, though Alasdair didn't know it at the time."

Hebrides looked at her godmother, her eyes wide, and a faint smile hovered around her lips. "You mean . . ."

"I mean that you and Iain may well be in love with each other. But you must take time to test your love. Next year you may feel quite differently."

"Next year," Hebrides wailed. "I can't wait till next year to see Iain again."

"Perhaps your parents would allow you to come for Christmas," Flora suggested. "All the family will be here. And we can see how you feel then. But don't make too many plans, darling. At your age your emotions are in a turmoil—"

"But we want to be together," Hebrides protested. "To . . . to marry as soon as we're old enough."

"Then that's something to look forward to," Flora said practically. "In the meantime take this separation as an apprenticeship for marriage. If you still feel the same way about each other when the time comes, then you will have proved your point, won't you?"

Hebrides nodded dully. "I just want to be with Iain," she whispered.

Flora hugged her. "I know you do. . . . Say, let's go into Perth and do some shopping. I want to buy presents for you to take back to the family and . . . something special for you. Wash your face and meet me in the hall in twenty minutes." She smiled into the girl's woebegone face. "How does that sound?"

Flora could see that, now that Iain had gone, nothing sounded good to Hebrides.

Planting a swift kiss on the girl's shining golden curls, Flora left the room. She sighed as she walked back down the gallery, remembering her own teenage emotions—her love for Robert that her parents had been unable to understand. And she determined that whatever else she could do for this cherished goddaughter, she would give her all the support she needed in this first real trauma in her young life.

Twenty-nine

"There's a letter from Josh," Alasdair announced. Placing a tray on the bedside table, he walked across to the window and drew the curtains. Laura stirred lazily.

"Josh?" she queried.

Alasdair sat down on the bed and began to pour the tea.

"Yes, Josh." He grinned, handing her a cup. "You know, that pianist chap who haunted the place till he went off on tour last July."

"You sound as if you don't like him." Laura yawned.

"I like him very much," Alasdair laughed, slitting open the envelope. "I said that to startle you into waking up."

Laura sipped her tea but did not reply.

"He's arriving on Saturday," Alasdair went on, his eyes scanning the letter. He frowned thoughtfully. "That's tomorrow. Says he'll let us know the time of his plane later."

Putting the letter down, he disappeared into the bathroom.

When the family had returned home from Annanbrae, Laura had reduced her classes at the Academy by half. This was a practical step she could take to carry out her resolve, formed by her talk with Flora, to put Josh out of her mind. In thinking about what changes she needed to make, she remembered Edwina's warning so long ago, before her marriage, that she should stop making music her god.

Once the boys went back to school, Laura and Alasdair had

settled into the comfortable, affectionate silence and regular routine that had characterized their marriage since they had moved to London.

But even so, Laura had wondered how she would react when she heard of Josh's return. Now she was surprised at how little the news of his imminent arrival affected her. She smiled to herself, confident that she had her emotions under control, stored away in a box with the lid firmly shut, only to be opened much later when perhaps, like Flora, she would reminisce with her daughter-in-law.

Hearing the splash of the shower, Laura picked up the letter and ran her eyes over it. But there was no reaction, no surge of emotion, no tangled feelings hammering inside her for release.

Suddenly a feeling of intense happiness coursed through her. She felt free and lighthearted, as if the last barrier had been torn down.

"It was only imagination after all," she assured herself.

"What did you say?" Alasdair inquired, appearing at the bathroom door, his face smothered in lather.

"Nothing," she replied, adding on a sudden impulse, "Would you like to invite me to lunch?"

"Sorry, darling." Alasdair grimaced. "Not today. Old Johnstone's still around. I have to dance attendance on him, I'm afraid."

"Never mind." Laura smiled. "I'll ring Edwina and see if she's free."

"If not, try your niece Polly," Alasdair suggested.

Singing under her breath, she entered the small kitchen giving onto the tiny garden filled with her potted plants. As she reached for the kettle, some words she had once heard and long since forgotten floated into her head: "God's in His heaven—all's right with the world." Laura leaned against the sink, idly watching the water tinkle into the kettle and felt that the last hurdle had been jumped. She had run the gamut of emotions, come full circle, and survived. All was truly right with the world.

Edwina had already left by the time Laura telephoned, but Polly was at home and delighted by the invitation. Over lunch Laura and her niece exchanged family news. Polly's father was now also at the embassy in Washington, and he and Philippa often met up with Deirdre and Ninian.

"It's odd, isn't it," Laura remarked, when Polly told her how much her parents were enjoying this posting, "how the two families have linked up."

And she remembered Flora's words: "I knew God had a pattern for my life. . . ."

"Do you think, Polly," she asked pensively, "that it's all by chance? Life, I mean. Or could there be some divine hand guiding everything?"

Polly crumbled a roll thoughtfully. "I don't know. Why do you ask?"

"Oh, just the way things work out," Laura answered vaguely. "Ninian could have been sent anywhere in the world. But he went to Washington where your parents are. It's almost as if some unknown force were planning our lives."

Polly didn't reply.

"As one gets older, one does see a kind of pattern," Laura reflected. "My mother-in-law firmly believes in a God who has our lives in His hands and guides and directs them."

Polly stopped crumbling and looked up. "Your mother-in-law is a very special person," she said quietly. "I noticed it all those years ago when Daisy and I were your bridesmaids. And how old was I? Twelve? Not more. She's got something about her. I can't quite pinpoint what."

"An aura?"

"Perhaps. Yes, I think that's what it is. She's different from the rest of us."

"Pity that aura didn't fall on Daisy," Laura remarked drily.

Then she realized that both she and Polly had been avoiding mentioning Daisy's name. There was a pause as if each was waiting for the other to continue the taboo subject. Laura looked at Polly, whose eyes had suddenly filled with tears.

"Whatever got into her?" Laura puzzled. "Abandoning her husband and child like that. She and Rupert seemed to be so happy."

"They were," Polly declared. "Until that ghastly man came on the scene."

Laura shook her head in bewilderment. "Daisy, of all people. She was always the shy, retiring one." She smiled mischievously at her niece. "Now, had it been you—"

"In a way I feel responsible," Polly cut in miserably.

"Older sister syndrome?"

"Could be. I was always very protective of Daisy. Then when Mark and I became engaged, she seemed lost."

"But didn't Daisy meet Rupert through Mark?"

"Yes, at our wedding. Don't you remember? Rupert was Mark's best man. He and Daisy fell madly in love the moment they set eyes on each other and were married four months later. It seemed to be a marriage made in heaven."

Polly sighed.

"But for Rupert it turned out to be just the opposite. And poor little Clarissa—she misses her mother so much."

"I can imagine," Laura murmured.

"I do what I can," Polly continued. "But Clarissa's very shy and gentle, just like Daisy was as a child. And my two boys are so boisterous they terrify her."

Laura smiled, and Polly looked at her aunt thoughtfully. "Daisy should have been *your* daughter. Mother always said she was more like you than anyone else—even to enjoying piano practice!"

For a moment Laura was shaken. The comparison was frightening. "Do you have any recent news of her?" she asked, hastily changing the focus. "I haven't heard a thing for ages."

"Not much," Polly replied bitterly. "They seem to bounce around between his penthouse in New York and the Bahamas. But as far as we can gather from the odd postcard, which is all we ever get, they're now sailing on his yacht around the Greek Islands."

"But what's going to happen?" Laura inquired.

"I think, in the end, Rupert will divorce her," Polly sighed. "That's what she wants, and there doesn't seem to be any other solution. At first he thought she'd come back. We all did. But it's been two years now, and she's apparently anxious to become the fourth Mrs. Whatever-his-name-is. Something 'opolopolous.'" Polly made a face. "Imagine giving up a nice, uncomplicated name like Haigh for that handle. Sounds like a disease."

"Poor Rupert," Laura murmured.

"And poor Clarissa," Polly broke in angrily. "How could Daisy do that to her only child?" She looked helplessly at Laura. "Whatever does she see in that dreadful man? He's old enough to be her father. And rich as Croesus."

"I didn't think Daisy was all that interested in money," Laura remarked.

"She wasn't—until he started dripping diamonds all over her." Polly laughed shortly. "The ironic thing is, Rupert introduced them. I was having lunch with Daisy when he rang to say they had to dine with this shipping magnate. Clarissa was running a temperature, and Daisy wasn't at all keen. But Rupert said he was a very important client and persuaded her to come. She went dragging her feet, but no doubt looking stunning, or the end result might have been different." She sighed. "Poor Rupert. I bet he now wishes someone else had brokered the wretched man's yacht."

Laura could think of nothing to say.

"Who's she like?" Polly went on. "Have there been any other bolters in the family?"

"What do you mean?"

"Any other females in our ancestry who've behaved in this outrageous fashion?"

"Not that I know of."

"I suppose it sometimes skips a few generations," Polly suggested. "I never knew Grandmother. But from what I've heard, she seemed to live a life of unsullied purity. And one can hardly call Aunt Edwina wanton—or Mother or Aunt Mary for that matter."

Laura smiled absently.

"That only leaves you." Polly grinned. "You could be another dark horse and surprise us all. But I shouldn't think so. You and Alasdair have a blissful marriage." She grimaced. "But that's what we thought about Rupert and Daisy."

At Polly's words Josh's face rose before Laura's eyes. And, seeing the comparison, that awful fear gripped her once again. But at that moment the waiter came to brush the crumbs from the cloth. By the time he left, the momentary panic had subsided, and Laura was able to steer the conversation to other topics.

As she mounted the steps of her house and turned her key in the lock, the telephone started to ring inside. Dropping her parcels on the floor, she ran lightly across the hall and picked up the receiver.

"Hullo," a man's voice with a North American lilt came down the line.

Hearing it, Laura's heart started to thunder in her chest.

"Hullo there. . . . It's Josh."

"Josh," Laura answered breathlessly, "where are you?"

"In Geneva," he laughed.

The line crackled.

"Just wanted to let you know my flight time like I promised."

"Yes," she replied, "of course."

There was a slight pause. "It *is* okay, isn't it?" Josh's voice came anxiously down the now crystal-clear line. "I mean, if it's a hassle for you to meet me—"

"No, Josh," she cut in, "of course not. We're all looking forward to seeing you."

"Should touch down at 3:30," Josh informed her. "But I gotta leave almost immediately. My rehearsals in Boston have been moved up a week."

So it was to be hello and good-bye.

A feeling of relief surged through Laura, immediately replaced by a terrible bleakness, as if the world had suddenly been dyed gray. At the sound of his voice, the old turmoil had surged up inside her as dormant emotions churned through her body with even greater force than before. Her throat parched and dry, Laura could not reply.

"Hey, what's going on?" Josh called as the line once again crackled ominously. "You've gone all weird on me."

Laura tried to force a laugh through her tightened lips. "N-Nothing," she stammered. "It's this bad line."

"It's not only the line," Josh insisted as the crackling ceased. "Is something the matter?" There was concern in his voice, the laughter gone.

"No, nothing," she answered dully. "When do you have to leave?"

"Sunday morning, first thing."

"So you'll be with us just one night?"

"'Fraid so," Josh replied. "Look, I have to dash. Got a rehearsal for tonight's concert in five minutes. Sorry about that, but I've been trying to get hold of you since noon."

"I've been out," she answered mechanically.

"Don't I know it," he said, the laughter back in his voice. "And so does the hotel operator. I've just about driven her bananas."

"See you tomorrow then, Josh, half past three," she repeated tonelessly and hung up.

Sitting down heavily on the chair beside the telephone, she looked up at the copper-green sky that still held an afterglow of summer, reflected in the tall, oblong window on the half-landing above her. As she stared vacantly through it, a veil seemed to pass over its surface. The pools of sunlight on the parquet floor vanished, leaving dark shadows flitting across the hall. And a jagged crack gashed her world, revealing a bottomless void beneath.

The telephone jerked her back to consciousness.

"Laura?" Alasdair's voice came down the line.

But she sat mute.

"Hallo . . . Laura?" he repeated.

Laura slowly dragged her thoughts together as if awakening

from a deep sleep. "Alasdair, hallo. I'm sorry, my mind was on something else."

"Darling, you sound very odd. Are you all right?"

"Of course I'm all right," she answered testily, then hated herself for her abruptness.

"I've been trying to get hold of you all afternoon."

"You're not the only one. Josh has just rung from Geneva." Laura compressed her lips into a tight line to hide her emotion. "He's arriving tomorrow afternoon."

"Good," Alasdair replied warmly.

"Alasdair," Laura broke in sharply, "did you ring for anything special? I've just come in. I'm surrounded by shopping bags, and I'm dying for a cup of tea."

"I'm afraid so," he said apologetically. "Old Johnstone's not leaving this evening as I thought. He's decided to take the Concorde back to New York in the morning, and he wants us to join him for dinner."

"Oh *no*," Laura groaned.

"Sorry about that. But he *is* my chairman. There's nothing much I can do about it." He paused. "If you're too tired, I can make some excuse. But he *does* have rather a soft spot for you, and if you could make the effort . . ."

"It's all right," she said resignedly. "What time?"

"Early, mercifully. Wear your black chiffon. He'll be completely bowled over. May even give me a partnership. Must go, darling. Bless you for being so understanding."

Laura slowly replaced the receiver.

Glancing down, she saw that her knuckles were white. Her taut hands still gripped the edge of the dark oak table, onto which a bunch of sulphur-colored roses, drooping in their pewter jug, had molted soft velvet petals, leaving behind a lingering scent of summer. She idly picked up the petals, one by one, and sat gazing at their dying beauty. A butterfly wafted in through the half-open window, shimmered momentarily above her, and then fluttered languorously away in a flash of blue and gold and scarlet.

From the church in the square a tumbling peal of bells rang out, crashing, bouncing, echoing around the silent hall. Laura pressed her face into the fading petals, slowly inhaling their elusive scent, breathing deeply in rhythm with the distant chimes. But then the pealing ceased, followed abruptly by a solitary melancholy clang, like the slow beat of a dying heart.

She closed her eyes. But Josh's face rose up before her, and the momentary anesthesia of the bell's hypnotic clang evaporated.

Nosing open the drawing room door, her sons' aging Yorkshire terrier padded across the floor and settled himself on her feet. Laura reached down blindly and, picking him up, nestled her face in his soft, warm coat as tears spilled over onto its silky strands. "Puddle," she choked. "Oh, Puddle!"

His kennel name was Ulysses. But her sons had abandoned it when the puppy refused to comply with even the most elementary rules of house training. And although this misunderstanding had long since been resolved, Puddle he had remained.

The dog stirred and growled, then settled contentedly in Laura's arms, gently licking the tears from her cheeks. She hugged him close, feeling security in the warmth and familiarity of his furry body—a feeling she knew would fade as soon as she turned to face the evening. The weekend. And all the pent-up emotions threatening to choke her.

The telephone rang again.

"Mum?" Andrew inquired. "What's happening tomorrow? Are you picking us up from school?"

"Can you make your own way home?" she answered. "Josh has just rung. He's arriving at half past three, and we've promised to meet him at the airport."

"Josh!" Andrew exclaimed. "Super! But can't we come to the airport with you?"

"No, darling. If we picked you up, we'd be late."

"Okay," agreed the easygoing Andrew.

How like his father he is, Laura thought, as she replaced the receiver. *Never any fuss.*

And a hot tear fell on her wrist. Brushing a hand impatiently across her eyes, Laura straightened up.

"This is *absurd*," she said angrily, walking toward the stairs. "You have *everything*. A loving husband. Three teenage sons. A home, friends, security. Yet you're behaving like a hysterical schoolgirl, threatening to ruin it all. And for what? A young man. No, a boy who is scarcely older than your own sons."

She took a deep breath and planted her foot firmly on the bottom stair.

"After tomorrow you'll probably never see him again."

But as the words left her lips, all her careful reasoning collapsed. Laura knew that whatever it was she felt for Josh, it was certainly not the love she felt for her sons. His voice had stirred all the buried emotions his letter had failed to revive, emotions she had convinced herself were all in her mind.

She reached the top of the stairs just as she heard Alasdair's key inserted into the lock. Crossing to their bedroom, she heard him call her name, but she didn't answer. Her heart was too full of suppressed emotion. A feeling of guilt and shame invaded her. How could she ever look him in the face again? Alasdair, who was so transparently honest, who had loved and cherished her for almost twenty years.

His footsteps disappeared into the drawing room, and Laura was suddenly pleased that they were going out this evening, that she didn't have to face him alone across the table at dinner. She knew that if she did, she would be unable to pretend. Her anguish and humiliation would come pouring out. And she couldn't bear the pain she knew she would see in his eyes.

Lying on their bed gazing out over London's rooftops, she tried to shut Josh from her mind. But his face kept blotting out everything else. She wondered whether Josh was also aware of this subtle change in their relationship. As this thought struck her, she heard Alasdair's step on the stairs.

"You look whacked," he said gently, sitting down on the bed.

In the dim light she saw concern in his hazel eyes. Over her husband's shoulder, she caught a glimpse of the oval photograph in the silver frame standing with the others on her dressing table. Daisy on her wedding day. Once again she was struck by the incredible likeness between them. It was true what Polly had said, what her sister Philippa had always said. Daisy was more like Laura than anyone else.

Suddenly, as if superimposed on the oval frame, another picture appeared—Daisy as she now was, sailing around the Greek Islands with her middle-aged billionaire lover, her wedding vows and all thoughts of her husband and child swept from her mind. And Polly's question about other bolters in the family rang clearly in her ears.

She stifled a cry and clung to Alasdair, afraid of herself, of her reactions, her heredity, afraid of this strangling emotion, which she thought had released its grasp, but had now returned to torture her. She was afraid too of the future and that uncanny resemblance between herself and Daisy, the shy, gentle niece who had changed so dramatically. She wondered just how much any human being was ever really in control of her life or her emotions—and what part heredity and destiny played in the overall pattern of each individual existence.

Her husband sensed her tension but mistook its source. "I'm sorry about tonight, darling," he apologized. "But it needn't be late."

He bent to kiss her forehead, stroking back her hair as he did so. "Stay there and rest," he said softly. "I'll call you when your bath's ready."

As Alasdair closed the door quietly behind him, Laura buried her face in the flowered pillow and wept.

Thirty

As she and Alasdair waited in the autumn sunshine for the plane to land, a light breeze caught the folds of Laura's dress, causing it to billow about her legs. She glanced up at Alasdair standing at her side, his large muscular frame propped casually against the balustrade.

"Just half past three," her husband announced, squinting at his watch. "Looks as if Josh will arrive on time."

Over the rattle of trolleys, a syrupy voice announced the arrival of the flight from Geneva. Shading their eyes, they leaned forward to watch the aircraft bump down.

The plane door opened, and a hostess appeared at the top of the steps, followed closely by a stream of passengers, the last of whom was Josh.

"Well, he's here," Alasdair announced, straightening up and taking his wife's arm. "Be nice to see him again, won't it?"

Laura didn't reply. But she was grateful for her husband's arm against her side as he steered her through the waiting crowd. Her life with Alasdair was so organized, so safe. Or it had been. Yet at that moment their years together seemed to have slipped away, forgotten, and she felt like a young girl in love for the first time.

"Welcome back!"

Alasdair gripped the young man's hand. Then Josh caught Laura to him in an affectionate hug. She held her breath and allowed her cheek to be kissed.

"How did the tour go?" Alasdair asked, as they made their way to the car park.

"Pretty well, I think," Josh replied. "Did you see the notices?"

"We certainly did," Alasdair enthused. "Laura's kept all the cuttings."

"Thanks, Mom," Josh said warmly, turning to her with a smile.

The word made her wince. Yet a few months earlier when he had adopted her as "his English Mom," she had been so touched.

Laura was very quiet on the drive home. Normally she would have enjoyed the beauty of the autumn-tinted landscape. The late afternoon sky was like a faded rose. Trees in the orchards bordering the country lanes hung low with juicy apples, and the smell of burning leaves drifted on the still air. But today her mind was restless.

As the car slid to a standstill in front of the tall, terraced house, three pairs of eager feet thundered down the uncarpeted stairs like a landslide and shot through the front door.

"Josh!" Jamie screeched, poking his face through the car window as Big Ben struck the half hour.

Josh laughed and pulled Jamie's tousled red hair, affectionately pushing him aside as Andrew yanked the door open.

"Good to see you, Josh," Andrew said warmly. "How did it go? Mum kept all the cuttings."

"Good old Mom," Josh laughed.

Again Laura winced.

Glancing down at her, Alasdair thought he had never seen her looking more beautiful. Her pale gold hair fell softly around her face, and her eyes were moist and shining, their deep blue reflected in the woollen coat that clung attractively to her slim figure.

"No one would think you were the mother of that lot," he confided, slipping his arm through hers.

He wanted to tell her how beautiful she was, even more beautiful than on that far-off summer evening when he had fallen in love with her. But there was now this invisible barrier between them. And whenever he attempted to put his feelings into words, they stuck in his throat. "More like their big sister," he ended lamely as they entered the house.

Laura smiled at him as she dropped her coat and bag onto a hall chair.

"I'm going to see about dinner," she said hurriedly and fled to the kitchen asking herself for the hundredth time that day the same question: How had it happened?

"What a pity it's just a stopover," Alasdair remarked after dinner, settling comfortably into his armchair. "I was hoping I could persuade you to accompany Laura to some concerts."

He leaned forward and took the coffee cup his wife was holding out to him.

"I wouldn't have needed any persuading." Josh smiled. "But I start rehearsals in Boston the day after tomorrow."

"You forget he's famous now, Dad," Andrew put in. "You can't boss him around anymore."

Josh leaned back in the deep chintz-covered armchair. "Hardly famous," he laughed. "But these months in London have sure opened the door to engagements—and contacts. And the tour was a wonderful bonus."

"But now you're deserting us for the New World," Alasdair teased, looking across at Josh with a twinkle in his eyes.

"Not deserting," Josh corrected. "Going home. It's been a fantastic experience over here, and I'm going to miss you all a whole lot. But it'll be great to be on the same continent as my folks again."

His words sank slowly into Laura's muddled brain.

Tomorrow everything will return to normal, she assured herself.

Then doubt crept in.

Or will it?

Looking up, she saw her husband's eyes upon her.

"You're awfully quiet, darling," he said gently.

But she avoided his gaze.

"Are you very tired, Josh?" Alasdair asked. "If not, I'm sure Laura would love for you to play one of the pieces that was such a success on the tour."

His words pierced Laura's heart. She didn't want to remember those sensitive hands on her keyboard, hands she had so often watched and now longed only to feel enclosing her in a physical embrace. But Josh had already opened the piano and was sitting on the long tapestry-covered stool they had once shared, idly stroking the keys.

"This isn't a tour piece," he said quietly, his head bent low over the keyboard as his fingers tripped effortlessly up and down. "But it's a piece of music that has come to mean a lot to me in the past few months."

He looked at Laura, and their eyes met.

Alasdair saw Josh's look. He glanced at his wife, then back to Josh. But the young man's head was turned away from him. As Josh struck a few random chords, Alasdair leaned back in his chair, his expression thoughtful.

A log sank into its bed of ashes with a lingering sigh, sending plumes of smoke spiraling up the chimney as the first haunting bars of "Liebestraum" throbbed through the silent room.

Laura bit her lip, memories of that May afternoon dancing before her. Through half-closed eyes she saw Josh's straight, dark hair sweeping his forehead—and willed herself to be emptied of every emotion but enjoyment of the cascading notes that rose and fell, pleading, sighing, caressing. And, with a quivering sigh, finally dying.

Then subtly, before any of them had time to emerge from the beauty of the music, the rhythm changed. Smiling toward her, Josh broke into "Laura," singing the words softly to himself.

A surprised murmur rumbled through the assembled family.

"Your tune, Mum!" Andrew exclaimed.

Jamie leaped up and began waltzing with an imaginary partner around the chairs. "'They say that falling in love is wonderful,'" he crooned, his eyes rolling voluptuously. He paused to dramatically place his hand on his heart. "Iain's in love with Hebrides, and Josh is in love with Mum," he moaned sensuously. "Tiddle-dee-dee. Tiddle-de-dum. Josh's in love with Mum . . ."

The music stopped abruptly. Josh didn't look up as his hands fell from the keys, and an embarrassed silence descended on the room.

For a moment Laura's composure deserted her.

"Stow it, Jamie," Iain barked, his face puce. He looked anxiously at his mother.

But the irrepressible Jamie was enjoying the sensation he had caused. Collapsing onto a sofa with a series of erotic gasps he continued his chant, rolling his eyes ecstatically toward the ceiling.

"Stow it, I said," Iain threatened, rising menacingly, his fists tightly clenched.

Startled by this outburst from her mild-mannered son, Laura looked quickly across at him, and their eyes locked. Before his penetrating gaze, she dropped her own. And suddenly a coldness enveloped her. Her flesh stiffened with goose bumps, and she shivered. Iain, her sensitive firstborn who was so like her, had been unusually quiet all evening. Had he guessed her secret? When she looked up again, his eyes were still on her. Now in their depths she saw the question.

For a split second her composure deserted her. Then quickly getting to her feet, she began putting coffee cups on the tray. "Jamie," she snapped, "get up and behave yourself. And don't let me hear any more such rubbish."

"Oh, Mum," Andrew broke in with a grin, "can't you take a joke? It's time you and Dad did something different. Got out of your rut before it's too late. You've been in love for nearly twenty years. It's hardly decent."

"That's enough, Andrew," Alasdair said sharply. "And that goes for you too, Jamie."

At his tone even Jamie fell silent.

Rising in his turn, Alasdair took the tray from Laura's hands and followed her into the kitchen. "The boys can be very stupid," he said. "But they were only teasing."

"Of course they were," she replied tartly, her voice hard and metallic.

She tried to smile at Alasdair, but her lips were taut, and the smile was forced and unnatural. "I've got rather a headache," she stammered, passing a hand across her throbbing temples. "I think I'll go to bed. Say good night to everyone for me."

Josh was leaving early the following morning, and the chances were that she would not see him again. But Alasdair did not suggest she say good-bye.

When he finally came to bed, Laura's eyes were closed. He slipped in beside her, but she didn't move. And for the first time since they were married, he didn't kiss her good night before turning out the light.

The house was silent. But Josh's music was everywhere, whirling round and round inside her head.

Josh, Josh, she cried voicelessly into the darkness.

He could almost be your son, that inner voice kept reminding her.

She knew he could, but it didn't matter.

Laura got out of bed. Alasdair was not asleep, but he didn't stir. Dragging on her dressing gown, she went downstairs into the dark drawing room and sat at the piano, softly picking out the notes. "Laura." The words rang in her ears.

Why had he played that tune? He'd never played it before. Had he been trying to tell her something? She remembered his expression as their eyes met.

Once again her fingers picked out the notes. In her mind she heard him softly singing the words. Abruptly her hands dropped to her lap, and she found that she was trembling.

After a while she got up and crossed to the window. Pulling aside the heavy velvet curtains, she stared down at the empty square. The houses opposite looked gray and lifeless, like empty shells, and the street lamps cast an eerie glow over the trees in the center. In the distance she heard the low hum of a car speeding down the King's Road.

Listlessly, Laura let the curtain drop into place and turned back to the room. The ashes were cold in the grate, and the room was chilly. She shivered. Drawing her dressing gown more tightly around her, she walked wearily toward the stairs.

As she put her foot on the bottom step, a door opened, and Josh came onto the landing wearing only his pajama trousers. He paused as if listening. She held her breath. Had he heard her picking out the notes of her song? *Their* song?

"Laura," he whispered tensely, as if sensing her presence. "Laura, are you there?"

She remained motionless, suddenly limp and drained.

"Laura," he whispered urgently, "I know you're there. I heard you playing . . . our song."

Tears began to meander down her cheeks as the words of the song danced through her head: "But you're only a dream, only a dream, only a dream." The last line echoed on and on like an old gramophone record caught in a groove.

"Laura," Josh pleaded. He paused, and a note of anxiety crept into his voice. "Laura . . . you're crying."

In the darkness how could he know? Once again she felt his heightened sensitivity and knew that was what had drawn her to him.

For one wild moment she almost ran up the few stairs dividing them and flung herself into his arms. She longed to bury her face in that hard, young chest. As she imagined the touch of those sensitive hands and his arms tightening around her, her body trembled, and she clung to the bannister for support.

"You're there, Laura," he whispered tensely. "I can smell your perfume. Throughout the tour it kept coming back to me."

Josh felt for the bannister and began to walk slowly down to the half-landing until he was standing just above her. But she flattened herself against the wall, hardly daring to breathe. Below him in the shadows he could just make out her slim body and reached out to take her in his arms. But she drew away. They remained rooted to the spot, staring at each other as the sailing moon again fleetingly lit up the stairs.

"I love you, Laura," he whispered. "I don't think I fully realized it until this evening. . . . But I love you."

For a few tense seconds there was an electric silence between them. Every fiber of her being cried out for him. Never before had such strong waves of emotion raged through her. Never before had she felt this craving, this burning desire to capitulate, to completely annihilate herself in another human being. Her head reeled, and she held her breath, not daring to move.

"I love you," he repeated softly, silently pleading for some response.

A low cry escaped her lips, and she made a movement toward him. But as she did so, in her mind she heard Flora's voice: "It was like a dream. Had it come true, it likely would have ended in a nightmare. . . . What I did, with God's help, any woman can do."

Laura drew back.

Her mouth once more assumed the fixed position it had taken on earlier that evening in the kitchen with Alasdair. Although she tried to speak, no words came. Then she heard a harsh grating sound rising from the back of her throat. "Josh, don't be so ridiculous. You could almost be my son."

Josh's arms, which had been about to enfold her, fell abruptly to his sides. He gasped as if struck in the face. "Laura!" His voice was a strangled cry.

As the moon once again illuminated the dark staircase, they stood face to face—his expression hurt and bewildered, his eyes pleading; hers set and cold.

"Please," he pleaded. "Please, Laura, say you don't mean it. I-I can't imagine life without you. Even my music doesn't seem to matter anymore. *Say* we can be together . . . someday. I'll wait for you, Laura. I . . . love you so much."

Before he saw the pain on Laura's face, the longing in her eyes, the moon glided away, and darkness shrouded them. *God help me!* her heart cried desperately as, trembling in every limb, she leaned against the bannister steeling herself to resist.

"How *dare* you," she said tightly, her lips white in her ashen face. "How *dare* you! One more word, and I'll call my husband."

"Laura," Josh cried brokenly. "Laura . . . please."

The heartbreak in his voice almost finished her, but her lips remained closed while her mind pleaded desperately with the

God Flora had promised would help her. From somewhere strength came. "I don't want to see you again, at least not until you have grown up—and learned how to behave."

With a sharp cry Josh staggered against the stairs as if winded. Once again that electric silence zigzagged between them. But Laura's face remained flintlike.

A shuddering sigh convulsed Josh's body. Then groping blindly for the bannister, he dragged his bare feet back up the stairs. As he reached the top, he turned and looked beseechingly in her direction. But she resolutely turned her back. After a few tense seconds he heaved himself onto the landing and crossed to his bedroom.

Mesmerized, Laura half turned and watched as he opened the door. He gave her one agonized backward glance and then closed it behind him. For a few moments there was no movement, and she knew he was standing on the other side of that closed door waiting for her, willing her, to join him. But she did not move. As life began to throb back into her weary body, she heard the gentle creak when he at last climbed into bed. Clinging tightly to the bannister to prevent herself from following him, she imagined the second creak as she crept in beside him. A dull moan rose in her throat, and once again she heard the tune. Their tune. Going mercilessly around and around in her head.

Would there ever again be a waking moment when Josh would not fill her thoughts? He had come into her life as unobtrusively as a pebble which, tossed into the water, drops to the bottom of the pool. And, like the pebble, he had remained there, sending out ripples in every direction.

Laura raised her head and saw the doors behind which her sons were sleeping. She knew that at the other end of the landing, her husband, the man she had loved for over twenty years, the man she still loved, was waiting for her. And once again words that Flora had spoken came back to her: "Just call on Jesus . . . and He will come."

With a heartrending sob, Laura lifted her face and cried out to this unseen God. As she did so, light flooded the dark staircase. It seemed that a smiling harvest moon, so unlike the pale silver sliver that had been gliding in and out of the clouds, filled the oblong window on the half-landing. It swept slowly across the aperture and then disappeared, leaving behind an indigo sky speckled with glittering stars.

She raised her eyes to the vast velvet immensity, and the sob died in her throat. Something snapped; the tension inside her melted, and a great surge of peace coursed through her body. She felt as if she were floating effortlessly in a cradle of love. "O God," she cried. As she yielded to this gentle caress, her anguish slowly faded. She heard herself whisper, "My *Father!*" and knew that she had at last found the loving father she never had. All the pain and grief of abandonment and loneliness rose to the surface, and she wept in great, tearing sobs. The grieving was like a cleansing flood, sweeping away years of hidden pain in the warmth of that great love.

At that moment she knew that her destiny and Daisy's were not inevitably entwined. She was not the slave of heredity nor of her turbulent emotions, being led blindly along a path she didn't want to take. She had surrendered herself to the God she had paid lip service to for most of her life but until this moment had never really believed in. She was no longer standing in the path of a roaring wave. Jesus had caught her up in His arms and lifted the burden from her shoulders. He would take charge of her future and guide her into safe waters.

As this realization penetrated her tired mind, a sob escaped her lips. "Jesus, I'm sorry," she whispered. "Forgive me for not trusting You, for shutting You out of my life." The sense of what she had missed struck her—God's loving plan for her. "God forgive me for choosing my own way," she cried. "I want to walk in Your way. Please, Lord, help me to change."

There was silence. But it was not an empty silence, and she was not alone. He was there, He had heard, and He would make all things new. She sank gratefully onto the stairs, drained but at peace.

The church clock chimed and ponderously struck two.

A door opened quietly, and Alasdair came and sat on the stair beside her. Gathering her trembling body in his arms, he carried her back to bed. She seemed to be slowly waking from a dream, and in her bewilderment she clung to him.

As her weeping gradually ceased, she lay helpless in his arms.

"You've been in another world," Alasdair said, tenderly wiping away her tears.

It was so close to the truth that she felt he had looked straight into her heart. She raised her head and saw the raw pain reflected in his hazel gaze. "There's something I have to tell you," she said, her voice scarcely above a whisper.

But he put his fingers on her lips. "Do you *have* to tell me?"

She dropped her eyes but didn't reply.

"Do you want to tell me?"

"Don't you *want* to know?" she whispered brokenly.

"All I want to know," he said hoarsely, drawing her back into his arms and brushing his lips through her long golden hair, "is that you're here with me now. Nothing else matters."

He paused, as if uncertain how to continue. "Laura, you're the most beautiful woman I've ever known, and you'll never know how much I love you. But . . . for a long time you've been so far away I haven't been able to tell you."

Abruptly his lips clamped tightly together as if afraid he had said too much. "Perhaps now it's too late?" he asked raggedly.

With a shock Laura realized what his words meant. Her husband had known all along, or certainly yesterday evening about her feelings for Josh. Suddenly, the leaden fear that had been dragging at her, the pain and humiliation surged in front of her eyes in a terrifying wave. Then, just as once before Alasdair's face had risen before her and been blotted out by Josh's lean features, so now Josh's face hovered fleetingly in front of her eyes, then slowly receded.

Tentatively, Alasdair's lips sought hers. She yielded willingly to his touch like a violin thrilling to the tremor of the bow. As she did so, she experienced once again that wonderful feeling of being cradled in the peace and love that had flooded through her on the stairs when, in her moment of deep distress, she had called on the God Flora had promised would answer her.

She suddenly had a tremendous longing to see Flora again to tell her that she had met her Lord and Savior and given Him her life, that Jesus had forgiven her sins, healed her pain, and set her free. At the edge of the precipice, her foot had been kept from slipping.

Turning her head on the pillow, Laura saw her husband as if for the first time. Again she remembered Flora's words as they sat together that August afternoon at the Fort: "I had found a new love with Robert. Our love, Robert's and mine, deepened and became even more beautiful through my idyll with Jaraslaw."

Laura couldn't believe what was happening. It was as if the doubts and anguish of the past months had never existed or had been swept away, leaving behind only a hazy, painless memory. The years when she and Alasdair had walked alone along parallel paths, each searching for the crossroads that would bring them together, yet lost in a fog of misunderstanding, might never have been. The years since Sandy's death rolled away, and she was back in her husband's arms, safe and loved and cherished as she had been on their tenth wedding anniversary, before that fateful telephone call that had shattered her world.

Laura closed her eyes and silently thanked Flora's Savior, who was now so real to her, making all things new as He had promised. She thanked Him for this new outpouring of love for her husband that was flooding her whole being with a warmth and tenderness she had never experienced before. She felt like a balloon abruptly released from a child's tight grasp, at last able to soar joyfully upwards toward a beckoning blue sky. And she sighed in deep contentment. All remembrance of past pain was gone.

"Alasdair," she whispered huskily, her blue eyes deep and lustrous as they scanned his face, "is it too late?"

Raising himself on his elbow, he lifted one eyebrow inquiringly. "Too late for what, darling?"

She put up a hand and stroked his cheek, conscious of nothing but tenderness and joy. Suddenly that telltale blush that had not stained Laura's cheeks for many years began to slowly mount until they were suffused with a soft pink glow.

"For us to have our little Elspeth," she whispered shyly.

Alasdair stared at her unbelievingly.

Laura slowly raised her eyes until they were looking straight into his, smiling that sweet, shy smile that had first captivated him.

As the meaning of her words struck him, he drew her tenderly back into his arms. It was much more than desire that throbbed through his body. It was rather a consummation of all the lost years of longing and hoping.

Laura nestled against him, eager for his embrace. And as they expressed their love, it seemed to Alasdair that their youth reflowered, and the barren years drifted away—those locust years. He knew that they had at last found the way out of the long, dark tunnel. The ghosts, the misunderstandings, the dark shadowy figures stalking them since Sandy's death had finally been laid to rest.

With this realization, Alasdair felt the woods, the lake, and the rolling lawns of Annanbrae stretch out green and russet arms and wrap them both in a vast embrace. It was one of those rare, almost mystical moments that happens only once in a lifetime. And sometimes never happens at all.

Dawn was stretching its pale gray fingers across the night sky as the church bell chimed and slowly struck five.

Alasdair smiled lovingly at the heart-shaped face on the pillow beside him, seeing again the girl who had captivated him all those years ago in the ballroom at Annanbrae. He knew that the evening had been cathartic for them both, and he understood how very nearly he had lost her. But he also knew that now he would be able to tell her how much she meant to him. And more. The words would no longer stick in his throat.

"You've been a long way away, my darling," he whispered, tenderly kissing her closed eyelids. "But . . . thank you for coming back to me."